A Horse Called Bicycle

Roxana Valea

A Horse Called Bicycle

The Polo Diaries Book 2

Prologue

I dreamed of it again last night: the farm in the middle of the Argentine *campo*, the place I came to one day by a twist of fate and which would become so central to my story.

My dream always begins with the traffic in Buenos Aires. I feel its grip as I struggle to get out of the city. And when I see the highway tolls and I know I have succeeded, I'm able to move faster. I drive on, passing by a small town. This is where I once broke my right arm playing polo. But that was another story and when my arm healed, my story ended. Or so I thought.

I carry on driving and soon there are no more towns, just the vast expanse of the pampas and the dirt road cutting straight through it. And the huge cloud of dust that gathers behind the car as I drive towards the farm.

But then the dream changes and I'm moving fast still, but I'm no longer in a car. I'm back on a polo field riding my horse, holding the mallet in one hand.

I grip the reins in my left hand as the mare picks up speed beneath me. I grip them tight as fear rises. The wind is on my face, the smell of grass in my nostrils, the thunder of the hooves hitting the ground in my ears, and that mingled taste of fear and excitement in my mouth. And nothing else. There's nothing else left as we fly together on that polo field. The world has melted away, replaced by a shot of adrenaline that makes my body dance in the saddle.

And then, in a blink of an eye, the dream changes once more and I'm back in a car, rushing through the entrance to the farm. The polo field appears on the left as the track bends towards the farm, and a big bell suspended on a stone arch just in front of the house tells me I've arrived. Five dogs will come to greet me soon, and the smell of jasmine from the pillars of the porch will hit my nostrils.

I know there will be greetings and the voices of kids playing and the sound of the horses' hooves hitting the ground as they're set free in the early evening into the fields behind the house. I listen for these sounds …

But my dream always stops there, with the sight of the bell and the smell of jasmine. There's more to it, I know, but I can't reach it. Instead, I wake up suddenly, and in a second all is gone into darkness—the dream, the road, the farm. And my polo horse has vanished, too.

October

I step out of the plane in Buenos Aires in the morning and I'm struck by the same old feeling. It's as though someone has switched on the lights and they're bright, really bright. It might be the lack of sleep, crammed into an economy seat for thirteen hours all the way from London, or maybe there's more light in Argentina than anywhere else I've ever been in the world. And I've been to quite a few places.

I'm the last one to leave the plane, just as last night I was the last one to board it after the final call. I suddenly heard my name called and I ran and ran, desperate to get into the plane before it closed its doors. I made it. And I'm here now. And yet I walk out shyly with small steps, slowly taking in the light, the buzz, the Spanish language with that sweet Argentine accent, heavy on 'j's'. How much I've missed it!

Once again I feel inexplicably but definitely home. I felt like this each of the other five times I landed in this country, even the first time. Maybe it's because Argentina is the land of polo, and I love polo. I still love it, despite all the bones I've broken. Four bones, to be precise. But I always come back to polo every time, and the game has never left its grip on me. I'm going to play again now, here in the *campo*. I'm going to play with my Argentine family, the friends I made three years ago and who kind of adopted me and made me feel part of their family. I'm going back there, to their house in the middle of the green fields surrounded by horses and cows, and we'll play polo again, and it will feel like I never left. All this is enough to make me feel I'm coming home.

But there's more to it this time. There's Rodrigo. He's probably here already, waiting on the other side of the huge immigration queues.

After our fling ended last February in the same airport, prompted by my imminent departure on a British Airways flight back to London, I thought that was it; I was never going to see this guy again. And better so, my rational mind told me. This whole story was impossible. Not only the age difference, but a whole load of other issues came into play as well—money, education, social class, ability to travel. My mind told me it was impossible to have a future with this boy fourteen years younger than me, a maintenance worker in a cable factory. A boy who couldn't afford to travel. Whose passport didn't allow him to come and live with me in Europe. Whose social class … but who cares about social class, anyway? My heart told me to hell with all these things. He called me *linda*—beautiful—and every time he did, my heart danced.

I thought it was over when I left in February, but Rodrigo came to London in June, on a stopover at Heathrow Airport between two flights. He was on a backpacking tour of Europe for a month. I went to see him. I thought it would be nice of me to show him a little bit of London for the few hours he was going to be here. No romantic purpose, just as a friend would do.

He left his luggage at my place, and I told him I had a lot of tourist attractions lined up for the few hours he had available, but that he had to choose.

"What would you most like to do with your day in London?"
I asked him.

"Make love to you," he answered, looking straight at me. And then, seeing the shock in my eyes, he added, "We don't have to, of course. But if you're asking me what I'd like to do, I tell you honestly. This is what I would like to do more than anything in the world."

And then he called me *linda* again, as he so often used to do in Argentina. And then nothing else mattered, because nothing ever does when he calls me *linda*.

So, we spent the day in bed. Then he came back, one week later, and we spent another four days together. All of them in bed, too. Things were like this with us. We tended to spend a lot of time in bed. Sex madness, my friends called it. Love madness, I corrected them. No, this wasn't just sex. It was never just sex with Rodrigo, not even at the beginning, when sex was all there was supposed to be. It's always been something more—a deep, authentic, and powerful connection between us. Something I hadn't felt in a long time and something I thought I would find only on the back of a horse, playing polo. But polo is a different story. I can't think of polo when I have Rodrigo on my mind.

So I didn't think about polo. I thought only about how I could see him again. We agreed to meet, in Barcelona this time, and by the end of that weekend I was solidly in love. He was too, he said. We discussed being together forever, living together, building a home, having children. We discussed the issues too.

First of all, the age thing.

"Can't do much about it, so let's not discuss it," he said. "And you're more *linda* than any girl half your age, anyway," he added.

Half my age would be twenty-one. I doubted I was more beautiful at forty-two than a girl at twenty-one, but hey, it's nice to be told so, isn't it?

We discussed money. I earned in two days as a freelance consultant about the same as he earned in a month as a maintenance worker in a cable factory. I spent money on expensive hobbies, like playing polo, and I was going to continue to do so. Nothing was going to take polo away from my life. And he was still going to continue to live off his salary. These were my conditions. I wasn't going to finance his lifestyle or give up mine. He said that wouldn't be a problem.

Then we discussed where we would live. He couldn't come to live with me in Europe unless I married him and I wasn't going to do that. Ever. I made that clear to him. I was divorced and so had decided never to marry again. So, we would have to live in Argentina. That suited me. Argentina just happens to be the best country in the world for polo. He said that wouldn't be a problem.

Whatever my rational mind could come up with, Rodrigo managed to dismiss with a shrug and an easygoing *no pasa nada*. I know this phrase well. I learned it in Argentina. This is what they say when they mean there's no problem. I've heard it enough times to understand it. But believing it, this wasn't as easy.

I laid out in front of Rodrigo all the objections I could think of and watched him cast them aside, one by one. And when the last one was gone, I smiled, relieved. Maybe this was the guy for me.

I told him I had no more objections. We sealed it with a kiss, and another *linda*. The next day he boarded his plane for Buenos Aires, and I spent the rest of the summer in Europe. Despite all our conversations of how the future could look, we agreed to leave it open. To not talk about it once he went back home, and just to wait and see where this story wanted to go. Then, once I came back to Argentina, we would check in with our feelings again. And if we decided to get back together then, it would be for good.

I told myself I should not build up my hopes too much—a lot could happen still. Another Argentine saying I learned last time was *después vemos*. "We'll see about it later." Four months is a long time. I might meet someone else. Or he may not be there when I go back. My mind told me to be cautious, but my heart told me to go for it.

In the end I persuaded myself I would be cautious, but I packed ninety kilograms of stuff in three suitcases, just in case I wouldn't be coming back from Argentina for a while. And twenty-five pairs of shoes. One definitely needs a lot of shoes when one is about to start a new life.

Te estoy esperando, sabés? he texted me a week before my flight. *I'm waiting for you, you know?*

Just as he's waiting for me right now, right here in this airport.

The knot in my stomach tells me I'm still not quite sure this is really going to work. But then, it has to. The lady with a crystal told me it would work and she must be right. She talks to angels, so she should know what she's talking about.

I don't tell many people about the lady with a crystal. Actually, the ladies with crystals, because there are more than one of them. Not all have crystals, but there's a whole army of astrologists, energy workers, card readers, angel whisperers, and so on, whom I consult on a regular basis—every time I'm lost about the direction of my life, which is something that occurs quite frequently. Shall I change jobs? Shall I go to Argentina? And if I go, will he love me? Whenever I don't know the answer to one of these questions, I call a lady with a crystal. Or a couple of them, just to be sure. They usually don't agree in their answers, but I feel relieved at least to have talked to someone. And, in any case, I only choose what I want to hear from their answers.

My life being the weird life that it is, it's hard to get advice from anyone else. I'm over forty, unmarried, no kids, and no stable career. Just freelance work, which pays well and gives me a lot of free time. No allegiance to a particular country, although I carry the passports of two. No place I can call forever home. Even my nicely decorated flat in London feels like it belongs to the past. One expensive and dangerous hobby—playing polo, which has resulted in two accidents, involving a total of four broken bones. These are accidents from which I've recovered, and I'm currently playing again. My family, friends, and acquaintances constantly move from pitying my life, assuming I must be heartbroken and lonely, to envying my life every time they hear about a new destination I've chosen to go to. No ties also means I can pick a new destination or a new hobby whenever I want. This constant move between pity and envy leaves me drained and I've stopped asking for advice. What's left are a few trusted friends who listen to my stories and restrain themselves from telling me what to do. And I love them for it.

But there's a time when one wants a little bit of advice, and not having anywhere else to turn to, I started turning to Upstairs. To the next level up—angels, guides, and so on. Basically, the guys who are meant to know better. Upstairs will always talk back to me, sometimes during the meditation routine I've developed slowly over the last few years. And whenever I catch their voices, they've always been proven right. But it's a hard job to stay on your bum and meditate and turn inside for advice. Because, you see, Upstairs talks only when you're listening. And listening is a hard job. So, I developed a shortcut. I thought maybe others would be more skilled at getting information for me and could deliver it painlessly in exchange for a reasonable fee per hour. I found a lot of ladies with crystals who would translate for me what Upstairs told me I should or should not do, or should do more of, or less of. They saved me the trouble of finding out for myself. It seemed like a good deal.

It was one of these ladies with a crystal who told me Rodrigo is the man of my life, he'll love me forever and we'll have an incredibly romantic love story with a big, shiny, happy ending. Bang! Finally. About time. I've been waiting forty-two years for it. Another lady with a crystal told me Rodrigo could be right for me, but he could also be wrong, and that I'm to proceed cautiously and check in with my feelings every step of the way. Hmm. That wasn't so easy. Actually, I was paying precisely not to have to check in with my feelings. She was the shortcut. But the shortcut this time would say no more. No magic solution. Shortcut dead-end. So I turned to a third lady with a crystal who told me planet Saturn was moving against some other planet, I forget which one, and this usually meant trouble. But not always. That is, it could work, but it might not work, too. And that this year is the year of endings for me, something about numerology, not new beginnings. But that if I really wanted, I could proceed cautiously and see how it works. Saturn will tell me quite clearly if it doesn't work, she added. And just to be clear: no rushed decisions, no moving in together and no weddings. Not yet. Maybe later. Or maybe not at all.

With these three conflicting pieces of advice from three ladies, each of them equipped with their own crystal, I did what I always ended up doing. I decided to listen to the one I liked—lady number one and her story of shiny love forever. So be it!

SUNDAY 30TH OCTOBER

Rodrigo is pretty straightforward when it comes to sex. He drives me straight home and we make love. There isn't much talking. There's no need. We're both busy trying to discover if the passion is still there. It is. As is the big unanswered question as to what exactly I'm doing here. But with a few kisses and a few *lindas* the tension eases a bit and then I stop thinking altogether, because thinking and making love to Rodrigo are two activities that can't happen simultaneously. My mind has a rest. My body feels alive. My heart starts singing again. I'm in love, it says.

Yes, the passion is definitely still there. And so is that feeling of connection, of being one, one body with two shapes. He reads my thoughts, answers my unasked questions, anticipates my desires and eases my fears. Maybe this is what love is supposed to feel like. I'm not sure, because my love life up to now has been a roller-coaster.

About three years ago I gave up on trying to find love and I found polo instead. And with polo, it was love at first sight. Who needs love when there's a horse to connect to, teammates you feel at one with, and a big, endless polo field waiting for you? The shot of adrenaline I got from these games left me peaceful and happy. I might not have found a man to share my life with, but I thought I had found myself.

But now I have the man too, I think, as we finally get out of bed and go for a stroll around the city. I inhale the spring air, marvel at the bright purple jacaranda trees just starting to bloom, and I feel home again. Back in Buenos Aires, the Palermo neighborhood, a different flat from last time but also rented from Airbnb. In my constantly-on-the-move-never-really-settled life, this is as close as home can be.

"I'm home and I'm in love," my heart sings, as we stroll the streets hand in hand. Considering both these states have been rather lacking from the last few years of my life, I feel pretty fortunate. I just can't believe how happy I am to be here, listening to Rodrigo telling me about the plans he's made for us, about the road trips we'll take, about going to Colombia.

We still haven't formally discussed being together forever, but as far as I'm concerned things are pretty clear. I'm in love. And I feel he is too. And he's making a lot of plans for us.

"I can't go away for Christmas and New Year, *mi amor*. In my factory they close production for two weeks, but I work in maintenance and we need to be there for the annual overhaul of the machines. But afterwards, in January, we'll go, *mi amor*. I want to travel with you; I want to discover new places; I want to spend a week on a deserted beach with you. And make love to you all day and all night."

I'm starting to believe this guy. The part about making love all day and all night is the most credible bit. We have just spent twenty-four hours in bed. I'm starting to believe life can indeed be as beautiful as this.

I even ignore Gabriela's repeated messages with her characteristic swearing. She can't help swearing, she claims, but she means well.

Where the fuck are you? We want to see you, too! When are you coming to Lobos? And how about polo???

They're like my family here and I want to see them, too. All of them.

First there's Gabriela, a half-Mexican, half-Swiss, kind of non-conformist lady, a bag and accessories designer, and a polo player in her spare time. Spare mum to me when I need one in Argentina. I came to know her through a friend of a friend and we bonded instantly. That was three years ago.

Then there's Patricio, an Argentine professional polo player, boyfriend of Gabriela and father of Gabriela's seven-year-old child, who is called Patricio, just like his father. Little Patricio is in the habit of riding wild horses without a helmet or saddle across the fields at their farm, just like his father does, and with the blessing of both his parents.

And then there's Rosario, Patricio's cousin and a soul sister to me. My Argentine sister. I met her at a Christmas party during my first visit to Argentina three years ago and immediately and inexplicably felt like I'd known her for a lifetime.

The three of them and the many members of their extended family are my substitute family here. I spent two Christmases, two New Year's Eves, and one complicated fortieth birthday with them. This is more than I've done with my own family in the last ten years.

They all want to see me and I want to see them, too. Ah, and there is polo. Patricio and Gabriela not only play but also have a polo field in the backyard of their farm and a string of exquisite polo ponies, which I've ridden on more than one occasion. Plus, they have a whole team of cousins, friends, and polo clients who are in the habit of playing the game too, and I'm itching to be back on a horse playing with all of them.

But for now Rodrigo comes first. I want to enjoy my time with him, connect to him, see how we can reconstruct this fragile link between us. He hasn't met them yet and I don't want to put him under pressure. And polo can wait too. I don't even miss it that much when I'm with Rodrigo.

Later. I text Gabriela. *Maybe next weekend.*

"For now I'm busy being in love," my heart sings.

LATER THAT NIGHT

But polo can't wait. It comes to me deep in the night, in one long dream. And I wake up sweating, feeling again its powerful grip as a reminder that nothing, not even love, can tear polo away from me.

"Push! Pu-u-sh!" I hear the scream from behind as loudly as if his voice is right in my ear. "Push as much as you can!"

I push. I really do. As much as I can and then even harder. I push with all my strength, with my horse breathing heavily under me, with my eyes wide open and my jaws tightly closed. I lean into my opponent, feel the weight of my body going down into my legs and then, for a few seconds, I close my eyes as I push. But he's bigger and his horse is bigger too, and all my efforts make only a tiny difference. We're getting close to the ball now and it's still on his offside, to the right of his horse, at the ideal distance for a perfect hit.

"Pu-u-ush!"

I hear the scream again. I know I'm not pushing hard enough. I need to push him over the ball so the ball goes under his horse and then he won't be able to hit it. Ideally, I should push him all the way to the right so the ball passes under his horse and then passes under mine. Then I'll be able to hit it instead, on my left side. But this is a distant dream for me. There's no way I will be able to achieve it. At least if I manage to push him a little bit more, I will ruin his angle and he won't be able to hit it.

"Pu-u-ush!"

Another shout, as if I hadn't heard enough. This time there's irritation in the Old Man's voice. No wonder. From where he is, far behind me, he can see perfectly well that my desperate attempts to push a much heavier player off course have achieved nothing. He doesn't need to wait to see what will happen. He's good at anticipating, the Old Man. Anticipation. That is what makes a good polo player, he once told me.

How can time expand so much? I'm locked in a powerful embrace with the other player. It can have been only a couple of seconds, but still I have time to register it all—the shouts of the Old Man galloping behind me, the heavy breathing of the mare beneath me. She doesn't like it. Horses never like these ride-offs, even though the horses aren't in contact with each other. It's us, the players, who are. Shoulder to shoulder, knee to knee, hip to hip, as the book says. We're the ones slamming into each other at high speed, trying to push each other off the ball.

I register the sharp cut in my lower leg somewhere halfway between my knee and my ankle, and for a second I wonder how this can be. It feels like the stirrup of the other player is cutting through my boot. I make a mental note that I need to buy new boots, really thick ones, three layers of leather this time. And yet … his stirrup can't possibly reach all that way. How can he be so tall?

But he is. Much taller than me. Much stronger as well. And his horse is much taller and much stronger than my little mare. And these two facts together mean I stand no chance.

Time expands further. The ball is in the distance, coming towards us in slow motion.

"P-u-u-ush!"

I hear one more desperate cry from behind and I know I've lost it. There's a sound of metal against metal, must be from the stirrups. A smell of sweat from the horses, or maybe it's mine, or his. The pain in my right arm as I push against him and the persistent feeling of a bruise somewhere in my lower right leg. And the smell of leather, wet leather, his saddle, my saddle, or maybe the reins. I push with my last *inch of strength, knowing I've lost, knowing he'll hit the ball now and knowing I've let my teammates down, and the Old Man will be upset with me again.*

And then he misses. His swing is perfect, the ball still at a comfortable distance as we reach it, locked in our ride-off like a mythical creature with eight legs and two arms, the two horses side by side and us two welded together in this forced squeeze. He misses by less than an inch, just as all misses in polo happen.

"Well done!" I don't even register whether the voice is meant for me. Surely not? I haven't done anything. I haven't pushed hard enough. Far from hard enough.

But he missed it. Maybe just trying was enough. Maybe I'd annoyed him with my desperate attempt to push him away and this made him lose the ball. Maybe it's enough. Maybe I am enough. Maybe I am really enough.

In the darkness of the room, I grab Rodrigo's arm with a feeling of urgency and fear, as if I want to make sure I'm still in the bed with him and polo hasn't taken me away. He turns around, murmuring a half-asleep *linda*, and gathers me close to his chest. And then I can finally let the dream go and hide my nose in his neck and fall asleep again, his arms warm around me.

MONDAY 31ST OCTOBER

Mi amor, I miss you so much I can't possibly be away from you another night!

I stare at the screen of my phone, and the letters of the message dance in front of my eyes. A wave of joy washes over me. He misses me! How can life be so perfect?

I miss him too. His solid arms around me. His big brown eyes looking straight into mine as he calls me *linda*. And he calls me *linda* about twenty times a day. This is the best thing about him. Only one day apart and I miss him too.

We'd agreed that during the week it would be better for him to sleep at his place. He starts work early, and to get to his factory from my place he would have to get up at 4:50am. It's a sensible decision. But sensible decisions don't last long with us.

How about tonight? I text him back.

Sos el amor de mi vida, sabés? he answers.

I am the love of his life. My heart stops beating for a second. This is it. The love I've been waiting for my whole life finally came out of a relationship I thought would lead nowhere, and which I'd decided to terminate last year when I left Argentina. And yet it is here and powerfully alive.

I will see you tonight, mi amor. And I will make love to you all night long.

Another wave washes over me and this time it's more than joy.

I take a deep breath, but before I can dwell on my happy fantasies about what exactly will happen tonight, I hear a chilly voice.

"Maybe you should wait a little bit," the sensible part of me says.

She does things like this, my sensible self. She comes in unexpectedly and finds something to say to ruin my joy, pretty much every time I feel I've hit the jackpot.

I know I should ignore her, but I just can't stop myself answering.

"Wait for what?"

"Wait to declare him the man of your life."

"It's him who says I'm the woman of his life. Not me, silly."

"Yeah, right. Like I don't know what you're thinking."

"OK, maybe I think so, too. What's wrong with that? I'm in love. Can you for once understand that feeling?"

"Yes, I can," she answers laconically. "Just don't lose your head completely."

"What's the point of being in love if I don't lose my head?"

I know I shouldn't engage with her, because it just gives her steam, but I'm irritated now and I just want to win this argument for once.

"You can be in love as a trial," she suggests.

"This is the most stupid thing I've ever heard."

"The ladies with a crystal say you should take it easy."

"I am taking it easy, silly. I'm not doing anything major. He's going to come back to see me tonight and I'm just happy he's coming. Floating off my feet, actually. Can you understand that feeling? Light as a feather and bursting with joy. This is love!"

"It's just the effect of too much sex," sensible me says, unimpressed.

"How do you know?"

"This is what your friends say."

For a second I remember Gabriela and her rational approach to life. She and my sensible part sometimes talk the same language. But I told Gabriela she was wrong; this wasn't just too much sex. It was much more than that.

"In what way more?" I hear the skeptical question, and this time I'm not sure if it's Gabriela or my sensible self who's talking.

"I can see his light."

"Give me a break. Bullshit!" she screams. This time it's Gabriela talking. My sensible self doesn't swear; she just talks plainly and boringly.

I take a deep breath and decide not to answer. I'm not sure who I'm talking to anyway, now that my sensible self has decided to merge with Gabriela. They don't understand, clearly not. And there's no rational way to explain that I really see his light.

I do. I see it immediately as he enters the room and takes me in his arms and murmurs *linda* in my ear. I see it when he cooks and chases me out of the kitchen with a wooden spoon, telling me I'm such a disaster at cooking—which I know is true—that we're lucky at least he knows what he's doing. I see it as we spend endless hours talking on the sofa and listening to music, and then I'm surrounded by his light deep into the night when he makes love to me. Maybe light and connection are one and the same thing. The connection I thought I could find only by playing polo, my love for horses and for the game, has now entered my life in the shape of an attentive, solid, and handsome Argentine boyfriend who calls me the love of his life. And this is something that my sensible self will just have to learn to get used to.

LATER THAT NIGHT

"*Mi amor*, we should be sleeping. You'll wake up in exactly two and a half hours from now," I tell him as I feel his lips on my ear in the darkness of the night.

"Shhh," he tells me, and then I can't talk any longer as his light shines bright for me in the darkness of our bedroom and I melt under his kisses, as I always do.

And then, just before we fall asleep, now less than two hours before he needs to wake up, I hear his voice again.

"*Mi amor*."

"Yes? What?" I murmur, half-asleep and dizzy with the feeling of his arms holding me tight.

"*Mi amor*, I want us to have a little girl just like you … as *linda* as you are."

My eyes get wet with tears, instantly. He can't see this in the dark. I hope he doesn't. Instead, I try to laugh.

"And why not a boy?"

"Boys bring trouble," he murmurs, half-asleep. "But a little girl, as beautiful as you are, that would be just perfect."

Maybe lady with a crystal number one is right to tell me not to be afraid to be in love. Maybe we should go for it. Making babies, I mean. Even though I'm not really sure I actually want any babies. And even though the other ladies with a crystal said I shouldn't make big decisions just yet. Maybe they've got their timings wrong.

How can I wait, when one loving, tender, passionate man, who's displaying a characteristic and very sexy unshaven Argentine look plus a pair of strong muscular arms, which right now he's using to hold me tightly to his chest, asks me to have a baby with him?

The sexy man in question is now snoring peacefully next to me, but I remain awake long afterwards. I'm staring into the darkness, where the picture of a perfect baby face starts taking shape. She's a little baby girl with big brown eyes, as beautiful as his. I stay there with her a long time, getting to know her and the new feeling of holding her in my arms. Maybe I want a baby, after all.

I'm slowly going insane. I'm over forty; I shouldn't be thinking of such things. My sensible self doesn't miss a single chance to step in. I dismiss her voice and try to go back to my little baby girl with brown eyes, but then she too is fading away, because I'm finally falling asleep.

And just before I do, one last thought flashes through my mind.

How would pregnancy fit with playing polo?

I have no answer to this, so I decide to push the question away for now.

November

WEDNESDAY 2ND NOVEMBER

Two more days in Buenos Aires and I'm completely settled in my old routines. I have a coffee at the same coffee place I used to go to every day last year. I join the same gym as I did last year. I walk the same streets, speak the same language, shop in the same places.

And Buenos Aires still has the same air of a big European metropolis with beautiful buildings and large boulevards. It has the widest boulevard in the world—*Avenida 9 de Julio*, with seven lanes in each direction, flanked either side by parallel streets with two lanes each. It simply doesn't get wider than this. The coffee places are still as stylish as those in Paris, and the restaurants still cook food that tastes as good as that in Italy. People are still kind, smiley, relaxed. And the number of dogs on leashes I see in this city is still overwhelming. I don't think any other city has more dogs per square meter.

All is just as I left it, with one big difference: the prices have doubled. The dollar exchange rate is the same, but everything is much more expensive. My gym costs double; a coffee and a *medialuna* (the Argentine version of the butter croissant) cost double; painting my nails costs double too. I've no idea what just happened to this country. It's more expensive than Spain, where I spent the last two months, and almost as expensive as London, which is incredible. After all, one of the reasons for leaving London when I'm not working on a consulting assignment is precisely to save money.

I walk around the streets of my neighborhood wondering how I can settle here for good, and how I can be with Rodrigo forever. I miss him again and it's only two days since I saw him last. Our plan to live separately during the week clearly doesn't work. Tonight he's coming back to spend the night with me. We need to find a more sustainable solution for our living arrangements.

Maybe we should move in together. To hell with my sensible self and all those ladies with their crystals. I can't be here and not see him, and the amount of text messages he's sent me during these past two days is proof that he can't be without me, either. I'll talk to him tonight.

He arrives and we talk, only for the discussion to take a surprising turn and go towards a big black hole I want to avoid at all costs. Marriage.

I feel uneasy about marriage discussions. I've felt like this ever since my divorce, after a very short-lived marriage nine years ago. Yes, I want a stable, loving, caring, amazing man in my life. But no, I don't want to get married to him. No papers, I mean. If there's a way to get married without papers, I could be persuaded. But papers, hell no, no way. Not another divorce, please. No papers. Papers make me freak out. They remind me of papers I signed and then other papers I signed after that and discussions with lawyers about papers I was supposed to sign. As far as I'm concerned, the surest way to kill love is with papers. So, no papers, please.

I thought Rodrigo understood. It was part of the long discussion we had in Barcelona about what we would do and what we would not do. But he clearly didn't get it. Maybe it's because he's never been married. He has no idea how much this whole topic freaks me out. But by the end of our short conversation tonight, five days after my arrival in Buenos Aires, I make sure he has a pretty clear picture.

"No way," I tell him again. "No way I'm getting married again. I told you so. Remember? In Barcelona. I told you I'm not getting married ever again in my life and you said OK."

We're sitting on the sofa after dinner. Rodrigo keeps his eyes stubbornly fixed on the floor. I wish he'd look at me.

"Yes, but I've never been married," he says. "What if I want to get married and I can't, because you're so crazy about this whole thing? Will you ever relax a bit, do you think?"

"Maybe in ten years' time," I say. "And anyway, why do we need to have this discussion right now?"

It's not exactly that he's asked me to marry him. We were just talking and he brought it up. He asked if one day I'd feel like marrying him. I'm confused. Is this a marriage proposal or just a pre-discussion about a potential marriage proposal? And then why do I react so badly? I'm the one who came here hoping to be with him for good. Which is much like marrying him. I should be glad, not angry, that he feels the same way. Surely that's why he brought it up? He loves me and wants to spend the rest of his days with me. I know I should be happy but I feel uneasy—one of those unexplainable emotions that build up inside sometimes. I've learned there's no use trying to either understand or fight them. So I just let them be.

Let's change the subject, I decide. It's the best way to get annoying topics out of the way.

"I went to the gym today," I tell him, cheerfully ignoring the whole conversation about marriage. "I signed up at the same one as last year. Everyone recognized me. But my old trainer isn't there any more. I have a new one. His name is Augustin. He's a nice guy."

Rodrigo looks at me, alarmed. The whole marriage discussion is forgotten in the face of the new threat.

"*Mi amor*, be careful. He'll try it on with you. I know how these Augustins are in the gyms. They'll all try it on with you."

I laugh and I tell him about the scene that unfolded at the gym as I was doing my sit-ups on the floor, under the careful supervision of the said Augustin. Two other guys came to sit with him on the same bench, watching me doing my sit-ups, until Augustin sent them away.

"*Qué pasa, chicos*? Are we having a meeting, or what?"

I'm used to the attention of Argentine men. I learned all about it on my previous visits, and I actually find it quite flattering. Especially after some time spent in England, where no one would line up to watch you doing sit-ups in a gym. Or chat you up randomly. But here flirting is part of life. No one takes it too seriously. No one but Rodrigo, it seems.

"*Mi amor!*" He sounds even more alarmed on hearing my story. "Do you really need to go to the gym?"

Yes, I do, because I'm going back to polo and I haven't been on a horse for three months, and I need to get my muscles going. And it's really important to get back on a horse and back to polo. Even though I'm in love with him, polo will never go away. I try to explain but I find it all too complicated, so I end up instead with the one phrase that says it all in Argentina.

"*No pasa nada.*"

But even this can't calm him down. His mind is racing.

"And this Augustin, he must have all the muscles in the world. I know them, these Augustins of the gyms. I know how they're built, how they look. He must look like a sex symbol. And I'm sure he will try to chat you up. Did you tell him you have a boyfriend?"

The marriage discussion is definitely off the agenda, since Rodrigo is now fully occupied with constructing his defense against Augustin.

"What? He calls you Ro? This is really not good news. Too intimate. Especially for the first week he's known you."

"*Traqui. No pasa nada.* Everyone uses short forms of names here. Ro for Roxy."

"No, no. I don't like this. I really think he's hitting on you."

They're like this, the Argentines. Jealous. Possessive. Passionate. I never thought I'd love it, but I do.

And then when we're done with Augustin, Rodrigo finds something else to be worried about.

"And polo. That makes me nervous, you know."

I know. Last year, at the start of our romance, I broke my arm playing polo and I spent six weeks in a cast while dating him. Rodrigo remembers the cast well. And so do I. But he doesn't play polo and can't understand why I would want to play again. And there are things I can't explain, no matter how much I try.

"I know, *mi amor.* But I'll be OK, I promise," I say instead.

"There's no way you can know that." He looks at me accusingly. "You said you'd be OK before and look what happened last year. And the year before that. I really can't understand why you need to do this to yourself."

"I'm not doing anything to myself. It's just polo. We take a fall sometimes."

"It's not polo." He looks at me again with an intensity that scares me. "It's you. You do it. You do it to yourself. You do it by going back to a sport that nearly killed you."

"*Mi amor*, you don't understand. Shall we leave this discussion now? Please. It's making me tired."

It really makes me tired when people who don't play polo try to put me off playing polo.

He strokes my hair and after a while says in a calmer voice, "I don't ever want to see something like that happening to you again."

"I know, I know. I promise, nothing will happen this time. I'll be fine. I played in England this summer and I was fine. I even played a tournament."

I omit to tell him that the memory of the fall and broken arm of last year is still playing on my mind. But I'm determined to get over it, and there's no way I can risk another full speech from him now on why I should give up playing polo.

"I'll be OK, I promise," I repeat. It's all I can say.

"You have to be OK. *Te necesito en mi vida, mi amor.* Nothing can ever happen to you."

Te necesito. He needs me. A bit too dramatic, I think. He means he loves me, surely.

And then later, in bed, just before we fall asleep, "*Mi amor?*"

"Yes?"

"I worry, you know," he says. "I sometimes worry that one day you will leave me."

It's too dark to see his eyes. I touch his lips.

"Don't say this. Why would I leave you?"

"Because I'm not enough for you. For a woman like you. You may want to have a man who can offer you a life like the one you're used to. And I ..."

He pauses, unsure. My heart shrinks. I want to tell him something, but I've lost my voice, just as he has.

"I won't be able to," he adds, finally finding his words.

The fear of not being enough. The classic fear each of us secretly harbors in our hearts dares to come out of him, exposed in the darkness of our bedroom.

"Don't be silly." I laugh. "I worry too, you know. I worry that you may want to be with a woman closer to your age."

It's his turn to touch my lips, trying to silence my words.

"But I worry more," he says.

Then we don't say anything anymore. The issues are still there in the darkness of the bedroom, as clear as they've always been. We know them well and there's not much we can do about them. He's fourteen years younger than me. And I have a lifestyle he can't afford. Not much more to say about either of these things. That's just how life is right now. But the worries are there and sometimes they don't go away with a kiss.

I don't want to think about this. I don't. It has to work. This time it has to work, even if it's against all odds. It has to work because I believe that it will. I came here to be with him. I will make it work.

Once again I stay awake for a long time, watching the darkness, long after Rodrigo's snoring tells me he is not worried any longer. We really need to do something about this snoring, I think as I try to fall asleep.

But I can't. Instead of sleep, polo comes once again to visit me, and it takes me back to the green field I know so well. The hooves of the horse hitting the ground ring in my ear, and the smell of its sweat fills my nostrils.

⁓∾

"Again!"

I hear Jonny's shout and I know I've missed it and he knows I've missed it too, and there's no way we'll finish this training session until I manage to put that ball through the goalposts.

I take my horse back into a wide circle canter and I try to void my mind and not think of anything. My body falls back into the rhythm of the horse effortlessly and I feel her strides gently rocking my body. I haven't lost it. At least I haven't lost this rhythm.

But I've lost pretty much everything else—my confidence, my physical condition, my grip on the mallet, with an arm that was broken four months before in Argentina after I hit a goalpost in a polo tournament. After having my arm in a huge cast, I'd thought it would be impossible to get back to polo. But Jonny promised me over a coffee we shared in Buenos Aires that he'd make sure I would. And one thing I know about Jonny is that he keeps his promises.

I take a wide turn and see he's placed the ball on the thirty-yards penalty spot, just in front of the goalpost. The ball is a minuscule white dot in the middle of the green field, peacefully waiting for me. If I were practicing a penalty shot, I would go slow, trying to control my horse so he doesn't pick up speed. I would swing slowly, keeping my gaze on the ball at all times.

But I'm not practicing penalties today. That would be too easy. I am going at it at full speed, as it happens so many times during play. I'm practicing a mad gallop, an attempt to hit, and then, as the horse runs wild, I'm practicing bringing him under control again, just as I pass by the goalposts.

And every time I pass close to the goalposts I remember it. The hit I took exactly four months ago, and the fall that broke my right arm.

"Again!" Jonny shouts, and I know I have not scored. I should have looked to see where the ball went, but all I could see was the goalpost as I passed by it at full speed with a horse still filled with the adrenaline of the run.

"And look at the ball next time," he shouts.

Yeah, right, it's easy for him. He's a professional player and, despite being only twenty-two, a very good one. Of course he would look at the ball, not at the goalposts. Even if he'd once run into one. But Jonny doesn't run into goalposts. He doesn't take falls or break bones. He rides like he was born riding. He also understands things without the need for too many words. He reads my fear, the fear of hitting a goalpost again, of falling, of breaking. The fear of pain. And he makes sure I do what I have to do to get over it.

I ride again in a wide circle, in a slow canter so that both the horse and I get our breathing under control. A wide enough circle so that Jonny has the time to place the ball back where it belongs, on the thirty-yards mark. I know this isn't going to end until I manage to score a goal. He knows that too but, unlike me, he doesn't worry about it.

"Faster this time," he shouts from far behind me.

I finish the circle and get my pony into a straight line. I pick up speed.

"Faste-e-er!" I hear the shout again.

I go in full gallop, get close to the ball, glance at the goalposts, panic, swing quickly and hit. It will go in now. It has to go in. And damn that goalpost, I will stop watching it!

"Again!" I hear his shout and I know I'm not yet done for the day.

FRIDAY 4TH NOVEMBER

I spent the past two days somewhat unsettled. I'm not sure what it is, maybe a few lingering thoughts after our midnight conversation about our big differences. But I don't want to think about it, not consciously at least. Or maybe it's this flat I've rented. It's very noisy and the bed is extremely old. Which makes sleeping really difficult. I decide to look for another flat.

Maybe the new flat will sort this unsettled feeling, I tell myself. Or maybe a few days in the gym. Or going to Lobos to finally see my friends. Or polo. Polo will definitely sort out any uneasy feeling, I know this for sure. And I'm going to go to Lobos and play some polo soon. Monday will be my birthday. Gabriela called and invited me to arrive the night before so I can celebrate my birthday there.

"I can't," I told her. I wanted to be in Buenos Aires with Rodrigo the night before my birthday. It's been some time since I celebrated my birthday with a boyfriend and I'm looking forward to being pampered by the man I love.

I offered to arrive Monday evening instead, the day of my actual birthday. It's all set. Rosario will host a dinner at her place; I'll get there early afternoon and spend some time with the girls; then Rodrigo will come in the evening, after work, and finally meet my Argentine family over dinner.

I tell Rodrigo about the plan and he agrees. Lobos is one and a half hours away from where he lives.

"No pasa nada," he says. "It's your birthday, *mi amor*. Of course I'm going to be there for your dinner. But I'm worried, you know," he adds. "Will they like me?"

"Why would they not?" I ask.

"Because I'm from a different social class."

We've talked before about age and about income, but not about social class. Although a world nomad who doesn't give a damn about social class, I was aware that Rodrigo's education and social environment would put him at a disadvantage next to my friends. But I didn't understand then how deep the social-class divide runs in Argentina and, anyway, I didn't want to go down that line.

"Don't be silly," I tell him. "Of course they'll like you. They're my friends and they're nice people. And you're the man I love. Of course they'll like you."

But I did think about it as I bought tickets for the *Abierto* later that day. *El Abierto*, the open polo championship of Palermo, the biggest polo competition in the world. The one I came to see last year and the year before that. The one people from all over the world come to see. I bought a full season ticket for me. I was going to see all the games. And just like last year, I was lucky enough to get the ticket next to Gabriela and Patricio's seats. And then I bought tickets for Rodrigo for the semi-finals and the final only. He said two games would be enough for him. He didn't know much about polo anyway. And I imagined he wouldn't feel too comfortable surrounded by people from another social class, either. Even though in Argentina polo is a popular sport, it still belongs to the middle and upper classes. And Rodrigo didn't feel comfortable there.

Well, he'll have to get used to it, I thought. I didn't intend to change my lifestyle. I also didn't intend to finance a new lifestyle for him. But there will be touch points like this one, the final of the *Abierto*, where I don't mind buying a ticket for him, and he shouldn't mind mixing with people from another class for a day. It was all part of the challenges this relationship was setting for us.

Buying the tickets did little to make me feel better. Whether it was the flat, the approaching birthday, or the differences between us that Rodrigo kept on bringing up, one way or another I was feeling restless. And as I usually do on these occasions, I dived head first into an activity that would keep me from thinking. In this instance, looking for a new flat.

My first appointment is at 3 pm, about the same time Rodrigo is supposed to come home from work. The good thing about starting work at 6 am in a factory is that by 2 pm you're done for the day.

I send him the address, then I send him another address where I'll be having an ice cream before the appointment, then I send him a third address when I've changed my mind about the ice cream and I'm having a coffee instead. Then I want to change plans again, but I decide not to send him another new address because he surely won't come that quickly anyway.

I end up going to see the flat alone, as he's nowhere to be found. When he eventually answers the phone he sounds as if he's swallowed a whole lemon. He's actually lost, confused by my many addresses, and has done a lot of walking between all three of them.

The problem with passion is that it goes both ways. When things are good, they're really good. When things are bad, they become pretty bad pretty quickly. In a matter of minutes after we finally manage to meet, we start arguing in the middle of the road. Intensely. Argentine style.

"Why did you give me the wrong address?"

"Why didn't you call me?"

"I didn't want to look like an idiot."

"Better to walk around like an idiot, then?"

Silence. Maybe that wasn't the right thing to say. He's so upset he's now walking two meters in front of me. I'm angry that a stupid thing like this can make me angry. I'm angry with him. I'm angry with myself. I'm angry at the stupidity of this whole situation. I'm full-blown, Argentine-style angry.

We reach home like two loaded but silent guns.

He stops in the entrance hall as soon as we close the door behind us. One hand on the wall, the other to his head as if he's thinking really hard. I watch him curiously. I've no idea what this is all about, but I've a sense it's going to be interesting.

"Do I have anything here?" he asks without looking at me.

"What do you mean?"

"Like any of my things. I don't think I brought any of my clothes or anything, right? No, I don't think I've got anything here."

He goes to the bedroom and takes a look around. Then goes to the kitchen and does the same.

A thought is slowly entering my mind, so absurd and so unbelievable that all I can do is watch it growing into shape.

"Why? Would you like to pick up your things and go?"

He still doesn't look at me. He's back from the kitchen now and looks straight at the wall in front of him.

"Actually, yes. I would like to go."

He's done this before. Gone home in the heat of an argument. But then he came back the next day as if nothing had happened and told me readily that he was sorry. But he hadn't checked if he had anything in the flat when he did that.

The unbelievable thought in my mind is still there.

"Do you want to go just for now, or forever?"

Silence. And then it comes.

"Actually, I would like to go forever," he says.

This man is telling me he wants to break up with me. Less than a week after my arrival. Less than three days after he made a big deal about me not wanting to get married to him. This man is actually telling me he wants to break up with me, and all this because of a missed meeting point somewhere in the city.

I consider this thought in silence while he goes to take another look around the flat. And when the thought finally finishes settling in my mind I feel a rage I've very few times felt in my life before. It comes from my belly, it rises slowly but surely into my hands and into my chest and it comes out in my breath. I could strangle him.

"OK," I say. Surprisingly, my voice doesn't tremble. "You want to go? Very well. Go. Look, the door is there. Go through it, right now. Go through it and close it behind you. You'll never see me again in your life."

I'm surprised at how angry I feel and how cold my voice sounds.

He stops and for the first time looks at me. "*Mi amor*, I did not mean—"

"What? What didn't you mean? Didn't you say you wanted to go? Forever?"

"But *mi amor*—"

"No *mi amor* at all. No longer. Go! Just go! Get the hell out of here. The door is there."

"No, *mi amor*. Actually, I don't want to go."

"So, why do you tell me you want to go?" *You son of a bitch*, I add in my mind.

"I didn't mean it."

"What did you mean, then?"

"Actually—"

"I don't care. You said you want to go. So go. Now."

"No, I don't want to go."

"What do you want to do, then?"

"Stay here with you. Be with you."

This makes me even angrier.

"So, why the hell did you tell me you wanted to go?"

"But, *mi amor*, why do you get angry like this? Please—"

"Let me tell you why I get angry like this. Let me explain this to you very clearly."

By now I'm incoherent in Spanish so I switch to English. "I'm not sure what type of women you have gone out with before, but let me tell you one thing. These types of games don't work with me. You hear me? Don't work with me!"

I'm shouting now.

"*Mi amor*, calm down. You're so angry."

"Yes, I am. And you will listen. The next time you ever open your mouth to tell me something like this, it's over between you and me, you hear me? It's over. I'm not sure what you expect and what women do here when a man says he wants to go, but let me tell you what I will never do. I will never beg you to stay. Is that clear? Don't you ever play these games with me again! Don't you ever dare, or it will be the last time you will ever see me. Is this crystal clear?"

I'm so angry that I could slap him. He's now sitting down on the sofa, watching me with round eyes. One thing is clear. He didn't expect this. I didn't expect to get angry like this, either. But I did and it felt good—the only good thing in this whole absurd situation.

He doesn't go. He tells me instead that he's scared of me.

"Why, what do you think I can do? I can't harm you. You're stronger than me," I tell him when I've calmed down a bit.

"But, *mi amor,* I wouldn't resist if you wanted to harm me."

Even for my tolerance levels to Latin drama, this sounds so wrong it almost makes me laugh. The levels of absurdity of this afternoon reach new heights.

He doesn't go away. But he has the sense to quietly disappear from my sight and he goes to take a very long shower, while I slowly calm down on the sofa.

Maybe it's just one big misunderstanding. Maybe this is how people react here. Maybe it's just the flip side of passion. He didn't mean it. He couldn't have meant it. And look, he didn't leave after all. My mind races around in circles trying to reassure me that this meant nothing and the love is still there.

LATER THAT EVENING

At 7 pm I have another apartment viewing, and dead or alive I have to make it. Rodrigo has spent the last couple of hours tiptoeing around the apartment while I tried to calm down, ignoring him. He says he wants to come with me to this viewing.

He's acting like nothing has happened. As if he didn't want to go just two hours ago. As if all is fine and I got angry with him for no reason. As if he's an attentive boyfriend who cares only about my well-being and things are actually OK between us.

See? It's nothing, I try to tell myself. It was really just a misunderstanding. But I can't stop feeling cold and distant and I walk around like a mechanical doll with a frozen mind. I don't understand what just happened. I don't get it.

We get to the viewing and the landlady asks a lot of questions. They always ask a lot of questions in Argentina. It's part of being polite. In her case, she also wants to know who exactly is going to stay in her flat, so the list of questions becomes even longer than usual.

I tell her I'm a freelancer, living in London part-time, the rest of the time in Argentina and Spain. My living situation is rather hard to explain. I'm a management consultant. I do projects for big companies. When I do them, I work hard and earn good money. Then I write books for which I earn no money. Yet. And I'm here to play polo. And write. And be with Rodrigo, I wanted to add, but I left this one in the air. Yes, the flat is just for me. Rodrigo has his own place. He lives in the suburbs, one hour away from here, and sometimes he'll be here with me, weekends mostly. Other weekends, we will travel. He wants to show me Argentina. Oh, and yes, we're going to Colombia, on holiday, in January.

And then she questions Rodrigo.

"We spend a lot of time travelling together all over the world," he says, indicating me. "We meet in various places and travel the world," he repeats. "And in case you're wondering about my accent, I've a strange accent in Spanish because I travel a lot and I speak other languages most of the time."

He doesn't mention anything about the cable factory where he works in the maintenance department every day. He also doesn't mention that his English is basic and actually we spend all our time speaking Spanish. And there's absolutely no weird accent to his Spanish. Can't be. The first time he left his native country was last year. I just watch him in shocked silence as he tells her all these things.

Maybe it's his way of dealing with the differences between us. Maybe it's just an innocent little lie that makes him feel better. But I'm not quite sure what is worse—the fact that two hours ago he wanted to leave me or that he's building a world of complete fantasy that he portrays as reality. And I'm not sure how to deal with either of these situations.

SATURDAY 5TH NOVEMBER

I do what I do best when I'm not sure how to deal with something. I ignore it, hoping it will just go away. We go home and I try to say something about why he said those things, but then he says, "Which things?" and looks like he's not really sure what I mean, so I drop it. Enough drama for one day, I think. I'll try another time.

But something has changed between us, and nothing, not even making love, can erase that uneasiness.

We wake up early at the sound of his mobile phone. Who on earth is calling him at 8 am on a Saturday morning?

"Yes. Yes. That's me." His sleepy voice pauses in between words. "Yes. I know. I'll pay. Likely today. Maybe Monday. I've not been paid my salary yet."

And then he tells me after putting the phone down, "Crazy people. They call me on a Saturday morning to remind me I haven't paid my internet bill. I know I haven't paid the internet bill, for God's sake."

"Why haven't you paid it?"

"Because I haven't been paid my salary. It should have happened yesterday but I've not been paid. They do this at my factory sometimes. The bastards. When pay day comes on a Friday, they often move it to the following Monday."

We try to go back to sleep, but neither of us can anymore. It's his problem, I tell myself. I'm not here to solve his financial troubles.

"What are we doing today?" I ask, trying to change the gloomy mood.

"How about we go to Tigre?" he suggests.

Tigre. I've always wanted to go there, and in my four previous trips to Argentina I've never made it. This delta, only twenty miles from Buenos Aires, is the favorite weekend destination of *porteños*, as the residents of Buenos Aires are called. It's made up of hundreds of tiny islands created by five rivers that come together before flowing into the great Rio de la Plata. Once upon a time its islands and forests were the playground of jaguars, hence the name of the delta—Tigre, meaning tiger—but these days the tigers are gone, replaced by the luxury weekend homes of the rich and famous overlooking the countless peaceful waterways.

"Tigre, that would be great! I've always wanted to go there." I jump out of bed.

Last year he didn't offer to take me to Tigre. Last year he didn't offer to take me anywhere. Except for our trip to Uruguay. But who suggested Uruguay? Was it him or me? Can't remember. Doesn't matter. It was a great trip anyway.

The gloomy mood doesn't change even when we get into the car and start driving to Tigre. I tell him I'm starting my Spanish classes again with Santi, my teacher of last year. He doesn't like this.

"Why do you need a Spanish teacher? You speak Spanish with me and you speak pretty well."

I don't tell him it's because Santi teaches me proper Spanish instead of slang. When we started dating, Rodrigo made an effort at first to clean up his Spanish, but then, seeing that my comprehension had increased, he relaxed back into what I later discovered was street talk. Initially, I had fun learning his way of talking and even shocked my teacher back at the language school with some of it. But I wanted to speak proper Spanish, and for this I needed Santi, his verb charts and his reading assignments from Jorge Luis Borges. I doubt Rodrigo ever heard of Borges.

But not mentioning the reason behind my decision to restart Spanish classes doesn't do much to ease the atmosphere in the car. The traffic bothers him, the news on the radio bothers him, the heat bothers him. When Rodrigo is in a bad mood, it's pretty clear. I've a good tolerance for his complaints, but half an hour into the drive I find myself screaming, "Eno-o-ough!" with enough violence to shut an elephant up.

"That's enough. Really enough! Is there anything that's to your liking today?"

He apologizes. "*Perdóname.*"

Another great thing about Rodrigo is that he apologizes pretty quickly.

"I'm sorry, I think it must be the heat. I don't know why I'm so restless today. And the bed. We don't sleep well. We really don't sleep well there."

This is true. Neither of us could sleep well in that flat.

"We'll move next week," I tell him. "I just need to decide which flat to pick."

I remember the two flats I saw the day before, and the memory of the uncomfortable conversation with the landlady kicks straight back.

I look at Rodrigo, trying to decide if this is a good moment to ask him what on earth he meant when he told her we were travelling the world together, but he's got that bull-in-a-fight type of look on his face that tells me he's still in low spirits.

Not now, I decide. Maybe later.

"The trouble is none of them have a car park," I say instead. "What are you going to do with the car when you come to stay with me?"

In Buenos Aires it's impossible to leave a car on the streets because of the constant police patrols and their fines. Hence, either the flats have parking underneath, or one rents out a parking space in one of the many private garages scattered around the city.

"I'll figure out something," he says. "Don't worry. It's not worth renting a parking space for a month: it's too expensive. Better to save the money for our holiday in Colombia."

"I'm not worried about that."

"You don't need to save anything to go to Colombia, do you? You have enough money for that anyway."

It's not really a question and I say nothing. No, I don't need to save money to go to Colombia. I also don't want to talk about this. It makes me feel pretty uncomfortable discussing finances with Rodrigo. And it's none of his business, anyway. He'd be better thinking about his own savings.

And then he asks me out of the blue, his gaze on the road ahead, his voice casual, as if we were speaking about the traffic:

"When you go back to Europe in a few months' time, are you going to take me with you?"

Llevar. He used the verb *llevar.* The same verb one uses to buy a bag. Or for a takeaway. A pizza to take home is *para llevar.*

"Look, *mi amor.* My Spanish isn't very good, but for me this verb *llevar* is for a bag, like a suitcase. Not for a man. You're a man. You take yourself wherever you choose."

I deliver my answer straight and without thinking too much, as if my brain had it in store already. Maybe I'd been expecting this question and the verb that came with it.

"That's not what I mean," he says, annoyed. "I'm not asking you to pay for me."

"So, what do you mean? I can't take you anywhere. You take yourself where you please. Isn't that what a man does?"

"Let's leave it." He waves his hand, irritated.

Indeed. Everything we say is going wrong today. And why does it all have to be about money, anyway?

We reach Tigre and go straight to lunch. It's hot outside, and the many misfired conversations between us this morning have left me very low on energy. I feel like fainting. I don't understand how I can feel so full of life beside him one day and so empty of everything the next. And I've been here less than a week.

But one big pizza and one hour on a boat in the delta do miracles for my energy levels. We board an elegant wooden boat that takes tourists all around the canals. The boat reminds me of Venice, but Tigre is everything that Venice is not. No stone buildings here, only lush vegetation and timber houses scattered on the shores. Everything around us is green—a deep shade, which makes me remember that in Argentina November is a spring month. The front gardens of the elegant summerhouses we pass are bordered by the canals. There are no beaches, just some trees or bushes rising straight out of the water. The guide tells us how the delta used to be one giant fruit orchard in the last century and how all the fruit would be carried to the main harbor, where it would be loaded onto big ships and transported further down the river to Buenos Aires.

These islands are the youngest Argentine territory and continue to be formed every year. The Parana River carries a lot of sediment, which it drags from the lands it has flooded upstream, depositing it here in the delta. Held up by the reeds on the shores, the sediment slowly begins to form ridges and then it develops into new islands. The landscape of the delta is constantly changing.

I'm peacefully floating on the waters, hand in hand with Rodrigo, listening to the soothing voice of the guide telling us of the Indians who inhabited the islands before the white men came, and how they used to make an ointment from the white fluff of the willow trees, and how that cream could be used to cure every pain in the body.

I should try it out one day, I think. Maybe it works for polo bruises, too.

Polo. In the very next second my mind drifts and I'm back on a polo field, the smell of the horses all around me. Their hooves hit the ground with that unforgettable thunderous pounding and there are voices around me. Shouts. There are always shouts in polo and there's always something to shout about.

"Go for it! Your ball! Leave it!"

And then one unmistakable loud scream, as if coming from the bottom of his lungs. It's the Old Man.

"Che-e-e-ck! Check! Che-e-eck! Control your ho-o-o-rse!"

Is this for me? I wonder. If it is, I must be going too fast. Slow down. Slow down. Too fast means I might fall. The fall … I don't want to fall. Not again. I don't want to break—Too fast. I'm going too fast—

"Mi amor, estas bien?" Rodrigo squeezes my shoulder and I come back. I take a deep breath.

"Si, si," I murmur. The polo field has vanished and I'm back in the boat with him, immersed in the lush green and the calm waters of the delta, which tell me that everything is all right, I won't fall from a horse again, this man loves me and we'll find a way to work through our differences.

LATER THAT EVENING

We're going out dancing. Finally. In all the time we've been together, he's never taken me out dancing. It was kind of difficult last year anyway, since most of the time we spent together involved one huge cast on my right arm up to my shoulder, and when the cast was gone the arm would stubbornly refuse to move. And when it did move, so did I—to another country.

But in Barcelona he promised me he'd take me out as soon as I arrived in Buenos Aires, and tonight was going to be that night.

"I'll come and pick you up around midnight," he said, as he dropped me at home after the trip to Tigre. "Wear high heels, please. I don't care that you will be taller than me. The highest heels you have. And a sexy dress. You will be the most *linda* in the *boliche* tonight."

So I make sure I am. I take out my gold platform heels, which make me exactly ten centimeters taller than Rodrigo, and a short black dress. I'm beaming. We're finally going out dancing!

He comes to pick me up dressed in his usual black T-shirt and dark jeans. He has shaved for the occasion, and I don't tell him I much prefer the standard Argentine unshaved look. He takes me to a nice place, a disco that's only just starting to fill up. People go dancing very late in this country.

We have a drink—Campari Orange for both of us, our favorite drink. We dance and it's kind of weird, given my new height, but we try to ignore it. We chat, dance, and drink some more. We're both tired. It must be the trip to Tigre and the heat of the day.

And yet, the memory of another night in a disco pops up in my brain and it doesn't want to go away, no matter how much I try to silence it. It was last year, here in Buenos Aires before I broke my arm, and even before I started going out with Rodrigo. For a second I'm back there and I feel the hungry lips of the football player I'd been dancing with all night meeting mine and I shiver. It all comes back to me—the lust, the dance, the music, the magic. Our bodies intertwined, dancing the sensual *bachata*. The disappointment in his eyes in the morning when I told him he wouldn't be coming home with me. My sadness as I got into a taxi and left him there. He promised to call. He didn't. In Argentina, a lot of men promise to call and don't, I was told.

Rodrigo was one who did. And because he called we've arrived here, in this disco, almost a year later, despite lots of conversations with my sensible self, who tried hard to persuade me to stop this madness. We're here, but there's no lust in his eyes tonight and we don't dance too much, either. By 3:30, just as the disco starts filling up, we decide to go home.

And that uneasy chill between us, the same chill that I felt the whole day, comes back home with us too.

Something isn't quite right. I'm not sure what, but there's definitely something.

SUNDAY 6TH NOVEMBER

I always get nervous the day before my birthday. That's because I get into a "How old am I and what have I done with my life?" train of thought, and I hate this train of thought.

So I suggest we go to the *Feria de Mataderos* today, just to run away as far as possible from these thoughts. The only good thing about my approaching birthday is that I'll spend it with Rodrigo and I'm sure it's going to be a romantic one. Things are always romantic with him.

The *Feria de Mataderos* is still where I saw it last year, but this year it feels a bit faded and looks like it's shrunk. Maybe I'm no longer a tourist and I've started to see things with the eyes of a local.

The stalls of the artisan market don't stretch forever as I remember them from last year. This time they just barely cover the main junction. The podium in the middle, where I admired folk dances last year, is still there but no one is on it. There's no show today, or maybe we're too early. The stands selling *gaucho* clothing, leathers, and *mate* cups are still there, but there are fewer than I remember. Someone is selling cheese in a corner and I ask if they have sheep's cheese. The thing I miss most from home is sheep's cheese. No, they don't. He tells me that sheep's cheese costs a fortune to produce, hence they don't make it. And yet Argentina has lots of sheep. Maybe they're missing the shepherds. Maybe there's a business opportunity to be had importing shepherds.

Rodrigo and I walk hand in hand under the scorching noon sun. He looks like he could do with some more sleep. I locate the *empanada* stand, the same one where last year I had my first-ever *empanada*. Fortunately, it's still there. I ask them if they have vegetarian ones. They say they do. Then I ask them if they have any with meat, for Rodrigo.

"*Mi amor!* You're in Argentina. Don't ask this ever again. It's embarrassing. Of course they have empanadas with meat." He looks at me with shocked eyes.

"It's not a big deal. I'm just a tourist," I say.

But I'm not. I've come to this country with three suitcases in the hope of making a life here with this guy. I told everyone I came simply for polo, like I have done every year for the past three years. But in my heart, I felt this time was different. Not a tourist any longer. Maybe I should learn the local customs then. No more questions about meat *empanadas*.

One last stroll through the stalls, I buy some bread and cheese for home and we're ready for the one-hour drive back. It wasn't worth coming all the way here, I think, as we get back into the car.

On the way back, the birthday blues return in full force.

"What shall we do tonight?" I ask, trying to guess if he has a surprise in store for me.

"Whatever you want, *mi amor*. It's your birthday night."

"Shall we go out, then?"

"Of course, *mi amor*. We'll go out. I'll come pick you up at 10. We'll go out for dinner."

10 pm is a very reasonable time to go and have dinner in Argentina. I've long ago stopped wondering why people eat so late here.

Rodrigo leaves me at home and goes to have a siesta at his place. I spend the next three hours in meditation, trying to calm my nerves. Why do I feel so restless anyway? No answer. Just my mind racing, my pulse beating, and my body cringing. Something is wrong; I'm just not sure what.

And then I remember how I went to a healer once, here in Argentina. The equivalent of a lady with a crystal, but this one was a man. He was actually a birthday gift from Gabriela, who doesn't really believe in such things, but she knows I do, so she booked me a session with the local healer in the town where they live—to sort me out, she'd said. This was two years ago and I had a lot to sort out. A polo fall that resulted in both arms broken, troubles at work, my home recently burgled, and my single status unchanged for a very long time. I went to the healer, who told me I should do everything I wanted before I turned forty-two.

"Why?" I asked, but got no answer.

So now, on the verge of actually turning forty-two, I remember all this with a sudden new thought taking shape. What if I'm about to die? Maybe he meant something will happen and I'll die at forty-two. I laugh at my fear, but the thought keeps coming back, no matter how much I push it away.

By 9:30 I'm ready, but Rodrigo texts me to meet him downtown. I get into the taxi, still trying to get rid of my paranoia involving a sudden end to my life at forty-two, the age I'll be in precisely two hours. I'm annoyed at myself for being such a nutter. I'm also annoyed at him for not coming to pick me up. Maybe he was busy organizing a surprise for me? Whatever happens tonight, sudden end of life or lovely surprise, I'm about to find out.

And I do find out. We meet downtown. We go into the first restaurant that takes our fancy as we stroll through Palermo. Rodrigo hasn't booked anywhere but he tells me we'll surely find something. And easily enough we do. We find a place that serves traditional *asados* and *empanadas*, with candles on rustic tables and low music in the background. We eat and hold hands. Midnight comes and goes with no events. No sudden end of life. No surprises from Rodrigo, either. No present. No flower, no cake, no candle, except the one that burns on the table as a standard decoration. Nothing. *Nada.* He hadn't prepared anything because he said he was out of money. He received his salary too late on Saturday. He barely managed to pay for the internet and that was urgent. You heard when they called me. But he will have a present for me, so I shouldn't worry about anything.

I say nothing and pay the bill at the restaurant. He asks me if I'm sure I want to pay it, because "*Mi amor,* in Argentina the birthday person usually doesn't pay anything."

I say OK then, does he want to pick it up? No, actually no, since I said I would pay it, why don't I go ahead.

I feel like throwing up as I pay the bill and we head home. He asks me why I'm so quiet. I say that maybe it would have been nice if he had a little present for me. He gets angry and tells me I've ruined it now, because he was going to have a present for me tomorrow. My nausea is intensifying. I desperately want him to go to his place but I can't bring myself to tell him, and he doesn't go. We go to my place together instead, and I have a distinct feeling that my dark predictions for the night have come true. Something in me has died indeed and it happened right at midnight, the second I turned forty-two. The same moment I realized Rodrigo had no present for me.

Nothing.

MONDAY 7TH NOVEMBER

I felt it when it happened. The break. The clean-cut break that restored us to two separate human beings with an abyss between them. No longer souls dancing together in the middle of a world that was melting around us.

Love, or what was left of it, decided to depart at some point after midnight on my birthday as we both lay wide awake in bed, pretending to be asleep.

I feel his move to touch me, and my body cringes and closes down as soon as his hand finds my shoulder. My body has never done this before, not ever with him. He withdraws his hand.

"I'm sorry," I whisper. "Give me some time, I'll be all right."

And we both know it's a lie.

Some minutes later a blast of cold air passes over us and we both shake. And then it's gone and we're left frozen, lying side by side, awake in the darkness, waiting for the morning light like inmates on death row.

At exactly 4:50 he gets up, seconds before his alarm goes off, and goes to work. I see him to the door. He tells me I should stay in bed, no need to see him off.

"Cuídate," he says as he gives me a brief kiss in the doorway.

What a weird thing to say, I think as I get back into the bed. *Cuídate.* Take care of yourself. They say that when someone leaves on a trip. But I'm going to see him tonight at the birthday dinner Rosario has prepared for me in Lobos.

The morning goes by in a blur. I answer happy birthday messages, go to a café to eat *medialunas* and catch the bus for Lobos at midday. Rodrigo sends me a grumpy text asking for the address for tonight. He slept badly, he says.

Yes, I know, me too. Go to sleep after work, then come to dinner, I text him back.

Dale, he says. This means OK. Still sounding grumpy, I register. I also register there are no happy birthday wishes from him. There was one last night, at 12 o'clock precisely, right before he told me he'd got nothing else for me.

I get on the bus with the distinct feeling someone has just stabbed me in the heart and the knife is still there, and that my heart is bleeding badly. I have no idea why that is and what I can do about it.

It takes two hours to get to Lobos by bus and, in the absence of anything better to do, I close my eyes and try to meditate. Meditation is like writing—whatever happens, you can go back to it. It's always there, waiting. Even when you have trouble actually doing it, it's still there, offering you a convenient escape from reality.

I focus on this feeling of a stab in the heart and try to have a conversation with it. It's so acute and so irrational that I doubt it wants to talk to me, but I try anyway.

"What is this?" my mind asks.

"Blood," my heart answers.

"Why is there blood?"

"Because it hurts, you stupid."

"OK, what exactly hurts? Can you please describe? Nothing happened. *No pasa nada.* Like they say in Argentina. He sent me a text asking for the address. I'm going to see him later and he'll probably have a gift for me this time. After all, it's still my birthday. And don't call me stupid, please. I'm not stupid. I'm just rational."

"You're clearly clueless," my heart answers.

"I really don't see why you make such a big fuss," my mind continues accusingly.

"Because you don't see, you just think. That's why you're so stupid. So busy thinking that you're missing the essence."

"And what is the essence, you silly?"

"The essence is that love is gone."

"And when did it go exactly?"

"Last night at approximately 1:30 am."

"Why then?"

"That is when the cold wind came and your body cringed at his touch."

"Ah, that. *No pasa nada.* We'll be fine. Next time it will be better."

"No, it won't."

"How do you know, you silly?"

"Because I felt like this before."

"No, you didn't feel like this. And he's not like the others."

"He's not, but when love goes, it feels the same. And don't tell me what I feel and what I don't. You're clueless about feelings anyway."

My mind is getting annoyed at all these insults.

"It's not gone, you imbecile. Love, I mean. He's only gone to work. He's tired. He will sleep. Then he'll wake up and feel better, put a smile on his face, and come to dinner with a present."

"Yes, it's gone, I can feel it. That's why there's blood everywhere and a big knife stuck right here in the middle of me," my heart answers. "As for him coming to dinner, do you want to bet?"

No, I don't want to bet. Betting against my heart is tricky business. I've done it a few times and it didn't end well. But I can't take this irrational shit as truth, either. There must be a way I can convince this imbecile that she's totally, utterly, and simply wrong. But after about one hour of this internal dialogue, I feel I'm getting nowhere. Deadlock between heart and mind. I'm familiar with this situation. There's no need to insist. It only makes the heart ache more and the mind get angrier.

So I give up. I open my eyes instead and look around, trying to find some diversion from all these thoughts. As soon as I do this, the woman two seats away to my left shouts out in surprise.

"Roxy!"

It turns out I've been sitting next to Rosario's mother the whole way.

After the customary hugs and kisses and *tanto tiempo*, so good to see you again, it turns out that Rosario's mother had been taking a nap while I was busy reconciling my heart and mind and woke up just at the same time as I gave up on my internal dialogue.

They're like this, the Argentines. They turn up from nowhere and land in your life just when you need them most. And a friendly conversation is exactly what I need right now.

When the bus finally reaches Lobos, Rosario comes to pick me up and finds me arm in arm with her mother. She also finds me with my mood significantly improved and the bloody heart silenced and left to sort out her own silly thoughts.

We go to Rosario's new place. It's the first time I've seen it. It's a lovely country house on the outskirts of Lobos, which she shares with her boyfriend and her teenage son. During one of my previous trips I'd spent two weeks with Rosario in her old place, a small house in the middle of the *campo*, which had a lot of pictures of Frida Kahlo, the Mexican artist who was very unhappy in love. I'd told her then that I thought Frida brought bad luck for love. But Rosario is an art teacher and she adores Frida Kahlo and she wouldn't take the pictures down. In her new place there are no photos of the crazy artist, and Rosario is very much in love with her new boyfriend. I must have been right about Frida.

Maybe it's because of Frida, but all my heartache comes back with a force that takes me by surprise as soon as we enter the house.

"Ro, he won't come. I can feel it. He won't come tonight."

"Why would he not come? He said he was coming, right?" She looks at me, her big brown eyes round with surprise.

"I don't know. It's irrational. There's this voice in me telling me he won't come."

I tell her about last night, about the chill in the air, the missing gift. She listens with that "things are going to be all right" type of smile. But then I tell her more. The journey to Tigre, are you taking me with you to Europe? About the drama of Friday afternoon when he wanted to leave and he'd checked if he had any of his belongings in my place.

Her smile is instantly gone. "What did he tell the landlady? Tell me again. That you and he meet in various countries and travel the world together? Roxy!" I detect alarm in her voice. "This is really not OK. The gift, yes, he can recover from that. But this … this is really not right."

"Oh, Ro, if you think so, I'm scared what Gabriela will say."

Of the two of them Rosario is the mild one. Gabriela is the tough one. Rosario is the one who would say give him a chance. Gabriela would say give him no fucking chance.

We're so lost in deep conversation about the pros and cons of the new love of my life, we don't notice that the gates have been left open and Rosario's dog has taken the chance to run away.

"Gordo! Where is Gordo?" Rosario is suddenly struck by panic as she discovers her dog has gone missing.

Gordo means fat in Spanish. In Argentina it's a very common nickname. Someone is either fat—that is *gordo,* or slim—that is *flaco*. There's not much room for any in-between category. Things are either black or white in this country.

Gordo is a sweet Boxer dog who's in the habit of running away from home. It's not the first time he's done it and he never comes back by himself. So, we prepare an expedition—Rosario and me in the car, Rosario's boyfriend on one bike, and her son on another. We all set out on the streets to look for Gordo.

Three hours later we still haven't found the dog, but the upshot is that we get time to have a proper girly catch-up in the car while we drive around town. We stop to order the pizzas for my birthday dinner and then we go to buy the drinks, and it's in that little shop that I get a text message from Rodrigo. He just woke up, still feels tired, and just realized it's more than an hour and a half's drive to Lobos. And it's 7:30 already.

No te preocupes, mi amor, I write back with shaking fingers. *If you feel too tired to come, don't worry about it.*

I'm setting a trap in cold blood and he falls into it.

But are you going to be all right if I don't come to your birthday dinner? I hate to disappoint you on your birthday.

Don't worry, I text back. *Have a rest. I'm fine. I'll see you when I get back home on Wednesday.*

No, I won't, I think as I press send. But damn him if I'll admit how much it hurts.

And damn that silly heart too, and her ways of guessing the future.

I show the text message to Rosario. "He won't come."

"Roxy, I'm so sorry." Her eyes open wide. "I guess you were

right in what you felt today, that he won't come. Incredible. You felt it."

I did. And I told him I was fine about it. Did I push him not to come? Does it really matter? The only thing that matters right now is that he isn't here.

"Let's go home," Rosario says.

We get back into the car in silence. There's no dog and no Rodrigo either, and it's about time we give up hope on both.

At home we all gather around the table—Rosario, her boyfriend, her son, her mother. And Gabriela and Patricio, who have just arrived.

"Hey, Roxy! What the fuck, I thought you'd never want to leave your love nest in the city. I thought you were never coming to see us again."

That's Gabriela and her characteristic swearing every other word. I give her one big hug. And one for Patricio too. I missed them lots.

"Where's your boyfriend?" They ask me one by one and I have to tell each and every one of them that Rodrigo isn't coming. Why is he not coming? Because he feels tired after work and doesn't feel like driving for one and a half hours. They don't say anything. They clearly don't want to spoil my birthday, not more than it already is, anyway. In their eyes I read a silent condemnation.

But there's no silent condemnation from Gabriela. She doesn't really do things silently.

"Why the fuck is he not coming? What do you mean it's too long to drive? It's your birthday, for fuck's sake."

So I give her a few more details—the night before, no birthday gift, I paid for the dinner. I don't even have time to say anything else because she's already furious.

"I had a bad feeling about this guy all along. All along, I tell you. Ever since last year. I really, really didn't like the sound of him."

"But Gabriela, you've never met him!"

"Don't need to. I have a sense for these things, you know? A good sense. Here, open your present."

She has two books for me. One is a cookery book. This is because Gabriela loves cooking and I hate it, and she has a secret ambition to turn me around on this one. "*Te vamos a sacar buena,*" she used to say. We'll make you good in the end. The other present is a relationship advice book. She actually bought the books before she knew Rodrigo would not show up.

"Gabriela! How on earth did you know he wouldn't come and that I would need a book on relationship advice?" I can't believe the foresight of her gift.

"Darling, it wasn't hard to guess that sooner or later this romance would turn sour. Not to me, at least."

Yes, she never liked him.

But I don't want to talk about this now. It's my birthday dinner. We eat pizza and have wine, and I eat too much pizza and have way too much wine, and I hope, desperately hope, that the tears I'm keeping in won't come out. I won't let him spoil my dinner, I won't, I promise myself.

Rosario brings in a huge birthday cake—the one she's spent the whole afternoon baking. In fact, I have two cakes, because Gabriela has baked one as well, and they both come in with candles. It feels like I have two birthdays in one. Just to compensate for the sorrow, I think. They start to sing, but I blow out the candles halfway through the happy birthday song because I can't afford to wait a second longer, otherwise the tears will come, and I really don't want to cry.

Hugs. Kisses. More gifts. More wine. More cake. More love pouring from each and every one of these people around the table. I feel it coming to me in waves and it feels soothing and healing. The pain of the empty chair to my right starts slowly fading, hidden by their voices and laughter, and the sound of the clicking glasses. My tears remain hidden.

Rosario talks about her love story with Tete. Tete is her parrot, a huge, green-feathered, talking parrot who lives in a big cage by the front door. He wasn't always sentenced to live in a cage. There was a time, several years ago, when Rosario and Tete were in love. Tete would fly all over the house and come to sit on Rosario's shoulder. She would feed him a little piece of everything she ate. She even gave him a little bit of wine from her glass one night and the poor bird collapsed, almost in an alcohol-induced coma. But there was no way she could not share things with him. He was jealous and possessive and wanted to try everything she ate. She took him driving with her, and Tete would sit on the wheel of her car and would wait patiently for her while she parked and went about her business. When her son was smaller and needed to be picked up from school, Rosario showed up with Tete on her shoulder, until her son asked her desperately to leave the bird at home otherwise his classmates would think he had a crazy mother. But despite what everyone said or thought, Rosario and Tete were inseparable.

Tete was a talking parrot and had learned to call Rosario by her name and imitate her quite well. One day, he flew away from home and didn't know how to get back. Tete had always lived in captivity. Tall trees were scary for him. All of Rosario's family went looking for him in the woods, shouting the bird's name, but he answered only to Rosario's voice. He heard her call "Tete," and he answered, "Ro," and then she called again and he answered again. Slowly, slowly, he came down from the tall tree where he had ended up and came to sit on her shoulder. She had been broken-hearted without him, and he seemed more content than ever to find her again. And their love story continued, until one day when the unthinkable happened. Tete bit Rosario's finger. It came about unexpectedly and it hurt a lot, since Tete has a big beak that could easily sever a finger. That day something died between them. Ro put Tete in a cage and never let him free again in the house. Tete dropped his head in sadness and accepted his punishment. Years have passed, and Tete remains just a bird in a cage, occasionally calling out Rosario's name. "Ro, R-o-o-o, R-o-o-o." She opens the door of the cage and gives him a piece of banana, which he takes delicately with his big beak, taking care to never frighten her again. But she could never forgive him, she said. The day he bit her, their love died.

I get close to tears as I listen to the impossible love story between a woman and a bird. Or maybe it's the wine. Or maybe just the care I feel from all of them. My big, caring Argentine family, who are all around me on my birthday, sharing crazy stories so that I don't have too much time to think of my own crazy story.

And when I simply can't have any more cake and wine, and I'm stuffed to the point of explosion, Patricio and Gabriela load me into their car and take me to their new house. It's the first time I've seen it finished. They've spent the last three years building it, and I remember having visited it in various stages of construction during my four previous trips to Argentina. Now it's finally ready. *El Puesto.* The place, as they call it, because every house has a name here. It stands tall and proud in the middle of the fields, some ten minutes' drive from the old family farm.

I fall asleep in the deep silence of the *campo*, too tired to think about anything. I don't even check my phone to see if there are any messages from Rodrigo. I know there are none. But I'm surrounded by friends and by the silence of the night in the middle of the Argentine pampas and, right now, this is all that matters.

TUESDAY 8TH NOVEMBER

I wake up in what feels like a modern art museum misplaced in the middle of the wilderness. Gabriela and Patricio's new place is a work of art. Decorated by Gabriela, it carries the mark of her unconventional, eclectic, artistic sense. Pretty unfriendly to a vegetarian, but I don't mind. There are cow hides on the floor as carpets and cow horns in the living room as decoration. A fox fur, complete with nose and whiskers, lies on one of the arms of the sofa. I have to admit it looks so real I almost jumped away in shock when I saw it. Bright silk curtains cover the wide windows of the living-room. Gabriela bought the sparkling fabric in Dubai and had the curtains made in Buenos Aires. The grey of the flowers on the bright blue background matches the exact grey shade of the walls and the huge stone fireplace. A tree branch decorated with light bulbs lights the guest toilet and it seems as though it's been dropped there straight out of a Harry Potter movie. A long wooden table, with several chairs of all different shapes, all reconditioned with different fabric, takes center stage in the kitchen. Next to the table is an old wooden cupboard, freshly painted in bright pink, that holds wine glasses and Gabriela's exquisite homemade jams. A brand new dishwasher and cooker are still wrapped up, waiting to be installed.

I walk around their house, marveling at the fusion of new and old, raw and refined, natural and high tech, Europe and Argentina. The house feels warm, welcoming, authentic, and a little bit crazy. Just like them.

In the morning Gabriela moves to a full-frontal attack. It's not my birthday any longer, so there's no need to go slow. She wants to know all there is to know about Rodrigo and "why the fuck he didn't show up last night." I lodge myself under a quinoto tree in front of their house and I tell her incoherent bits and pieces of the story as I eat the mini orange-like fruit directly from the tree.

I tell her about how well the first weekend went and that it was all perfect. Then about how things seemed to change on Friday. The moment when he said he wanted to leave forever, the trip to Tigre, the question about being taken to Europe—the verb *llevar*—the night before my birthday. I don't tell her about the comment to the landlady. She would explode if she heard about that one, too.

But she decides she's heard enough, anyway.

"A fucking scam, this guy. This is it. He was trying to take advantage of you and when he realized he couldn't, he dropped you. As simple as that. He dropped you on your birthday."

I suddenly felt a quinoto fruit stuck in my throat. "What do you mean?"

"Well, silly, let's recap. You come here and he says he wants to go to Colombia for a holiday. Right?"

"Yes, right."

"And what did you say?"

"That I'm happy to go if he can afford it. He said he could. Then I said all right, we'll go and buy the flight tickets as soon as he's got the money."

"Bingo. At least you're not completely dumb and you had enough sense of self-preservation not to offer to pay for his ticket."

"Of course I didn't. What do you think—that I would have paid for his holiday?"

"Not me, silly. He thought you would. Did he mention anything else about Colombia after this discussion?"

"Err, not really." I omit the remark about saving the money I was going to pay for a parking space so that we can spend it on holiday.

"Then tell me, who paid for things this week?"

"Well, we didn't do much; we only cooked and ate at home."

"Who paid for the shopping?"

"I did."

"For the bread and everything?"

"I did."

"Did he offer to pay?"

"No."

"Did he actually buy anything?"

"No. But wait. He did actually buy me lunch on Saturday. When I arrived."

"Did he pay for anything after that?"

"No."

"And the marriage question. Why on earth would he discuss

marriage on Wednesday, when you only just got here two days before and you were going to stay for three months?"

"I don't know. It was rather strange." I shrug my shoulders. I really have no explanation. But she has.

"I tell you why. Because the guy was evaluating the situation. Were you going to get married to him so that he could get the papers to go to Europe and were you going to finance his lifestyle, his holidays, and ultimately his ticket to Europe? And when you told him 'no' to all of these questions he decided you were a bad investment and not even worth a birthday present. So he conveniently enjoyed another dinner the night before your birthday, another meal paid by you, and then he disappeared."

I suddenly stop breathing. I stare at Gabriela but she doesn't see me. She looks at the quinoto tree, gauging where to pick next, and decides eventually to grab a branch high up, filled with the small ripe fruit.

"Here, have some." She hands me a handful of quinotos from the branch as I slowly recover my breath.

"But, Gabriela, he didn't disappear. He wants to see me on Wednesday when I'm back in Buenos Aires."

"So why did he not come last night, then?"

"I know that was bad. Maybe he was intimidated at the thought of meeting all of you."

"Of course he was. We're your family here. Of course he was intimidated. We would have asked him questions. We would have seen right through him. He wouldn't have been able to keep his fucking game up with us. Of course he knew this, that's why he didn't come. Plus, no show, no present, right? He didn't have to invest in a fucking present."

I'm silent. I don't even feel like eating quinotos any longer. She's harsh, but some of the things she says make sense.

"But, Gabriela, what if we've judged him badly, and he really was just intimidated?"

"And how about the show on Friday?" she launches back. "The fucking show when he said he wanted to leave? I tell you what that was. He wanted to see how hooked you were. He was testing you. Were you going to start crying and plead with him not to go? And what did you do? I'm actually so proud of you. You showed him the door and said, 'Fucking go.' So he realized, fuck, she's not as hooked as I'd hoped. So, basically, in one week you told him you're not giving him a European passport by marrying him, you're not paying for his ticket to Europe, and you're not paying for his holiday to Colombia either. And you're not even enough hooked emotionally for him to start playing games with you. Bad news for him. Really bad."

She picks up another quinoto fruit and throws it into her mouth, as if all there is to say about the subject has now been said.

"But, still, he says he wants to see me on Wednesday," I repeat, stubbornly.

"Well, darling, you still paid for the dinners, didn't you? Maybe he wants another free meal," she answers, chewing on the fruit.

"Gabriela, it can't be that bad." I've lost my appetite for quinotos. I'm busy trying to stop myself from bursting into tears.

"Oh yes, it is. Go speak to Patricio if you don't believe me. I'm seeing things so fucking clearly there is no way this guy is anything else but a scam. But go speak to Patricio, ask him what he thinks. He's a man. Maybe he understands the guy better."

I talk to Patricio in the car as we head over to watch a tournament in Pilar, where a few friends of theirs are playing this afternoon. They take me with them, even though I'm not invited. *No pasa nada.* Of course you can come with us, they say.

I plan to ask him, but he asks me first, as he's driving and Gabriela is soundly asleep next to him on the front seat. Gabriela always falls asleep in cars. I wonder how she does it.

"So, Roxy, tell me about this guy, then. What's going on?"

I tell him, all of it. No show, no gift, no payment for anything.

The marriage discussion. The scene on Friday evening when he wanted to leave. The question about being taken to Europe.

"So, this guy wants to marry you on Wednesday and then wants to leave you on Friday?" Patricio tries to get his head around my bits of information. "All because you didn't meet in the city, where you were supposed to meet?"

"Yes, well, we argued. And yes, he said he wanted to leave. But then when I told him to go, he didn't. He said he didn't want to go, actually."

"Roxy, this doesn't look right." Unlike Gabriela, Patricio is very calm in his assessment. "It doesn't look right to me. And he didn't come yesterday. I get it that maybe he was intimidated. But a man who says on Wednesday that he wants to marry you should have the courage to come and meet your friends three days later. This is really not good."

Silence. He drives on as I struggle to find something to say.

"Yes, but maybe there's an explanation. Maybe I can meet him again. Maybe we can still be together. Maybe it can still be fun."

"Fun?" Patricio throws me a quick, serious look through the rear-view mirror. "No, Roxy, not with him. If you want to have fun, do it with whoever else you want. Pick that guy in the street if you want." He points to a random guy we drive by. "Or another one. Whoever you want. But not him. Not a guy who treats you like this. Why didn't he come last night? He was afraid to meet us, that's why, and it's because he knows he's not treating you right."

"Of course he was afraid to meet us." Gabriela wakes up suddenly and catches the last part of the discussion. "We would see right through him."

Patricio doesn't say anything anymore. He doesn't need to. I get it. The verdict is not good.

Later, as we watch the polo game, the words of my friends are still going around in my mind. A new version of reality unfolds and I can see it more and more clearly. I came here with ninety kilograms of luggage to build a life with a guy who promised me the world and then vanished a week later, precisely on my birthday. A guy who has been a scam all along. This part is actually harder to digest than the vanishing part. His whispers, his caresses, the way he looked at me, the way he called me *linda*. How could all this be a scam? And yet my friends' words ring again in my ears and their cold, rational analysis slowly makes its way into my brain. A scam. Only a scam.

On the field a player manages to save a near-goal then takes the ball all the way to the other side of the field and scores. My jaw drops. I haven't seen anything like this before. My internal dialogue suddenly disappears. I can't think and watch polo at the same time. And thank God there's still polo. Nothing is going to take that away from me. A guy may be a scam, my ninety kilograms of luggage might serve no purpose at the moment, but polo—well, polo is always here. Waiting for me. No matter how bad things are, they can't be that bad. There's still polo.

I'll be on a horse soon, I think. I'll deal with this. I've had breakups before, and polo has helped me though them, too. It will help me again. It's here for me, it always has been and always will be.

I take a deep breath in. Thank God there's still polo.

And good friends, I add. I look round at Gabriela and Patricio, both absorbed in watching the game. They're here for me again, just as they were last year when I broke my arm. Just like they were two years ago when I needed to escape somewhere for my fortieth birthday. Just like three years ago when I hurt my back and couldn't walk for a few days. They're here for me again. And they come bundled up with polo too. Life is definitely not that bad.

Evening falls and it's time to go back to Buenos Aires. And I'm tired, too tired to think of anything any longer and especially not of the text message that arrives just as I reach home:

Will I see you tomorrow?

I don't want to see him tomorrow, but I've got no strength left to answer just now.

I'll do it tomorrow.

WEDNESDAY 9TH NOVEMBER

I wake up early and I call my lady-with-a-crystal number one back in England. I call her and not the other two, since she's been the most supportive of the story with Rodrigo so far. And I need urgent advice. I give her a summary of the situation. She laughs and tells me all is good. I tell her it doesn't feel good.

"All is good," she insists.

She tells me to meet with Rodrigo and make up with him because he really is the guy for me and he loves me, and that he didn't have a present for my birthday because he was planning to propose on my birthday.

This all sounds very wrong to me.

"But I told him I don't want to get married. Why would he still want to propose?" I don't get it. I just don't get it.

She tells me he's a romantic. I'm still not convinced.

"And how about my friends' suspicions that he expects me to pay for everything?"

She thinks my friends are wrong. They're not on the same path to enlightenment as I am. She thinks I'm on a path to enlightenment because I talk to her and she talks to angels. She says the angels tell her that things will be all right between us. That he loves me and I love him and that's all that counts.

"But how about money? This thing about paying for everything?" I urge her, still skeptical.

She says hang on a second, she needs to ask the angels. She spends a few minutes in a private conversation. Then she tells me that they—the angels—do indeed confirm that the guy expects me to pay for everything. Thank God they do. I was starting to doubt they could actually see things clearly.

"But you can talk to him about this and reverse this expectation. Don't worry," she says cheerfully, as if this is really not that big a deal. I guess she really likes Rodrigo and she's the only supporter he's got left.

I'm still not convinced.

"But he didn't make it to my birthday dinner," I cry, frustrated.

She tells me I'm an enlightened, powerful woman and that I'll find in my heart the strength to forgive him.

"But I don't want to forgive him. What happens if I simply don't want to forgive him for this and if I actually want a man in my life who makes it to my birthday dinner?"

"Ah. That is your free will." She can't interfere with my free will. Not even the angels can. If I don't want to forgive him, well, I shouldn't. But I'll lose a guy who truly loves me. Truly. This is what the angels say.

The allocated hour is up before I can persuade the angels of the contrary. She keeps her opinion. I keep mine. I apologize to the angels in my mind. I tell them I really want my boyfriend with me at my birthday dinner table. Ideally showing up with a present. I hope the angels can understand this.

And then I forget all about the conversation. That's the beauty of talking to a lady with a crystal. When she tells you something you don't agree with, you can simply ignore it and forget about the money you paid for the advice. Just wipe it away. No one will know, anyway.

As soon as I'm done with my lady with a crystal, I have another call, this time from Gabriela. She tells me I should go back to the farm with her and that I need to turn my mind to something else, and maybe playing some polo would be just what I need right now. She's discussed it with Patricio and they both agree it's a good idea for me to come and spend the rest of the week with them. She says she doesn't want me alone in the city. She doesn't want me to see Rodrigo again. She doesn't want me hurt. That's a very different perspective from that of the lady with a crystal. But I can see the sense in what she's saying.

"OK, I'll come. I don't want to get hurt either. I'll come back to the farm with you," I tell her.

Polo will save me once again. Polo, fresh air, the *campo*, and supportive friends. They're just what I need right now.

With this fresh conviction, I finally find the courage to text Rodrigo and tell him he shouldn't come tonight since I won't be there. I'll be back at the farm with my friends. And that I need a few days to think about how things sit between us because I didn't like how my birthday turned out.

This text message almost makes me faint. Basically, it's a breakup message, but I don't have the guts to say it. I just say I need time to think and hope he'll buy that. But he doesn't. Rodrigo, being Argentine, can read minds. They all do here.

You're going to leave me, he texts back. *And if you are, I'm not going to stop you. I just want you to know that I love you.*

That's a full-frontal blow about the height of my heart. I don't answer. I pack my gym bag instead and run out to meet my Augustin for an emergency training session, to help erase Rodrigo from my mind.

But no matter how hard I push on the bike or lift the weights, Rodrigo is still there, and the letters of his text message dance in front of my eyes one by one. *I love you.* Maybe the lady with a crystal is right. Maybe he truly loves me and this whole thing has been one big, terrible misunderstanding. Maybe I should call the other ladies with a crystal for some reinforcement. By lunchtime I'm almost crying. I check his message again and I notice he has changed his profile picture to the saddest picture I've ever seen—a small robot, disintegrating under the rain. The message is clear. He's suffering. I take another look at the picture and fight a strong urge to call him right there in the locker of the gym, to tell him I love him, I don't want to break up with him, and that things are going to be just fine.

But Gabriela's voice rings in my ears and is joined by Rosario's and Patricio's. No, no, no, they say. This isn't how you want to be treated by a man.

And, after all, I only said I wanted a few days to think about things. How about if I do just that? Give myself a few days to think about things and see how I feel? No need to make a decision right now. And with this thought, the pressure eases a bit. I put the phone back in my pocket. Little robot or not, I'm not going to call him right now. Instead, I call Gabriela and tell her I'll see her at the bus station this afternoon. I'm definitely going back with her.

Just before I leave my flat there's another text from Rodrigo saying he's at home. He got the day off because his boss found him crying at work.

I'm watching my hand shaking as I read this. I want to call him. I want to call him so badly, right now. I don't want him to suffer. I want to call him and tell him I love him. For the second time that day I see the faces of my friends lining up in front of my eyes. They all shake their heads. *Wait*, they say. *Wait!*

My hands are still trembling as I put the phone back into my pocket. OK, I'll wait. I can always call him tomorrow.

I meet Gabriela at the bus station finally and tell her about the messages in a choked voice.

"Bullshit," she cries. "It's all a scam. Be strong. Don't fall for this fucking shit."

"But, Gabriela, how do you know? Maybe the guy is really suffering. And the picture—look what a sad picture he put on."

I show her the picture and fresh tears appear in my eyes. I just can't bear looking at it.

"Don't you get it? This picture is a fucking message. Another one. Directed at you. He wants to manipulate your emotions. He wants you to feel sorry."

In this case he's done it. I feel sorry, so terribly sorry for making him suffer.

"But what if it's true that he's suffering?"

"Of course he is. He's suffering because his trip to Colombia is gone. Because his ticket to Europe is gone. Don't you get it, woman?

You were never meant to be anything else but this, his fucking check writer!"

"But Gabriela." I'm about to cry. "Maybe he did love me. He told me I was the woman of his life."

"And you were so stupid to believe this fucking bullshit," she concludes.

I close my eyes and say nothing else. He did love me. I know he did. I saw the light in him. And I remember his arms around me in the darkness of the night, and the way he stroked my hair. And our long conversations on the sofa, his soft brown eyes looking deeply into mine. And when we made love the whole world vanished. Gabriela doesn't know about these things, but I remember them well. They were part of my life until a few days ago.

Sos el amor de mi vida. You're the love of my life. His words still ring in my ears.

How could things change so fast? What happened?

My mind races, trying to understand, to discern the truth from falsehood in this game of mirrors. I know there's a part of this man that truly loves me. I know this for sure. I've seen it and it was beautiful. This is true. Definitely true. But it's not the whole story. Other things are true as well. Facts. Behaviors. Things he said. Things he did. Things he didn't do.

The bus is shaking and puffing, trying to negotiate its way out of Buenos Aires and the streets choked by traffic. Gabriela has fallen asleep next to me. I envy people who can sleep like this on buses. I can't. I go inside my own head and try to answer unanswerable questions instead.

Patricio comes to pick us up from the bus station in Lobos.

"Welcome back. It wasn't long this time. How are things?"

I give him an update as we take the dirt road towards the farm—the messages, the profile picture, Rodrigo crying at work today.

"Roxy, let me tell you one thing," he says. "No Argentine man will ever cry at work in front of his boss. Ever. Maybe only if his whole family had been killed in front of his eyes or something really serious like this. But not over breaking up with a girl, no way. I don't know about the rest of it, but this one particular message is bullshit."

"Are you sure?"

Patricio didn't usually give me definite opinions and this one sounded quite definite.

"Absolutely. It's a lie. Can you imagine one of the grooms working for me crying in front of me because his woman has left him? Can you imagine this?"

No, I can't. I picture Facundo, the solid middle-aged *gaucho* guy who grooms his horses, in tears. The picture refuses to take shape. I try again. No, definitely no shape.

"I'll have horses ready for you tomorrow morning. Go stick and ball. It will help get your mind on something else," he adds.

Ah, yes. When things are bad there's always polo. And that's enough to make things not that bad any longer. Tomorrow I'll be on a horse and I'll feel better, I tell myself, as I push away the thought of an Argentine man crying or not in front of his boss at work. Tomorrow I'll be on a horse. Thank God for that.

THURSDAY 10TH NOVEMBER

I wake up and check my phone immediately. No new messages from Rodrigo. His profile picture has changed again and the new one is from what appears to be a Halloween party. He's smiling and dancing, dressed as a doctor. There's another guy dressed as a devil behind him, half-seen in the picture. I show this to Gabriela, speechless.

"Fucking bastard. See? See how much he was suffering? It lasted only twenty-four hours."

"Why? Do you think he's actually out partying now?'

"No, silly, he's giving you a message. This picture is for you again. He couldn't get you to call him yesterday with the saddest picture and messages in the world, so today he's telling you, *Fuck you, I'm partying.* It's all designed to get a reaction from you, don't you see?"

I slowly start to see, even though I still don't believe what I'm seeing.

"Fuck him," she declares. "Just ignore it. Let's go ride."

There's nothing that can't be sorted out by the phrase, "Let's go ride."

But before we do, Rosario calls with good news. She has found Gordo. It's a small town and someone recognized the dog and brought him back. She wants to know the latest developments in my emotional drama. I give her a brief description of the party picture that replaced the sad robot picture of the day before.

"Roxy, forget about him. This guy is unstable. I think you should speak to a therapist. There's a good one in town. I can ask if he's got a vacancy for you."

Gabriela agrees readily. "That's a great idea. Maybe a therapist can sort you out. What the fuck you saw in this guy, I have no idea."

I take my polo bag and head towards the pony lines. I don't want to think about anything any longer. No Rodrigo, no therapist, no emotional instability, and definitely not about Gabriela's question about what I saw in this guy. I saw his light, but if I say this she will have me locked up in a mental institution immediately. Riding is the only thing that can help me right now.

Patricio is already at the pony lines talking to Facundo, the solid *gaucho* I tried in vain to imagine crying the day before. They're getting the horses ready for stick and ball. This is how we train in polo. We ride a horse and hit a ball with the mallet. We try to hit from different angles—forward hits, backward hits, angled shots or under the neck. This goes on until we're out of breath, which in my case happens quite quickly, or until the horse is out of breath, which brings that session to an end. Then we change horses and do the whole thing again. I never ride more than two horses, which is about one hour in total. Gabriela and Patricio ride five or six horses each and they're still not out of breath afterwards. I have no idea how they manage to do it.

I feel a bit nervous as I approach the pony lines. It's been three months since I last sat on a horse. Even though I've finally recovered from my fear of hitting a goalpost and I even played tournaments last summer, three months off a polo pony is still a long time. Tomorrow all the muscles in my body will ache. Even the ones I didn't know I possessed. But at least this will keep me from thinking.

Patricio is reading my thoughts, as usual. "Just take it easy today. Hit a few balls, go for a canter. Easy. It will come back to you, you'll see."

I tell him about the girls' verdict that I should see a therapist.

"Forget about it," he says, in his laconic style. "You don't need a therapist. You just need to stop thinking about this story. It's done. Finished. Now get on a horse and do some stick and ball. This is going to help you more than any therapy."

I open up my polo bag and take out my polo gear, item by item. I slip into my boots. I put on my helmet, which is bright blue and white, the same colors as those of the Argentine flag. I find my Oakley goggles and my riding gloves. I don't need the knee or elbow pads, as these are only for games. No one is going to ride me off as I stick and ball.

My right elbow pad has a stitch right through the length of it. Patricio had to cut it off my broken arm last year as I lay on a polo field, screaming in pain after my fall.

I show it to him. "Remember this? I sewed it back on."

He smiles. "It looks like new."

My arm looks like new as well. Luckily, I didn't need surgery and it recovered fast after six weeks in a cast and another three of physiotherapy. It didn't bother me and I almost forgot it had been broken. The other one—the one I broke two years ago—bothered me a lot more. I'd had surgery to insert screws in two different bones and then more surgery to remove them. In total I had four broken bones—two in each hand—in two separate polo falls. People asked me why I wanted to play again. It was hard to explain. Patricio and Gabriela didn't ask, though. They understood. They'd had their own falls, their own breaks, and their own scars. And they still played polo. It felt good to be with people who could understand.

But I still felt apprehensive as I watched Facundo bringing up one of the ponies.

"*Cómo se llama?*" I ask him. I always ask the names of the horses before I get on them.

"Amanda," he answers.

A mare. Most of the horses in polo are mares. They're more docile, they say. There are some geldings, too, but very rarely stallions. I can't imagine riding a stallion. Patricio has one and he keeps it tied up, separate from the mares. Poor thing, he always looks rather restless. What a price to pay to keep his balls.

But Amanda doesn't look restless. She looks *tranqui*—chilled—with her big brown eyes and long eyelashes. I decide I like her and that she's going to be an easy ride.

"*Tranquila?*" I ask Facundo.

"*Como una oveja.* Like a sheep. Super easy. Don't you worry about a thing."

Amanda waits patiently for me to get on and seems to submit peacefully to being described as a harmless sheep. I decide to call her Amanda the Sheep.

As soon as I feel the familiar touch of the saddle, my body takes over and shows me that yes, it remembers, and no, I don't need to think about it. Knees in, heels down, slightly rotated outwards, leg muscles tensed up, upper body relaxed. Stick lifted to my shoulder. Words I haven't used for a long time flowing out of my mouth in a whisper as I take the horse on to the field.

"Hello, sweetie. Nice to meet you. We'll be OK together. I promise. Just run with me. I'll look after you. And you'll be OK. I promise."

I always talk to the horses in my mind or in a whisper as soon as I get on them. They hear me, I'm sure. I can feel their body relaxing and I can see their ears moving. And I always make sure no one else hears me, otherwise they might think I'm a bit mad.

I lean slightly forward, bringing my left hand holding the four reins up the neck of the horse, and I think about running. The horse picks up on my thought, or maybe feels my body changing position, and she moves swiftly into a canter.

Feeling light as a feather, I take a long ride around the field getting to know Amanda the Sheep, giving her time to trust me and giving myself time to trust that I can still do this. Then I pick up a ball, one small, round white ball, and at the first click of the mallet as it strikes the ball my mind goes blank and I don't think of anything any longer. Once again, life has shrunk to just the field, the mallet, the ball, the horse beneath me, the wind on my face, and that intoxicating feeling of flying high.

The polo drug lasts a full hour and the two horses I ride that morning. But as soon as I jump off, the pain stabs once again, telling me it's still there no matter how much I try to cover it up. Gabriela is still on a horse; Patricio is busy with his grooms. Anyway, everything that could possibly be said about my broken-heart story has already been said. There's nothing more they can do for me, and it's about time I take healing into my own hands.

I take off my riding boots, head to a tree, and sit down underneath it to meditate. But before that, I need to talk to this pain inside. It's pretty clear it isn't going to leave soon unless I talk to it.

Two hours later I'm still under the same tree trying to talk to my pain. Unsuccessfully.

It goes like this:

"What are you?"

"Pain," it says.

No news there.

"Why are you here?"

Silence.

"Can I do anything to make you go away?"

"No."

"Do you want to tell me anything?"

"No."

"Come on, you can be a little bit more helpful than this."

"No, I can't. I'm just pain. I'm not supposed to be nice to anyone."

"OK, be grumpy then."

"I am."

After a while:

"And what am I supposed to do with you?"

"No idea, this is your problem."

"But look, I'm taking time to speak to you!"

"How very nice of you."

"Don't be ironic. It's not that easy, OK? You're not really pleasant to talk to."

"Then don't talk to me, you stupid. Go ride another horse. Get yourself busy with something. Anything."

"I will. In the afternoon. I'll ride again, don't you worry. So I can get rid of you."

"You won't," she says. "I'll come back to you. Disguised as muscle pain."

"Yes, I know, but that will be tomorrow. You won't come back until tomorrow. Tonight, I'll have a few hours of peace on the back of that horse."

"Perfect. You're sorted then."

"Stubborn bitch."

Silence. She doesn't like bad language.

"So, you still don't want to talk to me?" I try again, one last time.

"No, I don't. There's nothing you can do for me, anyway."

I give up and go to have lunch and a *siesta*. In the afternoon, I'll get back on the horse. I'll just ignore her. That will teach the bitch a lesson.

I manage to keep away from my phone until the evening. When I finally check it again there are no texts from him. There's one other message though, from Marco.

Happy belated birthday. Sorry, forgot. Are you done seducing young boys?

No surprise about the late birthday message. In the fifteen years I've known him, he's never got my birthday right. He's always a few days late. But a happy birthday message eventually arrives every year, and for Marco this is already a big thing. And I can't get angry with him, even if I try. He's one of those few people in the world who know me inside out and who have always been there for me, even when we haven't seen each other for years.

We met in Italy as fellow students on an MBA program and worked on a business plan together. The business never took off but our friendship did. He taught me Italian because he was too lazy to speak English and he taught me a lot of other things along the years, most notably about relationships and how to survive breakups. It would be impossible to imagine my life without Marco.

By "seducing young boys," he is referring to my love story with Rodrigo and the huge age difference between us. Nine months ago, when I saw Marco last, he told me to forget about this guy as soon as I left Argentina. I tried to follow his advice. Except Rodrigo came to London in the summer and our story started again, this time for good, or so I thought. Marco knew about it and this time restrained from giving me any new advice. But his opinion on the whole story never changed.

Thank you, I text back. *Yes, done. Story finished on my birthday.*

Can't say I'm not happy about it, he replies. *See you shortly. I'll be in Buenos Aires soon.*

One of the mysteries of my life will always be how Marco knows when I'm in a breakup situation and that I need him. He always shows up or calls. He has counseled me through many breakups in the past and will probably counsel me through this one as well. Except I don't feel like talking about it just now.

Maybe we'll talk about it later when he comes to Buenos Aires, and no doubt we'll go out for dinner, as we always do when we meet up in some corner of the world, both of us on business trips, or sometimes a polo trip for me. There have been considerably more polo trips than business trips lately.

FRIDAY 11TH NOVEMBER

I wake up in pain—muscle pain this time, but I'm happy about it. Muscle pain is better than heart pain. I can do things about muscle pain and I know it will go eventually. Heart pain is more complicated. It refuses to talk to me and I have no idea when and whether it will go away.

There's no message from Rodrigo. The party picture is still there. I put the phone away and go back to riding. I hear no more therapy suggestions, no more "fucking bastard" from Gabriela. Patricio makes sure horses are ready for me again. They give me all the space I need just to be in pain and I love them for it.

I ride two horses in the morning, despite the pain that's building up in my muscles. My polo swing comes back slowly. I hit balls, one after the other. Forward hits, backward hits, forward hits again. Don't think. Just don't think about anything. But fragments of conversations come into my mind again and again, no matter how much I try to focus on the ball.

"Colombia. We'll go to Colombia. I want to take you to this lovely beach I've researched. We'll spend a few days camping there." Rodrigo's voice rings in my ears.

"Look at the ball!" A new voice come to displace Rodrigo's. This one is the Old Man's, my trainer in England. I've spent so many hours on the field with him that he's always with me, even when I train on my own. "Look at the ball … Look at the ball!"

"I'm looking," I want to shout back, but then I swing and miss it. Maybe I wasn't looking closely enough. I turn the horse in a wide circle and prepare to take another shot at it.

"*Mi amor*, can you buy some bread? I have no cash with me. You didn't let me stop by a cash machine."

I didn't let him stop by a cash machine? When the hell did he tell me he wanted to stop by a cash machine and I said no?

Another swing and another miss. I have to stop this mental dialogue and just focus on the ball. That's it. Stop. Stop it.

"*Mi amor*, we can't live here. Not in Argentina, not right now. This country is a mess, you'll see for yourself soon."

And what if he was genuine and all he wanted was to live with me? In Europe?

"*Mi amor*, are you going to take me with you when you leave?"

Llevar. This verb is used for a bag, not a man.

"You take yourself wherever you want to go. Plus what are you going to do if you come to England? I don't even have a place there any longer."

Despite my mental dialogue I still manage to hit some balls. I hit them badly, though, and they head off at weird angles. The phantom of the Old Man shakes his head disapprovingly. "Not good, not good, Rosanna-a-a."

"Yes, I know it's not good. But look, what happened with Rodrigo isn't good either," I shout back at him, almost out of breath as I try to control my horse, who is starting to run just a little bit too fast.

Maybe he's really innocent. Maybe all he wanted was to be with me forever.

"And the birthday?" I'm not sure whose voice this is, maybe Gabriela's.

"He didn't have money to buy me a gift or pay for the dinner. What's the big deal? Can't I understand this?"

"Yes, but he should have got you a flower, a cake, anything. He could have cooked you a meal," says the voice with no face.

"He didn't think about it."

"He should have."

I stop the horse with one sharp move. There are too many voices on this polo field.

I can't carry on like this. I take the horse back towards the ball I've just missed. Focus on the ball, I tell myself. Nothing else matters. My arm goes behind my body to prepare the swing, my left knee pushes into the saddle, my left foot in the stirrup, my upper body rotates, my swing is now fully open, and the mallet comes down like a pendulum as I try to keep my head just outside the saddle, above the ball. A clear click and the ball heads in a straight line far in front of me. And all this because I managed to keep the voices away for exactly two minutes.

The Old Man's phantom smiles reassuringly, and Patricio shouts from the pony lines. "That's it! That's better. Your swing is starting to come back. Carry on like this."

Maybe I haven't lost it completely.

After riding I tell Gabriela I need to go under the tree and she waves me off without a word. I don't worry any longer that my meditation practices look weird. One way or the other I need to get to the bottom of this pain. There are so many voices in my head I feel I'm going slightly insane.

"Pain, are you there?" I ask, comfortably seated cross-legged under the oak tree by the side of the polo field.

"Of course I am," the bitch answers ironically. "Why, did you imagine I'd already gone?"

I don't ask her anything else. She won't cooperate, anyway. I'll teach the bitch a lesson. I start to visualize the energy field around my body. I'm going to get her out, whether she wants to talk to me or not. I've been practicing these meditation techniques long enough to feel confident they'll work.

So I look for it. For the bitch, I mean. With my eyes closed I scan my body and the space around it, trying to see if I can visualize any pain anywhere. I can't. I look for it again. Still nothing. I feel I'm slowly but surely getting angry, and it's no use meditating when you're angry.

I take a deep breath and try to calm down, turn my attention inside and look for this bloody pain again. I don't find it, but I find blood. It appears to be on the right side of my body, which is all drenched in blood. Right is the masculine side. Right is where I just had a breakup. Aha, we're getting closer now. I clean the blood in my imagination. I see more coming. I clean it again. It feels like a never-ending task. Where the hell is this fucking pain hiding and why do I see blood on my right side?

I take a deep breath, in through the nose, out through the mouth. This is what they say you should do in yoga classes. I have to calm down. I'm not going to achieve anything if I get angry. Another deep breath in …

Where's this fucking pain hiding?

I'm getting hungry now. The image of blood is gone, replaced by a big plate of cheese ravioli. They often cook cheese ravioli when I'm at the farm because they know I don't eat meat and they're too nice to give me just a salad.

Lunch must be ready. Maybe I can stop this hunt and go and eat ravioli instead.

But not before one more try. I'm now asking all the spirits to come and help me find that bastard pain and get it out of my system. I can't see it anywhere and it's clear I need some serious help.

Just as I do this I feel someone touching my face and for a second I think it's the angels I'm summoning. But, no, it's Vishnu, breathing straight into my nose.

Vishnu is one of the five dogs at the farm. Gabriela rescued her from a ditch and named her after a statue of the Indian god that she brought back to Argentina after playing a polo tournament in India. The dog is an unidentified, somewhat shepherd breed, but otherwise cute. She appears to be fascinated by my activities under the tree and takes advantage of the fact that as I sit cross-legged on the ground my face is at the same height as her muzzle.

But I'm in no mood for company.

"*Salí*," I shout. "Get away from here."

She doesn't get it. Why go away when she can stay and keep me company? Maybe even lick my face a bit, just because she loves it. I struggle with the dog for a while and all my beautiful visualizations go to pieces. Eventually she leaves, scared away by my shouts, and she takes all that's left of my focus with her.

I close my eyes again, but it takes only five more minutes until I'm interrupted again.

"Roxy, lunch is ready," Santos shouts from his bike. He was probably sent by the adults to rescue me from under the tree. I must have been there for a couple of hours already, in plain view of anyone from the house, dog fight and all.

Santos is one of the three boys living at the farm—little Patricio, the son of my friends, and his two cousins, the sons of Patricio's sister. The three of them are inseparable, playing together, riding together, sleeping in the same room, and going to school together. Santos is the oldest of them and already a passionate polo player at ten. I played against him once and realized that despite his age he played far better than me.

"I'm coming," I tell him.

I get up and bang my head hard on one of the lower branches of the tree I've been sitting under. "Shit." I mumble and try to hold my head with both hands, as the world appears to suddenly start spinning. I was wondering where the pain lives and now I have the answer. It's in my head.

As my vision slowly stabilizes again, I notice on my right arm the marks of the mosquitoes that have been feeding on me for the last hour. I bet this is where the blood in my visualization was coming from. Maybe this meditation thing doesn't really work here. I head towards the house.

The adults inside look at me with that silent, questioning expression in their eyes. Are you OK? But they don't ask anything. Only the maid asks me what I was doing under that tree for such a long time.

"Trying to soothe my bleeding heart," I answer. "You know, breakup with boyfriend."

"Aha." She nods. And then she pats me encouragingly on the shoulder. "It will pass, you'll see." I notice she doesn't give me the *no pasa nada* phrase. Maybe love troubles are the only ones that bypass this ever-present rule in Argentina.

Gabriela asks if I want to come with them to a nearby club, where she's due to play a polo tournament that afternoon. No, I would rather go under my tree again, I tell her. No comments. She nods approvingly and questions me no more.

They leave. I go back under the tree. There is no Vishnu this time, but no more visualization either. Only a sad girl struggling to hold back tears while giving up trying to make sense of it all. There have been no more messages from Rodrigo for the last two days.

Santos comes back after a while to tell me horses are ready for me. Do I want to stick and ball or do I want to go and ride in the fields? How does he know I wanted to ride? Patricio asked him to prepare horses for me before he left for the tournament. Ah, all right, let's ride in the fields then. I'm in too much pain for polo. But will I ride in the fields alone?

"Of course not," he says. "I'll be your guide."

I guess he has received strict instructions from his uncle about this, too.

Together, we ride out of the wooden gates and gallop through the meadow scattered with purple spring flowers. Santos is in front of me on a small horse called Illusion. Just like what I'd been fabricating in my mind about Rodrigo. I follow behind him on Amanda the Sheep, this time kitted for riding only. Which means I have only two reins, not four, and she has her tail free and no bandages on her legs. I bet she's happy. I'm happy too. No balls to hit, no phantom of the Old Man disapproving my bad swings. Just the never-ending fresh green fields, and us galloping into the horizon, all five dogs of the farm running wild behind us.

"Sto-o-op! Let's walk for a while. I'm out of breath," I shout.

Santos stops at once, although he's not out of breath. At ten he's a much better rider than I am. He's been riding ever since he was born. I remember Patricio telling me he'd fall asleep on the back of a horse when he was a baby and scream if he was pulled away from one.

He takes me to see the cows, a big group gathered by water-holes, and then we ride across the fields to see the newborn calves. Santos points to one of them.

"He was born this morning. Look there."

I follow his outstretched hand and I spot the placenta still fresh and full of blood on the ground. The calf is already on his feet next to his mother.

"Do they mind us coming so close?" I ask, apprehensive, as the mother cow stops grazing to stare at us.

"No, not at all. They're just curious." He sticks his ankles into the belly of the horse, leading him through the cows who have now gathered all around us.

I look at the peaceful faces of the cows and I can't imagine them getting aggressive. Plus, they have no horns. This breed has no horns, Santos tells me. He knows all about cows. He's been riding in the field with his grandfather for as long as he can remember. The cows are not really used to people, because they don't see that many. They live in the fields and breed in the fields, free until the day they're loaded up in trucks and taken to the slaughterhouse. I'm a vegetarian and I would normally feel uncomfortable living on a meat farm, but these cows look so *tranqui* and so happy that I can see nothing wrong in the fact that one day they'll simply die. We all die one day, anyway.

"Come, I'll show you the young horses." Santos urges his horse into a gallop across the fields again.

The young horses are in the same field, but a good twenty minutes' ride away from the cows. They all gather under a few trees and wait patiently for us to approach. There are five or six of them, all too young to be trained. They are all the result of Patricio's embryo program. It works like this: one of his polo mares gets pregnant—usually by the same stallion Patricio always keeps separate from the rest of the herd. Then the embryo is extracted from the uterus of the mare and implanted in the uterus of another mare, a surrogate mother. This way the original mare can still play polo, and the surrogate mother, who usually is a horse useless for polo, spends her time in the fields gestating the foal. After the foal is born, they are both left wild in the fields for about two years, and then the young horse is sent to the breakers. These are the guys who get the horse used to the saddle and bridle. It's a long process, and it's repeated a few times, with long periods of resting in the field in between. After it's broken in, the horse starts to be trained for polo. This takes a long time, as well. It takes about five years in total to have a horse ready to play polo, and not all the horses will be able to do it.

The young horses are curious, too. They come to sniff us, and I marvel at the light in their eyes. They look at me with the same intensity that I look at them, and with the same curiosity. They gather all around my horse until Amanda tenses up, letting me know with a few sharp movements that she feels uneasy in this crowd. I get scared all of a sudden, because a horse that's nervous makes me feel unstable in the saddle and then I remember my own falls very vividly. I look around to locate Santos. The boy has already seen the situation and he comes close to me, telling me it's best we carry on. His small horse isn't nervous at all, and this calms Amanda instantly. I wonder whether it's because he rides here often to see the young horses, and his mare is used to them. Or maybe he's just a much better rider, and a horse seldom gets nervous with a really good rider.

We move on from the young horses and break into a fresh gallop across the large expanse of pampas, with clumps of wild grass reaching up to our stirrups.

Santos turns around in the saddle and tells me to stay behind. He needs to go and check on a lonely cow he's spotted in the distance.

I pull my reins and let him go alone, watching his mad gallop across the field, his small body almost indistinguishable in the saddle, all five dogs running after him.

I slow down my horse to catch my breath, and we soon move to a trot, then walk. We're now alone in the pampas. I watch the cows on the horizon, the young horses back where we left them under the same trees, and the boundless green fields around me. Amanda's strong body feels alive between my knees. For the first time in the last few days I'm not thinking of anything and it's not because I have to hit a polo ball. The late afternoon sun warms my face. The smell of the earth is strong in my nostrils. It's dried mud and fresh leaves and a lot of other smells, too, but I don't know what they are—probably the herbs that grow around here. I can't hear a thing. Even the birds that are so loud in the trees around the house are silent now. Surrounded by this peace, I breathe.

Maybe it's not all gone. I wanted to make a life with Rodrigo here in Argentina. Rodrigo is gone now, but maybe my life here isn't. Here in the *campo*. And what if I buy a piece of land and build a small house? Somewhere close to my Argentine family? What if I buy a horse, too? Maybe even Amanda the Sheep. I'm sure Patricio wouldn't mind selling her to me. What if it's still possible to have a life here? Yes, the love story with Rodrigo is over. But was that the only thing that brought me back here? No, it wasn't just that. It was the immensity of the *campo* and this feeling of being at one with it—the connection I feel to this place and to these people. Connection. This is what polo gives me. This is what Rodrigo gave me. And this is what the *campo* now gives me, too. The connection is definitely still here. And maybe it's enough. I can see myself living here. And playing polo. Of course I'll play polo.

On the way back we take the dirt road, the same dirt road we usually drive on to get to the farm. We gallop fast, and a cloud of dust rises from the hooves of the horses. I watch the hard ground beneath, much harder than the soft grass of the polo field, and for a second I try to imagine how it would feel if I fall right now. I would break something again, probably. But then I push the thought away. I'm perfectly balanced in the saddle, my body following the moves of the horse, my head high, feeling the wind. I won't fall. Not anymore. Never again.

Santos has overtaken me and gallops in front of me on his small horse, the dogs all around him. In full gallop he turns his small body to look back every now and then to make sure I'm all right.

And for the first time in the last few days I actually feel perfectly fine.

SATURDAY 12TH NOVEMBER

The third day is the worst, they say. I wake up and I can't move. Two days of riding have done their job. My body is in pain. My heart is too, stubbornly, shattering my hopes that enough riding will sort it out.

I drag myself out of bed and back to the pony lines after breakfast. The best thing you can do for an aching body is to get back on a horse again. Same for the heart. At least Patricio says so. He must be right.

"Don't you think it's funny?" I ask him as I put on my riding boots. "I always end up here with a problem, and you always end up looking after me. Now it's heartbreak. Last year it was a broken arm; the year before that I couldn't walk because of too much riding, and you guys invited me to spend Christmas here. One way or the other, I always end up here with a problem. Maybe you and I had a deal before we were born that I'll come to you with a problem and you'll look after me."

He laughs. "You know what? Maybe you're right. But it's always a pleasure to have you here."

Amanda the Sheep is ready for me and I'm growing fond of this horse. I'll ask Patricio if he will sell her to me. She would be such a perfect start to my new dream. I talk to her in my usual soothing voice, and she waves her ears. I think she would like to be mine.

Once the agony of the first ten minutes in the saddle is gone and my muscles warm up, I get to hit the ball quite well. My mind starts its usual chatter. All the conversations I had with Rodrigo during the week we spent together come back one by one. I hit balls. I remember more words. I hit more balls.

And then I remember how he held me tight in his arms in the darkness of the night and I have to stop the horse because I can't ride and cry at the same time.

⁓ॐ

Rosario comes to visit that evening and we have a girls' counsel. Everything gets discussed once again, all the conversations, the facts, the messages. The final verdict is that he was a scammer. Rosario tells me the therapist has no availability to see me. Gabriela declares that maybe I'll be all right with just some polo. I tell them about my meditation and visualization technique and how I spent time under the tree cleaning up my energetic field. Gabriela looks at me skeptically, Rosario sympathetically, and then all that is needed to be said is said, and the girls decide the subject is now officially closed. Next on the list is a bottle of wine.

And just as all this is decided, a new text message comes through: *I need to know if you are going to give me the clothes that are still in your apartment. Can you leave them with the porter, please?*

The coldness of this text shocks me. I also notice the party picture is gone. There is no more profile picture. He vanished from my life just like that, in only three days.

I text back that I will, then I put the phone away and pick up a glass of wine instead and I try hard not to think about it anymore. Only much later, as I share a bed with Rosario, who has decided to stay over due to one too many glasses of wine, do I dare to tell her in the darkness that I still think of him and I still hope there might be a way for us to sort out this situation.

"I know, Roxy. But there isn't," is all she says.

SUNDAY 13TH NOVEMBER

It's pouring down and I run out to get into the car with Rosario, while Patricio stands in the rain holding the long wooden gate of the courtyard open for us.

We slept at Gabriela and Patricio's new place, but we all drive to the big farm for breakfast. The big farm is where everything happens—the meals, the riding, the polo, the conversations, the kids playing, my meditation tree, and the exquisite cakes of the housemaid.

"No more going under the tree today. You're coming with us," Gabriela declares after breakfast. Today is the final game of the polo tournament she's been playing these last few days at a nearby club.

With Gabriela things are quite straightforward. When she puts her mind to something there is no way to stand against it.

"And take your polo gear as well," Patricio adds. "You can stick and ball there. I'll make sure I have horses ready for you."

The horses are all loaded into a truck and sent to the polo field hours ahead with the grooms. They'll have a few hours to prepare the horses for playing. Polo is hard work and not only while playing. All the preparation of the horses that goes on behind the scenes is actually the hardest part.

We're just about to leave when Patricio receives a phone call from Facundo. His face changes. The connection is bad and the call gets cut. Phone connection is always bad in the *campo*. He gets into the car and disappears without a word.

"What's wrong?" I ask Gabriela.

"He's worried there's something wrong with the horses. Every time Facundo calls, it's bad news, and it's usually about the horses. He never calls otherwise."

It turns out there is nothing wrong with the horses, only a truck that had trouble starting. Patricio decides to go with the truck. Gabriela and I follow in a car, the three boys on the back seat, and all the saddles and bridles in the back of the pickup.

We reach the nearby polo club without further incident. Everyone is ready for the final two games of the tournament, and everyone knows everyone. There are cousins of Patricio there, many of them. Friends. Extended family. I've long ago given up marveling at how extended an extended family can actually be in Argentina.

I spot Rosario's mother and sister further along the sidelines of the polo field, and I go to say hello. Rosario's sister is married to a polo player, and her teenage son is a polo player, too. Polo runs in the family here.

We kiss in the Argentine fashion, one brief kiss on the right cheek. They ask about my love story. I tell them it's over. And I tell them about the most recent messages, and the one about when his boss found him crying at work and gave him a day off.

Rosario's sister looks at me with a straight face for a second and then she bursts out into uncontrollable laughter. Her body shakes silently. I watch her without a word.

"Oh God, I'm sorry, Roxy. But this is so funny. A really good one. Crying at work. Incredible. And you believed him?"

"Well, Gabriela said I shouldn't believe him, but—"

She wipes away her tears. "Roxy. Let me tell you one thing. No Argentine man will ever cry at work. Not over a woman, anyway. Maybe for football in extreme cases, but not for a woman. It's just not done."

For a second Patricio's words echo in my mind. He said the same.

"Never?"

"No, Roxy. Never. This guy must think you're completely silly to believe something like this," she adds.

Maybe I actually am. Completely silly. More silly than I ever thought I could be.

But there's no time left for additional explanations. Facundo holds Amanda the Sheep for me, and Santos gets onto another horse, instructed by Patricio to come stick and ball with me. The ten-year-old boy is very proud of his guarding task, but I don't even notice him, and this time it's not because I'm busy having conversations in my head. This time it's just anger, pure boiling anger. I can't believe how strong and fresh this anger feels, but it is there, and all I can do is hit balls with it.

When evening sets in, I feel empty inside. Gabriela lost the game and declared she has played the worst she ever did in all her polo playing history. I don't agree with her, but then it's a hard business not agreeing with Gabriela. Patricio and his groom manage the complex logistics of getting the horses un-tacked and loaded into the truck and the saddles and bridles nicely fitted on the back of the pickup truck. We all have a drink with the rest of the players around a huge barbecue holding a lump of meat about the size of half a cow. There's nothing else to eat, just the meat straight from the grill with fresh bread, and everyone is quite happy with this. I eat only the bread, thinking I must remember to bring some cheese next time I come to a polo *asado*. Kids run around; players in white jeans, dirty from the grease of the saddle, talk about the game; people mix and mingle; and everyone is just one big family around the fire. My anger is gone, lost in the balls I've hit, or maybe Amanda the Sheep cleansed it for me and took it away to be discarded into the fields. I chat to Patricio's many cousins, I listen to Gabriela reminding me of who is who, and I finally relax, surrounded by one big Argentine family. If there was some cheese for the bread, life would be just perfect.

TUESDAY 15TH NOVEMBER

El frío de mi cuerpo pregunta por ti-i-i! the old lady cries in the middle of Sol's hair salon, concluding her dancing moves with a hand held high in a pose she manages to hold for a few minutes.

The coldness of my body asks for you, it means. She sings along the lines of the newest Latino hit with dramatic lyrics. All Latino hits have dramatic lyrics. I've come to know this in Argentina.

I'm back in Buenos Aires and back in Sol's shop. Sol is my hairdresser of last year who washed my hair every other day, as I couldn't do it with my arm in the cast. Almost in tears, I tell her the whole breakup story.

"See? I told you!" she cries. "*Qué hijo de puta!*"

This is the most common Argentine swear word. It means approximately the same as Gabriela's favorite. *Fucking bastard.*

Sol never liked Rodrigo. Last year, as my story was unfolding, she kept telling me to be careful and that she didn't like the sound of this guy. Just like Gabriela.

The old lady is her aunt. I don't remember her name and it's embarrassing to ask since I'm supposed to remember it. I can't find out from conversations, because Sol and her three kids call her *Madri*, a short form of *Madrina*, or Godmother. She's the godmother of Sol's children and she helps her out, both in the shop and with the kids. As a single mother with three children under seven and a small hairdresser's shop to run on top of that, life isn't easy for Sol.

When all the details of the breakup have been exhausted, Sol takes a look at my hair and declares I need an emergency color change.

"Who did your hair last? What a disaster. Why so dark? You need lighter highlights."

And then, as she puts the light back in my hair, she asks me in a serious voice, "Roxy, tell me, has this guy ever given you a sign he can turn violent?"

"Violent? No, he's never—" I think hard. "He's never done anything wrong, but maybe—ah, but that is nothing."

"Yes? What is it?"

A brief memory comes to my mind of us arguing in the street after that missed meeting point on Friday, emotions running high. Emotions always run high in Argentina. Me, shouting. Him lifting his hand to pull my arm, suddenly and violently.

"That hurts," I screamed.

"You were about to cross on red," he answered. "Cars will run over you here if you cross on red."

"There are no cars around," I said.

He had grabbed me violently. My arm hurt. And exactly ten minutes later, he crossed on red in front of me. I tell all this to Sol.

"See? Trust your instincts, girl. Argentine men can get violent with women when they break up. Have you got any idea how many women have died in this country this way?" Sol's face is all gloom.

"What?" I think Sol must be paranoid. But then she tells me about a huge campaign that swept the country just weeks ago. *Ni una menos*—Not one less. Some 300,000 people gathered in the central square in Buenos Aires to march against violence towards women. Every thirty hours a woman is killed in Argentina, most of them in sexual attacks, a lot of them by ex-boyfriends.

"Don't joke about these things, Roxy. Men can go crazy here. If this guy gave you one single sign he could get violent, be careful. He may come after you."

"He can't," I tell her. "I left the old apartment yesterday as soon as I got back from the *campo*. I left his stuff with the porters. I sent him a message saying I was going back to my friends in the countryside and wouldn't be back for a few weeks."

"What did he say?"

"He asked if he's ever going to see me again. I said not for a few weeks. Maybe longer. I told him I'm not going to be in Buenos Aires."

"Good, but be careful, OK? Don't agree to meet him again. Whatever he says. He could get dangerous."

There was one more message from Rodrigo, but I didn't tell her about this one. It said, *Espero que algún día vas a poder perdonarme.* I hope one day you will be able to forgive me. This was yesterday evening. I still get tears in my eyes when I remember it. What if I could actually forgive him?

But Sol wouldn't let me dwell on these thoughts.

"Was there nothing? You felt no warning sign? In all these months while you were waiting to come back here to see him? I can't believe you felt nothing wrong."

"No, not really. He always told me he was waiting for me and that I was the love of his life."

And yet. In the back of my mind a new thought takes shape. About a month before I came to Argentina, Rodrigo had changed his WhatsApp profile picture to a picture of graffiti. He loves graffiti. This one said, "real eyes realize real lies."

He said it meant nothing. It was just a cool piece of graffiti. But I felt it was a warning. Maybe he wanted to tell me something. But I didn't listen.

It's too late to think about that now. Maybe there was an honest part of him, and that part loved me. And maybe it was the same part that tried to warn me.

Enough maybes. I don't want to think about it any longer.

With that Argentine secret power that lets them read thoughts,

Sol gets it and finishes my highlights in silence. Madri plays back the song about the cold body asking for the departed lover.

"Ah, beautiful." Sol admires my new shiny blond highlights. "Now you're back to being the Roxy of last year. Much, much better." And then, just before I leave, "And don't worry, Roxy. Buenos Aires is full of men. We'll go out and have fun, I promise you."

"OK, deal. When I come back. I'm going to Lobos again to spend a few more days at my friends' farm, training for polo. But next week I'm back and we'll go out. I promise."

Sol gives me a kiss. Madri gives me a kiss too. For a second I contemplate the client seated with her hair already washed, patiently waiting for Sol to do her haircut, and I wonder whether we should also kiss. But my highlights and the accompanying questions lasted a long time, and maybe she's pissed off from too much waiting, although she looks quite entertained by the story. I'm not sure, so I decide just to leave the shop without any further kisses or delays.

Tomorrow I'll go back to Lobos. I've spent only three days in the city, but I've done everything I have to do—changed flats, had my hair done, had my first language class with Santi, my Spanish teacher from last year, got a Jorge Luis Borges assignment to read and had to suppress my laughter. Santi loves Jorge Luis Borges and some things simply never change.

THURSDAY 17TH NOVEMBER

I'm back at the farm and this time I'm determined not to look like a broken-hearted silly girl. It's done. I've changed apartments. He doesn't know where I live. I've changed hair color and I haven't replied to his good-bye message. Done. I don't even want to talk about him any longer.

But Patricio does, just to make sure everything really is fine. "Have you heard from this guy again?" he asks as he gets the horses ready for my stick and ball session.

"Yes. But it's over. He said *adios*," I say briefly. But there was something more.

"He also said he hopes one day I'll be able to forgive him," I add after a while.

"He's not stupid, you know," Patricio says. "He leaves his options open with you. Careful, Roxy. He may try to contact you again."

"You think so?" I ask, in a voice where hope mixes with fear.

"I think so. And when he does, don't fall back. He's not good for you."

Not good for me. I know this. Maybe precisely that's why I'm in danger of falling back. I have a pattern of getting myself into situations that aren't good for me.

⤜⤏

Amanda the Sheep doesn't care about my mental patterns, though. By now she knows me well and she starts happily cantering around the polo field for a first round of warm-up. Then I find a ball and start knocking out every single word of that phrase: *I*. Hit. *Hope*. Hit. *One day*. Hit. Long hit to account for two words. *You will*. Hit and hit again since the ball bounced back. *Be able*. Hit. *To*. Hit. *Forgive me*. Hit and miss.

Wide circle canter, go back and pick up the ball. Again. *I*. Hit. *Hope*. Hit …

I'm starting to hit much better, I tell myself, satisfied, as I jump off the horse thirty minutes later and straight onto another horse. My body has recovered from the initial riding pain, too. My muscles start working well. My hand-eye coordination comes back.

"Good." Patricio nods approvingly from the pony lines. "Tomorrow we'll play some chukkas. You're ready."

There's nothing a good polo training can't get rid of, I think, as I sit under the same tree of last week. This time it's for a stretching session. Screw the meditation. Screw the broken heart. Screw him, too. I'm going to get myself back to being a good polo player and this is my top priority.

In the afternoon we train again, and this time the little boys join us, each one in their cute, little helmets, riding full-size polo ponies. The boys remain in the field much longer after we're out of breath. We jump off the horses and go and find a sunny spot in the grass to watch them train.

Patricio shouts at the boys, giving them advice. They're fully kitted for polo, with helmets, mallets, and whips. They don't seem to mind the big horses, which are far too big for them. They ride around the polo field, passing the ball from one to the other. This is how top polo players are made, I think, as I watch them. They start at the age of seven on a big horse, running around their polo field at home under the expert eye of their father, or uncle in this case.

"You almost have a full team here." I point to the kids. "They'll be amazing when they're old enough to play."

He smiles, proud of them. We're lying in the grass, three adults resting after riding, watching three kids learn to play polo. Gabriela's little terrier dog comes to lie with me. The sun is mild, getting ready to go down for the day. I can smell the grass. On the field in front of us the three little boys run wild on their big horses, and the clicks of their mallets on the small plastic ball sound clean and reassuring. I love being here. I really love it.

FRIDAY 18TH NOVEMBER

Today I'm going to play chukkas again. I feel ready. Patricio and Gabriela have stuff to do in town, but I head back to the pony lines for my morning stick and ball session full of energy.

"You'll ride Laucita today," Gabriela says, smiling. "She's my favorite, this small mare. I love playing her. She's my little motorcycle."

Laucita means Little Mouse. That's because the mare is very small. Gabriela loves small horses. I like them bigger but don't mind trying her little motorcycle. Afterwards I'll ride Amanda as my second horse for the morning.

The mare is too small for my sticks, and little Patricio tells me with a knowledgable air that I need a fifty-inch stick. I tell him I don't have one that small, but he says, "Mama does," and he runs inside the house and produces one of Gabriela's sticks for me.

"This will work better," he says, with a serious look on his face. Then he gets his own helmet and his own sticks. The boys will stick and ball with me today and they're all getting ready.

Facundo brings Laucita and tells me not to worry. She's like a sheep, too. "Gabriela said motorcycle," I correct him.

He laughs. "With me they're all sheep."

Of course they are. Facundo is a real *gaucho*, the South American version of the Wild West cowboy. Once upon a time he used to do rodeos, where he rode wild horses into submission to the delight of audiences. He's a sturdy middle-aged guy dressed in traditional *gaucho* clothes as if he's come straight out of a movie. White shirt, long beige cotton trousers called *bombachas*, with a button at the ankle. A sash around his waist, with a long knife in a silver sheath nicely tucked into it at his back. I saw him before as he left the knife on the table to go and ride the horses. Facundo probably learned to ride a horse way before he learned how to walk. No wonder they're all like sheep with him.

But Laucita proves to be a sheep with me as well. I whisper to her as we start a first round of warm-up and she nods her head docilely. Motorcycle, Gabriela called her. Who else called a horse a motorcycle? Can't remember.

A second round of cantering and I pick up a ball and take it all the way to the other end of the polo field. Good. I didn't miss a shot so far.

I hit a backhand and turn the horse sharply to go and get the ball again. Laucita stumbles and it seems as though she's about to come down. Then she regains her balance and I regain mine too, but she stumbles on the other leg. In a split second I see the horse's neck, then the saddle, then the ground, then the saddle again as she wobbles on her legs, trying hard not to fall, and then I definitely and painfully feel the ground. I have left the saddle and landed on my shoulder. Thank God I didn't put my arms out this time. If you put your arms out, they will break. I learned this from my previous two falls. This time I kept them nicely tucked into my chest and took the fall on the shoulder.

The very same shoulder that hurts a lot right now. But there was no crack. I heard no crack. I take a deep breath and I try to get back on my feet and onto the horse, who has come to a halt right next to where I'm lying on the ground.

But I can't. I make it to sitting up, but I can't do anything else. There is a sharp pain in my right shoulder.

I take another breath. Come on, let's try again.

Nope. Can't move.

But I didn't hear a crack. Please. Please, God, I say, as I sit there on my bum, cradling my right arm to my chest. I heard no crack this time. And it didn't hurt that much. Not like last time. Definitely not. Please, God. Please, make it that it isn't broken. Not this time.

Can't be.

It is.

The silly thought arrives from nowhere and settles calmly on my mind.

No, please, God! Make a miracle happen. I'll do anything. Anything you want of me. Just make it that it's not broken. Can't be. Not like this. This was nothing. Before, when I broke other bones, I was playing tournaments. Tournaments are fast games. I fell at speed. Big falls. I hit the goalpost once. The other time the horse fell as well. I put my arms down. That's why I had broken them. But not this time. This time, it was nothing. Gabriela took a fall just yesterday and she was fine. The kids fell too … See? Nothing. It's possible to fall and do nothing.

God isn't answering.

I look around. On the other side of the polo field I see Facundo galloping madly towards me on a horse that appears to be Amanda the Sheep. Of course it's her. She was already saddled, waiting for me to be done with Laucita.

I watch Facundo approaching and all I can think of is whether he had time to take off the long knife he carries in his sash before he got on the horse.

He jumps off, throws the reins away and in one big leap arrives on his knees right in front of me.

"*Qué pasó?* What happened?"

I have no idea what happened. I only know I have tears in my eyes and an arm I can't move.

He takes my helmet off. I remember my fall last year and Patricio's hands taking my helmet off as I had my eyes firmly shut, lost in the agony of pain.

There is no agony of pain this time, just an arm that won't move, and my other arm cradling it protectively to my chest.

"Can you stand up?"

I shake my head. "No. I don't know. Facundo, do you think … is it possible that it's broken?" My voice is trembling. *Please, God, please*, I add in my mind.

"Yes," he says. "Your shoulder is down. Likely broken."

God is definitely not listening to me today.

"But don't worry," Facundo adds. "*No pasa nada.* We'll take you to the hospital."

No pasa nada. I've heard this before. Last time I heard it on a polo field it resulted in six weeks of cast plus three of physio afterwards.

Facundo takes his phone from his pocket. I still can't see the knife anywhere. He probably had enough time to leave it on the table.

"Oh, no. Please don't call him."

We both know I mean Patricio. I remember his reaction to Facundo's calls. There's usually bad news when this guy calls, Gabriela said.

He looks at me with apologetic eyes.

"I have to. Of course I have to call him."

Patricio picks up at the first ring.

"Yes? *Qué pasó?* What happened?" I hear his worried voice as clearly as if he's next to me.

Facundo says one word only.

"Roxy …"

On the other side of the phone I hear a very succulent and explicit Argentine swearing. I've never heard Patricio swearing before. And then again, "*Qué pasó?*"

"She's on the ground. Here, on the polo field. Likely broken. Shoulder … yes …"

I don't hear anything else. I've suddenly remembered who called a horse a motorcycle. It was the Old Man, my trainer in England. Whenever we used to turn the horses sharply, he would scream. "Not like that! You're not on a motorcycle! They will trip and you will fall!"

I now know he was right.

Facundo puts the phone down and talks to me reassuringly. I'll be OK. I'll recover. I'll play polo again, please don't think otherwise. I'm doing well. They'll take me to the hospital. Gabriela and Patricio will be there soon. All is fine. All will be fine. And once again the general words of Argentine reassurance. *No pasa nada.*

But all is not fine. They get me in a car and back to the pony lines, and this proves to be agony. The kids take my polo boots off and replace them with my white trainers. Facundo places a strong painkiller under my tongue and tells me to keep it there until it dissolves. Patricio's father appears from the house, probably alerted by a phone call from his son, and he takes charge of operations.

"Don't you worry, *hijita*. We'll take you to the hospital now. You'll be fine."

Hijita. Little daughter. He pats my healthy shoulder reassuringly and keeps his hand there all the way to the town.

We arrive at the hospital and I feel like a character in a movie I've already seen, and someone has pressed play again and there's no way to stop it. *Déjà vu* scenes run one by one in front of my eyes. Hospital. Receptionist filling in forms—what's your name, nationality, date of birth? X-ray room. Patricio and Gabriela rushing though the front door of the hospital about two minutes after I get there.

"I'm sorry. I'm so sorry." I burst out crying as soon as I see them.

"Shhh. You'll be OK. We're here. We're going to look after you. What happened?"

I just fell like a sack of potatoes because I turned the horse sharply and it tripped. No glory this time. Not a fall in a tournament while actually playing polo, no fall at speed. Just a stupid fall that should have been nothing.

But the X-ray shows a bad fracture of the collarbone.

"Wait to speak to the doctor," the radiologist says. "You'll probably need surgery."

❧

With Patricio on my right and Gabriela on my left, we wait. I can't eat or drink anything, just in case I need to go straight into surgery. They don't eat or drink anything either, because there's nothing to eat or drink in the hospital, and they won't be persuaded to leave my side and go and have lunch. If they faint due to lack of food this won't help me, I tell them. They should go and eat and come back, and they will find me right here. I won't move from this chair, I promise.

No luck. They stubbornly refuse to move. We all starve for the rest of the afternoon, stuck on our chairs in the waiting room of the hospital. The doctor is still in surgery, we're told. I'm not sure if this is good news—that he's in demand and has a lot of patients—or bad news—that a patient has just died under his knife.

We don't talk about my arm, the horse, or the fall. We don't talk much. We are each busy digesting our own shock, in silence. All we can talk about are the immediate next steps.

"Roxy, if you don't like the look of this surgeon, you tell me and we'll take you to Buenos Aires, OK?" Patricio says.

The look—does he mean whether he's handsome enough?

"If you feel you don't trust him," he clarifies. "For us it's better if you have surgery here, because it's close to where we are. We can keep an eye on you and look after you here. But if you want to go to Buenos Aires we'll take you there, don't worry. You decide."

"Let's see after we meet the doctor," I say. I have no idea how one decides on such things. I know nothing about this doctor or about this hospital. But I know nothing about any other doctor or hospital, either.

The surgeon eventually arrives, and my first reaction is to turn to Patricio and whisper, "I think we should go to Buenos Aires."

I'm in a panic. This can't be the doctor. He looks like a teenager. What if he's a student, and I'm to be his first training patient?

But then he speaks and the sound of his voice instantly reassures me. He's done a lot of these operations, he says. He's seen a lot of these fractures. I'll be just fine.

I'm still not sure whether to trust him or not, but there's something in his voice that makes me trust him.

"What happened?" he asks.

I open my mouth to speak, but Patricio and Gabriela jump in at once, their voices united in one word.

"Bicycle. She fell off a bicycle," they say with straight faces.

We'd discussed this as soon as I got to the hospital. I wasn't sure my insurance covered polo. I was riding actually, not playing polo, but I didn't want to risk it. So we agreed it was to be a bicycle this time. Luckily, I didn't have my riding boots on. They'd been removed by the kids before I left the polo field and replaced with my white Converse trainers. The blue jeans and the Ralph Lauren polo shirt I wore looked casual enough for a bicycle ride.

"Ah, bicycle. Yes, very typical fracture for a bicycle fall. The collarbone. And the wrist. These are the usual breaks," the doctor says.

I don't tell him I'd broken both my wrists falling off a horse. Playing polo, actually. Very similar to falling off a bicycle.

"She needs surgery," comes the verdict. "We need to insert a metal plate to hold the bone together. Otherwise it won't heal properly."

"When?"

"Tomorrow morning, if you manage to get the metal plate and the screws."

"What do you mean?"

"You need to buy the screws in advance. Once you have them, I can operate."

He's talking to Patricio now. Procurement, transactions, buying something, all this is a man's business, obviously. I'm clearly not in a position to do anything about it, and, in any case, in Argentina men talk to other men about these things. What would have happened if I were here alone?

"Where do I get this metal plate from?" Patricio's mind has already started tackling this new challenge.

"I'll give you a phone number. It's a company that deals with medical devices. You can choose which one you want to buy."

"The best one, obviously." Patricio says.

"The best ones are imported. But they're expensive. You need to call this company and ask them if they have them in stock and arrange with them to have the plate and screws delivered first thing tomorrow morning. Here at the hospital. Once we have them, I can operate."

"And what if we don't get them?" Patricio asks.

"Then we wait. We can wait up to a week for this type of fracture. We wait until you get it."

"We'll get it. Can I call them now? Are they still open? It's Friday afternoon already."

"Come, I'll give you all the details," the doctor says.

I'm not sure what else he says. My mind is fixed on one word only. Screws. I'd had screws in my left wrist. It was a nightmare. My wrist refused to move and fourteen months later I had to have another operation to get them out. I don't like the sound of screws, I really don't.

But the doctor says there's no other way. It's a bad fracture, the bone is displaced. It won't heal without surgery.

"For now, I'll put you in a cast until tomorrow morning," he adds. "And get the plate today," he turns to Patricio, "so we can operate tomorrow. There's nothing I can do without it." And then to me, "Come. Let's get this cast on."

I follow him into another room, with Patricio and Gabriela walking behind me as my double shadow. Wherever I go, they go.

The new room is bare and dark, with a chair sitting awkwardly in the middle of it and a small desk in one corner.

I head towards the desk, but he motions me to sit on the awkward chair. I don't like that chair. Not sure why, but I really don't like it.

"Now you need to put both arms on your hips," the doctor says.

There's no way I can put both arms on my hips. The left one has been cradling the right one to my chest, ever since I left that polo field. There is no way they're going anywhere. He must be joking.

"It's going to hurt, but you need to do it," he says, reading my thoughts. "I can't put the cast on otherwise. I need to immobilize your bone when it's straight, and right now it's not straight."

I now know why I don't like that chair. It's the torture chair.

The doctor takes off my necklace with delicate movements, giving me time to get used to the enormity of the idea that I'll have to move my arms backwards and it's going to hurt like hell. He hands over to Gabriela my moonstone gem necklace. I wonder how long I won't be able to wear it for, and, for a second, thinking of that necklace gives me relief from all other thoughts.

"I need to cut your T-shirt off," he says. "Is that OK?"

Pointless to say no, he's going to do it anyway. There is no way that T-shirt can come off any other way. It's a Ralph Lauren T-shirt with a big polo player logo on the left shoulder. I wore this T-shirt a lot while training. Never for playing, though. We have team shirts for playing, with numbers and team names, but this dark blue T-shirt was perfect for training. I remember the Old Man once telling me that I should get a T-shirt with the logo of his polo club when I come for stick and ball, instead of this one with another club's logo.

"But this isn't another club's logo. This is Ralph Lauren's logo," I said.

"Same thing, same thing, Rosanna. Get yourself a proper one."

Well, he'll be happy now, I think, as I hear the scissors cutting though the fabric. I'm now left in my bright pink Victoria's Secret push-up bra, the one I always wear under polo shirts instead of an ugly sports bra.

"Wow, woman! Sexy bra! I didn't expect this under that plain T-shirt. Did you know you were going to fall today?" Gabriela says. "I like it. See? When I like something I say it."

Gabriela and I have very different ideas about what dressing sexy looks like. I'm glad she at least approves of my bra.

The doctor doesn't seem impressed with my bright pink push-up bra, though. For a second, I fear he's going to cut it off as well, and it would be really embarrassing to be left topless in front of the two guys. I hope Gabriela will find something funny to say to ease the situation. She always does.

But, no, my bra remains untouched. The doctor just lifts my hair up and then gently but firmly grabs my injured arm and starts pulling it back. As my first scream comes out, Gabriela's face goes white.

"Gabriela, go. Go out. I'll scream … a lot worse … don't want you to faint here," I manage to say.

She goes without a word. Patricio steps forward, takes my hair from the doctor's hand and holds it up as the doctor rolls the cast around my shoulders and in a figure-eight on my back, with quick precise movements. I scream. They carry on undisturbed. I'm lost in the darkness of the pain with only a silly thought for company.

"These jeans are really tight. I probably look quite fat, the waist of these jeans is too low. I should have worn the other ones."

Big tears roll down my cheeks and I cry for it all—for my broken bone, for the pain, for the trouble I'm causing my friends again, and for the wrong jeans I'm wearing today.

With the cast securely in place, the doctor gives me a hospital gown to put over the whole construction and sends a nurse to inject me with a painkiller. Why did he not do that before the torture started?

My arms are suspended, with the cast freshly fitted under them. There's no way I can take my trousers off. Gabriela has just returned to the room and does it for me, commenting on the pink shade of my underwear as well. I like matching underwear.

The doctor is gone now, replaced by a nurse, and my friends hold me, one on each side, as I stand up, my ugly jeans pulled down a little, just enough to expose the upper part of my bum to the needle. One last scream and it's done. We can go home now.

We get in the car and start to drive towards the farm across the dirt road, which causes the car to shake badly. But with the strong painkiller I got at the hospital, I now take the shaking quite well. And the cast, as bad as it was to have it fitted, is nicely supporting my shoulder. For the first time since the fall I relax a bit.

Patricio, on the other hand, isn't at all relaxed. He's on a mission to get the metal plate and he starts calling the number the doctor gave him as soon as we are on the way. He drives with one hand and holds his mobile in the other.

"I don't care. You hear me? I don't care that it's Friday afternoon and you're about to close for the weekend. I need these things tomorrow morning here at the hospital. Send them over. I don't care how you send them over, but this girl needs to have surgery tomorrow morning at nine." His voice is angry enough to carry the message. He's been telling them the same thing over and over. It's not entirely clear to me what the issue is and why they don't just agree to send the bloody plate over.

Patricio puts the phone down and brings us up to speed. It's payment. They don't want to send the metal plate and screws over to the hospital in the absence of payment.

"I told them we'll pay tomorrow when they deliver. It doesn't work. They want the payment beforehand!"

"How about a credit card over the phone?" I ask, hopeful that some things might be as easy as in England.

He shakes his head. "Only if the holder is there to sign the receipt."

By "there" he means in Buenos Aires, two hours' drive away. Impossible for me.

"And they'll close the shop before we can get there anyway," he adds, his expression grim.

All my relaxation is gone. I really don't want to wait until Monday, not with this very uncomfortable cast on my back.

"Don't worry." Patricio reads my thoughts. "We'll sort out something."

He calls them back to plead again with the same girl. Then he asks to speak to her boss. He manages to persuade the boss to take a credit card payment over the phone if the card works.

It has to work, I think. In the rear mirror of the car I see a cloud of dust rising towards the sky from the dirt road behind us. Patricio drives fast. We're going to reach the farm soon. My credit card is in my purse, which I left just next to my polo bag. We'll sort this out.

But my transaction for just over two thousand dollars over the phone doesn't go through.

"Call Visa," they tell Patricio. "Get them to approve it. And then call us back."

Seated at the kitchen table at the farm, Patricio dials again and again the number for Visa Argentina and keys in all the digits on my credit card as instructed. Time and time again the call fails. After thirty minutes of this useless exercise, he again calls the company that sells the metal plate. This time no one picks up the phone. It's 6 pm already. They must have closed the business for the weekend.

"Oh, God," I think.

Patricio looks at me with a determined glint in his eyes.

"Don't worry," he tells me again. "We'll sort this out. You'll have the surgery tomorrow. Whatever it takes."

He calls the doctor and gets the number of the owner of the company that imports the plate and screws. Then he calls the guy directly and tells him he needs to have the plate tomorrow, no matter what.

"We'll pay cash. Tomorrow morning. At the hospital."

"But I have no cash here with me," I say, while he's still on the phone.

He hangs up, a look of relief finally on his face. "I do. I'll pay them. You don't worry about anything. You'll have that surgery tomorrow," he says.

"But Patricio—" and then I stop. "Thank you."

He brushes off any further expression of gratitude with a quick gesture.

"Now we need to go back to town to have the cardio test." His mind has already moved on to the next thing on the list.

I need a cardiogram before the surgery tomorrow and it was too late to do it in the afternoon when we left the hospital. So Patricio has arranged to have it done with a cousin of his, one of his many cousins. I suspect half this town is more or less related to him. The cousin was on a *siesta* when we left the hospital, and *siesta* is a very powerful concept in Argentina, especially in the rural parts. Nobody can disturb someone during an afternoon *siesta*. But at 7 pm the cousin would return to his practice and start seeing patients again.

We get back into the car—Patricio at the wheel, Gabriela in the back, and me in the front seat, sitting on top of a big white pillow, which is supposed to help with the bumps in the road and accommodate my cast, which looks like a huge hump on my back.

We drive in silence. We're too exhausted to speak. It's been a long day and it isn't over yet.

"We should maybe tell Rosario," Patricio says out of the blue.

I nod. He dials her number with the phone on loudspeaker. I don't want to imagine what Rosario will say. Unlike Patricio and Gabriela, she doesn't play polo. People who don't play polo usually have a low tolerance for polo-related injuries. People who play polo are more understanding. They're likely to have experienced injuries themselves.

"*Ro, cómo estás?*"

The short form of Rosario's name is Ro, just like the short form of my name in Argentina, which just adds to the feeling of sisterhood I have with this girl.

"Listen, we have bad news," Patricio continues on the loudspeaker. "Our friend, Roxy—"

"Yes, what happened?" I hear Rosario's worried voice.

"She's pregnant."

"What?" I open my eyes wide and for a second I wonder about the blood tests they did in the hospital. Maybe the doctor told them something he didn't tell me.

"What?" Rosario's voice echoes my question. "How is this possible? Oh my God. No-o-o. The guy she broke up with! Oh, no! It's not possible."

"No, it's not that." Patricio decides this was enough of an introduction. "Something else. She's broken her collarbone today. Falling from a horse."

A juicy Argentine swearing comes through, and this time it involves the genitals of a parrot. Why parrots? For a second I think about her story with Tete but no, *la concha de la lora* doesn't involve Tete in particular. Just the genitals of an unspecified female parrot and Rosario's utter shock at the news.

By now I'm already laughing. Pregnant? How did he think of that? After all the stress of the day, how can he possibly think of something so crazy to say? But it's like that with Patricio. He has a way of making things seem not so bad in the end.

But Rosario is almost in tears. "Roxy, please, never—you hear me? Never get on a bloody horse again!"

This, I can't promise.

We arrive at the cardiologist's private practice. He gives me a kiss on the cheek and I feel so exhausted I can't remember if I've met him before at one of the many parties, lunches, *asados*, or dinners I've been invited to involving Patricio's huge family. His consulting office is full of plants, and a Verdi opera is playing loudly from the speakers tucked into the corner of the room. He has a picture of Padre Pio, an Italian saint, overseeing his desk. Besides this, he has all he needs to give me a cardiogram and reassure me that my heart is just fine. He has no idea, I think. My heart has been badly broken, and only last week. But this doesn't show up on the cardiogram.

Then he waves off any suggestion that we pay for the appointment. He's Patricio's cousin after all. It must be bad business having so many cousins in the town where one is trying to make a living.

We spend some time in small talk before we go. Argentines love small talk. It's what glues and holds their society together. I learn about his passion for gardening and the trees he's buying one by one at a local garden center.

"You know what?" Patricio says, as we get back into the car. "We'll get him a tree. He won't take payment, but he's not going to refuse a gift. A palm tree for his garden would be just perfect. What do you think?"

I think it's a wonderful idea. The night has fallen, my painkiller is wearing off, but the pillow on the front seat is comfortable enough, and with no more pressing things to sort out Patricio is now driving slowly back towards the farm on the dusty dirt road that cuts straight across the lush green fields.

SATURDAY 19TH NOVEMBER

In Argentina things have a mysterious way of sorting themselves out in the end. Late in the evening we were informed that the metal plate and screws were to be delivered to the hospital in the morning, and Patricio was told to leave the money with the doctor, in cash, in an envelope, right before the operation. The invoice was to follow later.

I didn't sleep the whole night. The cast on my back made lying down impossible. So, to save me attempting it, Gabriela brought me all the pillows she could find in the house and tucked them behind my back, and I sat upright in bed the whole night. Just like an economy class flight to Argentina, all thirteen hours of it.

I lay awake thinking about what I'd done to myself.

"Not you. The horse. Polo. Polo is like this," said my rational mind.

"But it's the third time."

"Others have broken bones too, and they still play and are fine."

"But I'm not others. Maybe I'll die next time."

"Don't be stupid."

"Maybe I'll die tomorrow during surgery."

"No, you won't. You've done it before. Surgery. It will be fine."

"I didn't even write a will. If something happens, my parents will have a hard time dealing with all the mess I left back in England."

"They won't, because you won't die."

"And what am I going to do now? Without polo? I need polo. Now, with Rodrigo gone, I absolutely need polo. There's nothing left. Nothing. I can't live with this abyss."

Even my rational voice had nothing to say to this.

Morning came eventually and I was loaded straight into the car by my friends and taken back to the hospital.

I arrive in a bad mood but I have no time to dwell on my fears or lack of sleep. The plate and screws are already with the surgeon, we are told. And the doctor is in the surgery room, so I should hurry. I'm rolled to the surgery room in a wheelchair, with Patricio walking behind me holding an envelope full of cash.

"I'll tell the doctor it was a horse you fell from. Maybe he needs to know this for the surgery. I'd better tell him, just in case." I hear him talking behind me as we make our way across the long corridors.

I don't know what else Patricio tells the doctor in the door of the surgery room as he hands over the cash. I'm busy trying to lie flat on the surgery table with a huge cast hump on my back, like the two nurses are telling me to do. Impossible. The anesthetist starts cutting my cast with a huge pair of scissors and I start screaming. It hurts.

"Can't you do this later, after I'm asleep?" I ask him.

"No. I need you to lie down to put you to sleep, and you can't lie down with this thing on your back."

I know I can't. I tried in vain all last night. There's some more fiddling with the cast and more suppressed screams. I don't like how this surgery is starting.

My doctor comes back from the door where he was talking with Patricio. There is a look of amusement in his eyes. Maybe he's smiling too, but I can't see his mouth because it's covered by a surgical mask.

"Aha, so tell me. How did this happen? This horse you fell from, was it called Bicycle?"

They all laugh as I cringe. I wish they would put me to sleep. Some more chit-chat in Spanish follows. I'm now slowly starting to tremble, because the surgery table is cold and with the cast now removed I can actually lie flat on it.

And then it comes. The blissful feeling of the drug injected in the vein and the lights in the room dim all around me. The silhouettes of the doctors and nurses still talking around me become softer and softer. And between them I begin seeing—or maybe I just imagine—other silhouettes, and I know these are my angels and they're here, as they have been during my previous operations, and I know they will look after me this time as well.

And Patricio and Gabriela are just outside the door and they will look after me too. And with this thought, I disappear once again into the abyss of nothingness.

✎

I wake up later, trembling. I always feel extremely cold after surgery and I always feel grumpy as I come round. It's like I've been pulled away from a world of exquisite beauty. I have no idea where I was, but it felt like a busy day of business meetings. It reminded me of work, when you visit another office and you have to schedule one meeting after another to make the best of your short time there. I felt as though I'd been having a one-to-one review with each of my angels and there had been quite a few of them queuing up to speak to me.

Gabriela and Rosario are there when I open my eyes. Gabriela takes pictures.

"Stop taking pictures, woman. I must look half dead."

"You do, but you're alive and this is good news, darling."

"How did it go?" I ask, remembering the most important question.

"Good, all done. Fixed. All you need to do now is rest."

There are no "fucks" in her answers. When Gabriela doesn't swear it means something is wrong and she's worried. Maybe she's just shocked. But she recovers quickly.

"You look like a fucking corpse, darling. Have a sleep. Don't talk too much. We'll be back soon."

Ah, that's better, I think, as I fall asleep again. If the swearing is back, it's not so bad.

I sleep the whole afternoon. The doctor comes back in the evening to check on me. He looks relaxed. He spent the whole afternoon playing with his kid in his swimming pool, he says. Wow, so he has a kid already. He can't be that young. And he's got a swimming pool at home. Maybe he's not just starting his career. Looks can be deceiving here. I learned that last year when I went on a date with a twenty-seven-year-old guy, thinking he was close to forty.

Now that the doctor is back at the hospital for his evening rounds, I really hope he'll let me go home. My friends, who have been patiently waiting beside me for the whole afternoon, hope so too. We all have a party to go to. At midnight it's Rosario's birthday. But the doctor doesn't need to know about that.

I like this doctor. He smiles a lot and he's very friendly. He also chats a lot and he starts his check-up with a little small talk with Patricio and Gabriela. He mentions his father owns a butcher's not far from where my friends live. I hope this isn't where he learned his skills.

Then, once the small talk is finished, it's time for serious matters. He turns to me.

"All is good. The surgery went well. I fixed all five broken pieces with a metal plate. I had to use a bigger one than I thought initially, so the cut is a little bit longer, I'm afraid."

Five pieces. I didn't know my collarbone was broken in five pieces. He didn't know either, he says. The X-ray showed only one break, but when he reached the bone he found the other fractures.

"Here, do you want to see what it looks like?" The doctor holds his iPhone out to show my friends a picture. "I took it during surgery," he adds.

I see Gabriela's face turning white. This isn't good news.

"Can I see, too?" My curiosity is stronger than any sense of self-protection.

He turns the phone to me and I see a large, fresh cut surrounded by blood. Inside the cut, a bright green piece of metal is firmly fixed with a number of screws and something that looks like ordinary wire. I suddenly feel like vomiting.

"You don't mind a little bit of blood, do you?" the doctor asks me gently.

I take another look at it. It resembles a piece of meat on the grill, like an *asado*. They sometimes fix the meat with wire here. I can't get my mind around the idea that what he's showing me is my own body. The bright green color of the metal shocks me most. Why so bright? Will it show through the skin?

Patricio brings us back to practicalities. "Can she go home now?"

"Well, it's better if she stays overnight," the doctor says. "But if she's well cared for …"

He appears to be giving in easily, I think.

"Don't worry," Patricio says. "We'll look after her."

The doctor nods and proceeds to put a huge bandage on my right arm. He discharges me from the hospital at 10 pm. There's no cast this time, as there's no need for one. I have a twenty-centimeter piece of metal keeping my bone together.

We get into the car and go straight to Rosario's birthday party. I've had so many painkillers pumped through the intravenous drip throughout the day that I don't feel any pain. I'm just a bit dizzy.

Several of Patricio's cousins are gathered at Rosario's party. They all know what happened to me, in detail. They know about the hospital, the surgery, the horse called Bicycle. News travels fast in this small town. Everyone is supportive, they all come to talk to me, feed me, and pour drinks for me. I feel surrounded by my own family. Maybe the doctor wouldn't have approved of me going straight to a party after surgery, but the care I feel coming from them helps me more than any painkiller pumped through that drip.

At midnight we sing "Happy Birthday" to Rosario and then, when no one notices and the party is going on in the garden, I slip into the house and I find a quiet spot. For the first time that day, I let myself cry.

What have I done to myself? The question is there with me, no matter how much I've tried to silence it. And what will I do now? Now with no polo, no love … nothing. Silent tears roll down my face and I don't even try to stop them.

But in Argentina you can't be alone for long, no matter how well you hide. It took Rosario only five minutes to notice I was gone and another two to find me. I have no idea how she did it, surrounded by dozens of guests, but she sensed exactly where I was and what I was doing there.

"Roxy." Her voice is soft, her hand in mine. "You'll recover. We'll all look after you. You'll be fine."

I know they will look after me. They did it before, last year and the year before that. It's the third time I've been injured here and this family has looked after me.

"Let's get this invalid home." Patricio comes in, echoing my thoughts. "Enough excitement for the day."

The night is dark as we get back into the car. It's well past midnight. We're all exhausted, but they still talk to me all the way home, trying to divert my thoughts from the bright green piece of metal I now carry inside my shoulder.

Thank God they're here, I think. And thank God there's no cast on my back. I'll finally sleep tonight.

SUNDAY 20TH NOVEMBER

"You know, last year you also fell on the eighteenth," Patricio tells me over breakfast at the big farm.

Breakfast at the old farm always takes place around the big round table in the kitchen as the inhabitants of the farm wake up one by one and come to take their places around it. The smell of toast fills the room. On the table there's a jar of Gabriela's exquisite marmalade. This one is made of peaches. I'm savoring a cup of well-brewed espresso. They might be in the middle of nowhere, but the farm has all the luxuries of civilization.

"What? On the same day? How do you know?"

"I write these things down. I have a file, like a journal, with everything that happens on the farm. A guy came to cut the wool of the sheep, a new foal was born. Roxy fell … Look, I have it all here. All on the eighteenth of December." He shows me a Word file open on his iPhone.

I believe in things like that. Coincidences. Except I have no idea what this one means.

"Next year on the eighteenth you must stay away from horses. And I don't care what month it's in."

Next year. So he thinks there will be a next year.

"So you think I should be playing polo again, Patricio?" I ask in a small voice.

"I think so. It's up to you, of course. But polo is like this, sometimes you take a fall—"

And sometimes you break a bone. I finish the sentence in my mind. But the trouble with me is that I seem to break a bone all the time.

"If I really thought you were bad at it, I would tell you, 'Roxy, give me your boots and never touch them again.' But no, I think you're doing well, I think you should play."

"First, she has to find out why she keeps on breaking bones," Gabriela jumps in. "It must be because you're vegetarian. Eat some fucking meat, darling, it's not going to kill you."

"Gabriela, you sound like my parents."

"They're right, your parents. You can't come to Argentina and still stay a vegetarian. We have the best meat in the world here."

I smile. This is exactly what my parents told me. "Go to Argentina. They will cure you of this disease." Being vegetarian, they mean.

The trouble is that Argentines have a deeply ingrained sense of hospitality and respect for their guests. Which means that instead of them curing me, I seem to turn all of them into vegetarians. Gabriela always makes sure the maid cooks vegetarian when I'm there, and more than once I'd been embarrassed to see the full family around the table eating meat-free dishes, just because I was there.

Gabriela comes up with another idea. "Maybe you should get yourself one of those riding vests. Like the Michelin man ad on TV. So you don't break another fucking bone next time."

She means next time I fall. It goes without question there will be another fall. There always is another one in polo. If there's a next time I play, there'll be a next time I fall. The vest she refers to is an ultra-protective piece of equipment used for eventing and other horse-related disciplines. An inflatable vest is attached to the saddle, and every time a rider falls, the vest automatically inflates like an airbag and protects the person from breaking any bones.

Except with polo being the elegant sport that it is, nobody wears these things. We wear only helmets, boots, and knee- and elbow-pads for protection. Sometime goggles and occasionally face guards, but it's mostly girls who wear face guards. No professional polo player would ever play with a face guard. And no one, absolutely no one, ever wears an inflatable vest while playing polo. I just can't imagine how I would look in it. And polo is all about the looks.

MONDAY 21ST NOVEMBER

The plan was to go back to Buenos Aires with Gabriela this morning. After all, I felt surprisingly well yesterday, just one day after surgery. I chatted with everyone and spent the day at the big farm. But morning came and I woke up hot with a fever after a restless night, and everything in my body hurt and I couldn't even bear the thought of getting out of bed.

"You're going nowhere," Patricio declares after touching my forehead. "You've got a fever. I'll call the doctor. Gabriela has to go, but you must stay. I'll look after you."

Gabriela is stuck in the doorway, speechless, looking at me with big open eyes. She's always very expressive, this girl. When she doesn't say anything, it's bad news.

"I'll be fine, woman. Go. Just go. I'll be OK. I'll stay in bed and I'll be fine. There's nothing you can do. It's just how one feels after surgery." I'm trying to convince her, or maybe just convince myself.

"Are you sure? Roxy—" But she doesn't finish the sentence. "You look like shit" is what she probably wanted to say.

"Yes. Please. I've messed up your lives enough. Please don't change your plans for me. Go. I'll be fine."

She nods. I take a deep breath, relieved I'm not ruining her plans for the day. Patricio tells me he has to go and play polo, but he'll send someone from the farm with breakfast for me.

They both go. I stay in bed the whole day. Patricio's sister comes with breakfast and then with lunch, driving across the fields from the big farm. I eat and then go back to bed, my mind blank, the time suspended.

The house is bathed in the light of the afternoon. Through the large windows of my room I can see the fields all around, empty and silent. Alone. *Sola. Sola* in Baires last year. *Sola* in the *campo* this year.

A woodpecker with a beautiful red head comes to the windows and attempts a shy knock. It's not a good idea. I remember Patricio saying he shot a woodpecker a few weeks ago. The poor bird took to knocking obsessively on the windows and they couldn't sleep for days. So, at one point he decided he'd had enough of it, and he took the gun out and shot it. It's like this in the Argentine *campo*. People have guns and they use them.

"This will teach the others a lesson," Patricio said. He also said they had not been disturbed since.

But now this little bird is playing with fire. Don't worry, I won't tell Patricio. If you go quietly now and don't come back, you might just live. It probably hears my silent whisper, because it goes and the windows stay empty for a while.

The house was built next to a group of huge eucalyptus trees. They always build houses near a group of trees in the *campo*. Otherwise, the scorching sun of the pampas would be too much for the inhabitants to bear. I spot other birds in the trees and I know if I go outside I'll hear their songs. Early in the morning is the best time, or the hour just before dark.

The fields are empty, with just a few cows grazing in the distance, but I know there are many more inhabitants of the pampas hiding in the tall grass. There will be foxes and pheasants around, and a weird animal with scales on its back and hedgehog-like needles on its belly called an armadillo. And skunks. Gabriela told me there were many skunks nearby, and one night when we drove back I could smell them too—a mixture of sulphur, coffee, and garlic. It was weird, but not as bad as I expected.

My mind rests on the skunk smell for a while until it decides to issue a red alert flag.

"You need to take a shower. You probably smell like a skunk by now."

But I can't take a shower by myself as I have a fresh cut on my shoulder the size of that bright green piece of metal. And the last proper shower I had was three days ago, the morning before my fall. With Gabriela gone to Buenos Aires, maybe I can ask for Rosario's help.

The sun is going down. I slowly venture out of bed and even step outside for a few minutes. But I'm feeling dizzy and my shoulder hurts like hell. I get back into the bed and take one more painkiller.

Text from Gabriela. *Have you got food?*

Yes, mummy.

Text from Patricio. *Will be late, polo game delayed this afternoon.*

Don't worry. I'll be asleep.

Text from Rosario asking for updates.

Please come help me shower!

She'll come tomorrow. Thank God.

No more text messages. No one else knows. Not my parents in Romania, not my friends in London. I'll tell them one day, but not now. It's too early. They'll make a fuss and I can't handle it. Especially my parents. Last year when I broke my arm here playing polo, I didn't tell them. My arm healed and there was no scar, so I didn't need to say a word. This time I'll have to tell them. One day. But not now. For now, all that matters is that my Argentine family is here for me and I don't need anyone else.

I go to sleep at sunset. I hope I'll get at least a few hours' sleep before I wake up in the middle of the night. Because I will, no doubt. It happened last night, and the night before, just after the surgery. I woke up in pain, as if a train had just run over me. I have no idea why the pain comes back so strongly at night, but it does. It'll come back again tonight, I'm sure. I'll sweat again and I'll feel the blood pumping in my temples, and that thirst that burns my throat. And once again I'll feel too weak to reach for the glass of water on my bedside table, and I'll just lie there thinking about it with a dry mouth and heavy breath. I'll feel my body cut in two, at about the height of my chest, the shakes coming and going, and then the little lights dancing in the darkness, and I'll wonder once again if this is how one feels on one's deathbed, just as I have wondered these past few nights.

It all comes, just as I expect. And the question that comes with it is the same one from the night before and the one before that. Am I going to die this time?

I've never thought of this before. I am not quite sure why I'm thinking of it now.

They say every person has seven lives. Seven opportunities to pass by death and mock it. In the darkness of the room my mind is counting them all, my body sweating with fever, then shivering with cold.

1. The Romanian revolution. I ran away from home when I was fifteen to join the Romanian revolution against communism. My parents locked me in my bedroom, but I escaped out of the window. Many people died on the streets of Bucharest that day. Luckily, I wasn't one of them.

2. The parachute that wouldn't open. Aged sixteen, I tried skydiving. My parachute didn't open during my second jump. I came down calmly, in free fall, without doing anything, blissfully unaware that my trainer and the other people down on the ground were anxiously monitoring me through binoculars, paralyzed with fear that I'd crash. Eventually—and much too late, as my trainer informed me in a scream of anger very shortly after I landed—I'd turned my head to check what was going on and why the parachute hadn't opened. That small move helped the parachute detangle from my helmet where it had got stuck, and it eventually opened. Just in time, as I was about to hit the ground.

3. Gunpoint at the Turkish border. Aged nineteen, I got myself in trouble arguing with the border patrol on the Turkish-Bulgarian border. It's a long story. Too long to recount it all. A soldier escorted me to the no man's land in between the two countries and left me there with no money, no mobile phone, and no documents, apart from my passport, which he'd thrown at my feet just before he threatened me with his orders to shoot if I attempted to cross the border. All a terrible misunderstanding, but I spoke no Turkish and he spoke nothing else, and I ended up being picked up in a state of near fainting a few hours later by a stranger and shoveled into his car. He then drove 700 kilometers, taking a big detour from his own route to take me to my parents' home in Romania, and he left before I could even thank him. I spoke no Turkish and he spoke nothing else.

4. Car crashes. A number of car crashes in my twenties, one after another, which resulted in me being officially forbidden to touch any car belonging to my parents or extended family. But maybe the car crashes don't count, and there were more than seven of them anyway.

5. Gunpoint in Africa. I definitely used up a few of my lives during my journey across Africa at the age of twenty-eight. A bazooka was pointed at me and my travel-mates somewhere in a sandstorm on the border between Chad and Niger. And there were a few more arrests at gunpoint in the Congo. And maybe one in Angola. But I didn't think they'd actually shoot—not the policemen and their arrests at gunpoint, anyway. They were just for show. Except for one incident. I remember a guy yelling, completely out of his mind, pointing a gun at me that had no safety pin on. I know this for sure. I wasn't able to sleep the whole night afterwards, remembering every single detail of that encounter. So, maybe Africa counts as one brush with death, on account of this particular mad policeman. Not the other incidents. There were more than seven of them, anyway.

6. The tsunami in Thailand. I was on a scuba-diving boat, all kitted up, ready to start the dive. Just before we jumped into the water the captain told us we should wait. They'd had a weird alert on the radio. The tsunami wave passed right under our boat.

So, six times so far. Or maybe five, if I don't count the car crashes. What next? Not a lot. My thirties were less eventful. A desert trip to Libya, but that was before the troubles started. Some civilized safaris in Africa. Getting married, getting divorced, almost getting married again. These don't count. They were only heartbreaking, not life-threatening circumstances. Or maybe one was, but then I met a nice guy who pulled me out of depression. No, it's not worth counting anything here.

Then polo came along. And polo is definitely worth counting: one fall in England, two arms broken, one fall in Argentina, one arm broken, another fall now. I've reached nine. It can't be. Maybe not all the falls could have resulted in me being dead. I'm alive, after all. Let's start again.

With my eyes firmly shut I count again.

1. The Romanian revolution;
2. The parachute that didn't open …

I don't even try to stop my mind from running in this mad circle anymore. I tried it the night before and it didn't work. It only made things worse. If I don't count, the panic sets in and tells me this is the seventh time and I'll die now. Post-operation infection, or something. Maybe I got a bug from the hospital. That would explain why I sweat like crazy, have a fever, and feel like a train has run me over. So, I don't try to stop my mind from counting. I just follow it through all the memories of when I shook hands with death.

Late in the night I hear Patricio coming back home. He stops at the door of my bedroom, which I've left open so I can see a little bit of light from the corridor. I was too afraid to count my lives in total darkness.

"Roxy, are you all right? Sorry I'm late, our game got delayed and it was a long way away. I brought you pizza."

"Already ate, thanks. Your sister was here earlier and got me some food. I'm fine, I just need to sleep," I lie. "I'll be better in the morning."

"Anything you need, I'm here, OK? Just across the corridor. I'll leave the door open so I can hear you. Just shout if you need anything."

"Don't worry, I'll be fine," I lie again.

He leaves, goes to his bedroom, and switches off the light in the corridor.

I wish I'd told him to leave it on, that it helps me a bit when I'm not completely in the dark. But there's no way I can admit to him or to anyone else how terrified I feel.

It's pitch black in the room now and I carry on counting lives in the darkness.

TUESDAY 22ND NOVEMBER

I did get a few hours' sleep in the end, just before sunrise, and they were enough to make me feel better. Or maybe the fever has done its show and decided to leave. Whatever the reason, as morning comes, I feel I could actually get out of bed and even venture outside.

A quick look around and I see Patricio in the garden by the little vegetable patch they've set up behind the house. He's planting cherry tomatoes and talking on WhatsApp with a polo client in Europe. Argentines love WhatsApp. Almost no one calls on their mobile here.

I go to my quinoto tree and start having breakfast straight from its branches, using the only healthy arm I have.

Now what? Feeling better means I can get back into planning mode. Let's think of what I need to do right now. My mind is still blank, as if it can't fully take in the new reality I find myself in.

Eat another quinoto. Think again. Nothing comes. More quinotos. Still no answer. I'll finish the whole tree before I get my answers, and Gabriela will get mad at me. She likes making marmalade with the fruit of her trees.

I came to Argentina to be with Rodrigo and play polo. Both these activities are closed off for the time being. What's my next dream? What am I going to do now?

"Mend your arm," my sensible part says.

"OK, I know, but I have no more fever and I'm feeling better now. I need to have a plan. What am I going to do next? Stay in Argentina? Go back to London? Start looking for work? Maybe I can call some head-hunters. With no polo and no Rodrigo, what on earth am I going to do here?"

I pick some more quinotos.

"You've just had surgery, for God's sake. Three days ago. Can you put off planning for a while?" sensible me says.

"No, I can't. I need to know what I'm doing next."

"Go nuts, then. You won't know. Not now. No matter how much you try."

I have a solution for this. Sensible me might not like it, but I'll do what I always do when I don't know what's next. I'll talk to one of my ladies with a crystal. Or maybe to all three of them. This situation requires an emergency counsel.

Talking to a lady with a crystal is my secret fallback option. She'll know for me. She'll tell me what to do. And then I'll evaluate the situation. If I like what I hear, I'll follow the advice. If not, I'll ignore it.

I pick two more quinotos and go back inside the house. I like putting things into practice immediately. Plus, a quick glance at the backyard confirms that Patricio is still kneeling next to the cherry tomatoes, digging with one hand and holding his phone in the other. It's going to take some time until he's done with both activities— enough for me to set up some appointments.

Ladies with a crystal work by appointment only. You can't simply call them just like that, because you found yourself without a life plan under a quinoto tree, one early morning in the Argentine pampas.

I pick up my iPhone and I email all three of them, requesting emergency appointments. I add for clarification that I've broken a bone—again—and that I desperately need to understand why I broke the bone and what I am to do next. And for this, I need a consultation.

Just as I finish sending my emails, Patricio comes back from his gardening activities and tells me it's time to go for breakfast to the big farm, if I feel I can face the ten-minute drive across the fields.

"Yes, definitely. I feel a lot better this morning."

And then, as he changes from his muddy rubber boots into trainers, I ask him the same question I asked the day before, just in a slightly different way. It's the same question I've been asking myself over and over again when I'm not busy counting my close encounters with death.

"Patricio, what will you do next year? If I call you again and I say I'm in Argentina and I want to play polo and I ask you for horses, what will you do? Will you give me horses or will you delete my number from your mobile phone?"

He lifts his head from the muddy boots he's pulling off and says, looking straight at me, "Roxy, if you ask me for horses again, I'll give you horses. Of course I'll give you horses. It's your decision, not mine. I'll do it," he repeats. "And then I'll look after you," he adds.

He doesn't say, "I'll look after you if I need to." He just says, "I'll look after you." Like he did the first year I came here and I hurt my back playing polo and stayed at their farm for Christmas. Like he did last year when I broke my arm playing polo and I ended up spending Christmas with them again. Like he's doing now. Does this mean he expects it to happen again?

"But, Roxy, you're the one with a broken bone and a piece of metal in your shoulder right now. You have to think if this is what you want. I can't tell you not to play polo. Polo is my life, I love this game. I know you love it too. There is no way I can tell you not to play polo again. I've had injuries, Gabriela has had injuries, and we still play. But this needs to be your decision. For my part, this is all I can say—if you ask me for horses again, I'll give you horses."

I don't say anything. He's right. I can't outsource this decision. I'll have to decide for myself if I'll ever play polo again. Or maybe I'll ask my ladies with a crystal.

We go to the old farm, and by lunchtime I feel so good and so upbeat that it sounds like a good idea to join Patricio and two of his polo clients as they get ready to drive to Buenos Aires to go and watch one of the polo games at the *Abierto*. Given the break-up with Rodrigo and then the break of my collarbone, I haven't seen any games so far. Neither have Patricio and Gabriela, who were busy looking after me on both occasions. Now one of the games has been postponed from the weekend to a weekday, and they've decided to go and watch it.

"You can come with us if you feel strong enough," they say, and I agree. I want to go back to the city, to my flat, to start planning my life again. The fever has passed and I'm feeling well. And I don't want to be a burden on my friends forever.

I get into the car and last only until the end of the dirt road, some twenty minutes later. The car is shaking badly, my fresh surgery wound hurts, and my whole body is in agony again. When we hit the tarmac road I feel close to fainting, although I try hard not to say a word.

"You're not going anywhere," Patricio says, taking a quick look at me. Reading minds is an Argentine trait. Maybe it's not that difficult in this particular case. I must look like a corpse again.

If they turn around to take me back to the farm, they will be late for the game. So Patricio finds another solution. He calls his sister, who by chance is in town, offloads me into her car and sends me straight back to bed. Maybe Buenos Aires and a game of polo aren't such good ideas for me right now.

His sister takes me to the old farm, feeds me lunch, and from there her fourteen-year-old daughter drives me on to the little house across the field.

"Where did you learn to drive?" I ask her.

"Dad taught me, here on the dirt road. I only drive in the farm and round about, though. I need to be eighteen to go into town," she says, her eyes focused on the dirt road ahead.

Soon I'm back in the same bed I left this morning feeling so well. This time, no amount of painkillers can ease the agony I feel.

To distract myself, I start playing with my phone. There's no one to send messages to—not about my current condition, anyway—so I start googling collarbone post-surgery care instead. They say recovery takes three months. Screw them. They have no idea. There is no way I can stay an invalid for three months. It's depressing. Better to change the subject. I google polo injuries. I come across a page that says Prince Charles had more injuries, due to playing polo, than did a boxing champion of England. Broken arm, broken rib, fractured shoulder, lost consciousness on the field. Enough. This is depressing as well. But he hasn't died. Maybe they wouldn't have let him play if there was a real danger he could die. He's a prince, after all.

I'm out of googling ideas, so I switch to emails. There's one reply from a lady with a crystal. She's lady number one, the one who talks to angels and believes in the happy-ever-after ending with Rodrigo. Well, she was wrong about that one. But still … Maybe it was only a glitch in the system and she's now got her angel connection sorted and this time she'll tell me something useful. She's happy to talk tomorrow afternoon. I say OK.

There's also a reply from lady with a crystal number two, the astrologist. She's got a session available in three weeks' time. Would I like to book it? Yes, please. I go straight to PayPal and I make the payment. That's because lady with a crystal number two always wants payment in advance to confirm the booking. Maybe she's had bad experiences with her customers. I have no idea, but anyway, it's her business. For my part, I just comply. She tells me to pay in advance, and so I do.

There's no reply from lady with a crystal number three—or the chief healer, as I call her. That's because she has a personal assistant who schedules her appointments, and the personal assistant works only occasionally, and at random times. I take a deep breath and send a prayer that the personal assistant gets off her lazy bum and does her job, because I am in desperate need of a consultation.

Then I receive several text messages: from Gabriela, Patricio, his father, his sister, the husband of the sister. I reply one by one, saying I'm fine, I'm in bed and, no, I don't need anything. Thank you.

Then I go back to the internet. What now? Rodrigo. For the first time in a few days, Rodrigo comes back to my mind. What about Rodrigo? There is no more Rodrigo.

"We know that," my heart says. "But is Gabriela right about him? Was he really that bad?"

"Look, it's not only Gabriela who thinks so. It's Patricio and Rosario, too. And Sol."

"What do they know?"

"They know. They can see clearly. They haven't got a silly heart desperately sad about losing him," I say. "And it's not just them. I know too. Deep down I knew, my body knew. Even you knew, silly heart."

"I did." My heart sighs. "And yet … Why?"

"Why what?"

"Why did things happen that way?"

"Because it was a scam and because I'm a silly girl and I believe every idiot who comes by and calls me *linda*."

"Now maybe you're too tough on yourself." My heart jumps to my defense. "He was nice."

"Yes. And a scammer. A narcissist."

"Where does this come from?"

"Gabriela called him that. And look. Look what they say about narcissists on the internet."

In an attempt to silence her, I google "relationship patterns with narcissists."

Roller-coaster. A relationship with a narcissist is a roller-coaster, they say. One moment great, the next moment terrible. No stability. No way of forecasting the future. Unexpected surprises. They don't love. They can't love. They just need others to validate their fragile ego.

Phase one of a relationship with a narcissist: they will be amazing, excessively caring, loving, and attentive.

Hmm. Like calling you *linda* a thousand times a day. I carry on reading.

In phase one the narcissist is enthusiastic and full of hopes and dreams. But then overnight, phase two appears to kick in and the narcissist reveals his true colors. The mask falls and his real motives are laid bare.

The verb *llevar* and a particular question spring into my mind. I read on. They start withdrawing. Ah, yes. No gift for my birthday. That makes sense. It actually all makes sense.

The victim usually becomes clingy at this stage and tries to win the narcissist back. Thank God I showed him the door when he said he wanted to leave. Fascinated, I read on.

Phase three: either they leave you an emotional ruin or, if you have any strength left, you decide you don't want to put up with this shit any longer and you leave.

Leave. This is what I've done. I remember his text messages and the desperation to get me back after he didn't bother to come to my birthday dinner.

I want you to know that I love you …

It was all a game.

Because, I read on, narcissists can't feel anything. It is all a façade, a mask, a means to an end.

And one more thing: a narcissist always reserves the right to revisit a former victim. They want to end things on a positive note so that they don't lose the opportunity of you serving them again sometime in the future.

The words of Rodrigo's last text message come back at me with a blow.

I hope one day you will be able to forgive me.

Wow. I close my iPhone and decide to read no more. This is really depressing.

Salvation arrives in the form of Rosario. She comes to give me a much-needed shower, girl chat, and a shoulder to cry on if I need one. I decide I don't need the shoulder, because I won't cry, no matter how much stuff I read about on the internet. But I'll take the shower.

"Ro, thank God you're here. I was going insane in my own little mind. And I smell like a skunk." I give her a kiss. "Sorry about this. You really don't have to give me a kiss. Everyone gives me kisses here, morning and evening, and all I can think of is that I really smell like a skunk."

She laughs. "You smell just fine, Roxy. Relax. Everything is going to be fine."

And everything turns out fine just by magic, just because she's here, my Argentine sister, and with a healthy dose of girly laughter my gloomy mood lifts a bit, and after the shower it goes away completely.

Then Patricio's niece turns up too, when I'm half-dressed and Rosario is putting my bandage back on my shoulder. She's come to bring me *chipas*, she says. She took her father's car and drove across the fields to bring me some of the housemaid's delicious freshly baked scones.

Then they leave, and I receive another surge of evening-time text messages. Patricio will be late, he's playing polo. Gabriela, from Buenos Aires, suggests Rosario and I open a bottle of champagne, and she gives us precise instructions as to where we can find one in the house. Patricio's sister, brother-in-law, and father all ask how I am, if I need anything, and if they should come and check on me.

I go to sleep surrounded by this warm, fuzzy feeling. It tells me I'm not alone and people care about me. It feels soothing. Maybe it can help me sleep tonight.

But nothing can help me sleep these nights. I wake up in a couple of hours, as I've awakened every single night since the surgery. The sweat is back and so are the shivers and the dry mouth and the feeling that a train has run me over. Why does this come back only in the middle of the night? My mind is alert, blood pounding in my temples, replaying over and over a comment Rosario made casually about a girl who died after she had surgery in the same hospital. She picked up a virus in the operating theater, my friend said.

I lie in bed sweating, then shivering, then sweating again. The light from the corridor comes into the room through my half-open door. Thank God for this little light, otherwise I would start to see the mysterious white lights dancing in the darkness again, and I'll imagine once more that they're my angels and that they've come for me because it's my time to die. I'll die … maybe tonight. That's it. Maybe I've got the same virus as that girl.

My mind goes back to counting lives in a desperate attempt to silence this thought.

Patricio comes back late, and just like last night he stops at the door of my bedroom to check on me.

"I'm fine," I say. I don't wait for his question.

Nevertheless, he comes in and sits by the bed.

"Fever?" he asks, touching my forehead.

"Don't know."

"Don't think so," he says.

What does he know? I'm drenched in sweat. Maybe it's the fever. Or maybe it's because of counting lives, and the fear, or maybe I'm just going to die.

I lie there in utter terror, feeling with every little cell of my body that my life is ending. I've never felt like this before. Maybe this is why they say people who die know when it happens. This is where it will all end, right here.

Patricio picks up my hand, the healthy one, and stays there for a while, in silence. It feels good. I'm not alone. At least if I die, I won't die alone.

"You all have been so nice to me. And your family … they all came in today, one by one, and sent me messages. I'm so grateful."

"Shh, it's OK," he says.

"No, it's just that … I don't want to do this to you again. I don't want to be a burden. It's the third time. Last year, and the year before, and now. I really—"

I stop. My throat is burning. I don't know what I'm trying to say. I don't know if it makes any sense.

He continues to hold my hand, in silence.

"I don't want to die," I say finally.

He squeezes my hand.

"Shhh, it's OK," he says. "You won't. You won't die."

And just like this, he picks it up for me—the large lump of fear I have finally forced out of me. He takes it and holds it for me safely, away from my mind, just as he holds my hand until I fall asleep again.

And for the first time after surgery I sleep all throughout the night.

WEDNESDAY 23RD NOVEMBER

In the morning I'm fine again. No fever. No pain. No fear of death. I have no idea why this fever and the irrational fear come only at night, but I give up trying to understand it. The important thing is that I feel well again. So well that I decide I'll go back to the city today. Enough with this invalid posing. Five days of it is more than enough.

But before I go I have another emergency to deal with—an email from my insurance. They say they won't be able to settle the bill with the hospital directly. I'm supposed to pay the hospital and they'll refund me the money once I'm back in England.

The bill? Ah, I forgot about that. How much is the bill? I call the hospital but the line goes dead. The phone signal is bad at the farm. I suddenly remember the few figures scribbled on a piece of paper after the doctor finished putting the cast on my back. I get the paper from Patricio. He's got all the documents from the hospital. I haven't seen any in these last five days. I find out the total bill for my surgery comes to about five thousand dollars, of which Patricio has already paid half with his own money. That's because unlike last year, when I was treated free of charge in a state-owned hospital, this time I had the surgery in a private hospital. And private hospitals issue bills.

I don't have all that cash with me and they wouldn't take credit cards. I need cash for the hospital—dollars, to be more precise, and a lot of them. Argentina's economy revolves around American dollars, although the national currency is the peso. I also need to repay Patricio and I need more cash for the upcoming expenses. Where on earth am I going to get all this cash from? I doubt I can take all that money out from a bank in Buenos Aires. Argentina has just legalized foreign currency transactions at the real rate of exchange, instead of the artificially low rate the previous government imposed. Still, it's a big hassle drawing cash out, and dealing with international transfers is a nightmare I don't want to have to think about.

Marco! The thought comes out of nowhere. Of course. Marco said he would be coming to Argentina. Maybe he can bring me some cash. It would be the perfect solution. He always turns up in my life when I'm in trouble. He always helps. Maybe he can help now.

I send him a text saying I've broken my collarbone and had surgery. Is he going to be back here soon?

He calls me straight away.

"How can you pick up the phone if you have a broken neck?" he screams at me.

"Not the neck. Are you crazy? The collarbone."

"What is that?"

"A bone in the shoulder."

I hear a deep breath in on the other end of the phone. "*Cazzo*. I thought—*collo* means neck in Italian. I got so scared."

"Marco, I was texting you in English. Collarbone. Not *collo*."

It's complicated with Marco. We speak Italian, but sometimes I text him in English or half and half. And since my Spanish clicked into place last year I'm mixing in a lot of Spanish words, too.

"*Imbecille*. Are you going to give up that stupid sport now?"

"Marco, please. I've no strength for this right now."

"And where the hell are you? In a zoo? I can hear birds all around you."

The line goes dead.

Reception is bad, I text him back. *When are you here?*

This weekend. In three days. Do you need anything?

Yes. 5000 dollars in cash. Please.

No problem. You'll have it on Saturday. And please don't break anything between now and Saturday. Seriously.

Just like that. Marco has a special way of making problems disappear.

I laugh. Marco also has a special way of making me laugh, even with a big piece of steel in my torso.

THURSDAY 24TH NOVEMBER

I wake up after the first night back in my bed in Buenos Aires feeling like a train has run me over once again. I can't move. I can hardly breathe. I can't imagine why it hurts so much, as if something has suddenly gone very bad inside my chest.

Yesterday I felt everything was perfect. I finally arrived back at my flat in the city after a relatively easy journey in Patricio's pick-up truck. My cleaner agreed to come by every day to help me out. It felt good to be back to my own life, and I thought the worst had passed. But I was wrong.

I grab the phone in desperation and send a message to the cutie doctor who operated on me. Doc, I've decided to call him. He's given me his phone number, and everyone uses WhatsApp here, anyway.

He calls me back immediately.

"What are you doing in Buenos Aires? That's two hours' drive from Lobos! Who said you could move?"

He's pretty angry, Doc. I can't picture him angry. All I remember of him is the carefree chitchat and a smiley teenager's face. But maybe I was on a high dose of painkillers and my memory can't be trusted.

I tell him I felt good and I decided to come home. I was all right last night, but the morning came and I feel like something has broken inside me again.

"Don't worry, nothing is broken. You've got eight screws keeping that metal implant in place. But you shouldn't have traveled, you hear me? You had surgery five days ago. A pretty big surgery. This isn't a joke, do you hear me?"

"OK, I hear you. But I'm here now. And I need to come back to see you on Friday for the check-up, right?"

"No. Now that you're there, don't move. Absolutely do *not* get out of bed. Don't come to see me. We'll stay in contact on WhatsApp and then you can get an X-ray there in a week's time and send that to me. You're not supposed to move, do you get that?"

Yes, Doc, I get that.

"Do *not* get out of bed," he repeats before he hangs up.

Stranded in Buenos Aires. I'm alone, in bed. I can't go back to the farm. I can't see my friends. What am I going to do with my life?

There's only one answer to this question under the current circumstances—call a lady with a crystal. And luckily I have an appointment booked with lady number one and I expect it'll cost me about a hundred dollars. Expensive but still a good deal for moments like this, when one doesn't know what to do with one's life.

Lady number one is the same lady who told me Rodrigo was the man of my life. I didn't agree with her last time we spoke, but now I'm coming to her with a new problem—my broken bone, the fifth one in three years. Why does this happen? And what can I do to stop this pattern?

The lady with a crystal doesn't want to talk about my bone, though. She wants to talk about Rodrigo. In her deep and caring voice she asks me if I've seen him. No, I haven't. Why not? He's never been in touch after that emotional *Adios* message, and because in the meantime I've broken a bone.

"But why didn't you call him?"

"Because I've broken a bone," I say again. "And had surgery. And actually I want to talk about the bone."

"Are you sure you don't want Rodrigo back? He's the man of your life and you can still make up with him and—"

"No, I don't."

I tell her I don't want to get back with him. That I've taken him out of my mind, one word at a time, hitting a ball on a polo field before I fell and broke—my bone! Why do I break my bones?

"But maybe you want to meet up with him one more time? Just to see what he has to say? And maybe see how you feel?" she suggests.

"I can't meet up with him. I'm in bed. With a broken bone! And Doc doesn't let me get out of bed, and—"

"Are you sure about this? He does love you, after all."

"And what if he strangles me? When I meet him? Assuming

he'll want to meet, which I'm not at all sure he will. Sol says women die in this country, and have you heard about *Ni una menos*? Do you know how many women get killed by ex-boyfriends in Argentina? Do you understand that I feel this guy isn't right for me and that I'm over him?" I am trying hard not to shout at her.

"But he's not over you."

I'm seriously losing my patience with this lady and her crystal. Maybe Rodrigo is secretly paying her to plead his cause.

I'm telling her that as far as I'm concerned, Rodrigo's wishes right now matter far less than the shit of the horse I fell off. And that I don't want to talk about him. Hear me? He's gone from my life. What's left is one broken bone, with a big metal implant attached with eight screws, and one unanswered question as to why this is happening to me.

She pauses. I sense she gets it that one more plea for Rodrigo will result in a broken phone line. She finally agrees to talk about my bone.

"This happens to you because the power of your thoughts has gone wrong. Like a boomerang, all the negative thoughts you send out there will come back to you."

I tell her that I'm not aware I'm sending any negative thoughts out there. I'm expecting her to mention Rodrigo again, and I get ready to hang up just in case, but, no, she can probably sense I've reached my limit in that respect.

"You sent negative thoughts to Jim. Six months ago."

The guy she mentions was a colleague at work. She knows about him because six months ago we had a session and I told her about him and the trouble I had with him. The situation was long ago resolved, and Jim and I had remained in polite contact ever since.

"What?" I doubt I've heard correctly. Or maybe it's the painkillers. Maybe they interfere with my ability to understand.

"It's because the negative thoughts you had about Jim have come back to you," she repeats.

I've definitely heard correctly.

"And they made me fall from that horse and break my collarbone in five pieces?" I check again, just in case there's still a misunderstanding.

"Yes, precisely. It's because of the power of your own negative thoughts that you have broken your bone."

Yes. Right. I take a deep breath and I ask her how much I owe her for this session. She tells me it's free because I was in an emergency situation and she wanted to help. She hoped she could.

I thank her and hang up. I think she's actually helping. Although dizzy with painkillers, I'm pretty clear about one thing—I'll never call her again. I hope her crystal tells her this, so I won't have to explain. And maybe this is precisely the kind of help I need right now.

My third call of the day goes to a friend. I have to start telling people about what happened and I'm practicing with friends before I talk to my family.

"What do you mean, you don't understand why you broke a bone? I'll tell you why," my friend shouts, once she recovers from the initial shock of the news. "You broke a bone because you went on a bloody horse and fell off. Because of polo. You don't need to spend hours trying to figure out what you can do to avoid breaking bones any longer. Get off the freaking horse!" she adds, just for clarification.

They don't get it. People who don't play polo can't understand these things. Life seems easy to them—you get on a horse, you break bones. If you don't want to break bones, you don't get on a horse.

"It's not that clear cut," I try to explain. I tell her other people play polo and don't break bones. I mean they don't break that many. And definitely not five bones in three years. I've never heard of someone breaking five bones in three years. Not even in polo. Maybe there's a pattern here. Maybe there's a meaning in this and I need to find out what the pattern is so I can stop it before I break any more bones. Or worse.

"Roxy, you need help," she says. "You need to talk to a psychologist. I'm not sure why you do this to yourself, but I can put you in touch with a friend of mine who might help you figure it out."

I tell her I've got enough ladies with crystals.

"I mean a psychologist," she shouts again. "Not a fortune-teller. Therapy. Have you heard of therapy? Like for people who self-harm?"

"I don't self-harm, I play polo," I shout back. "Sometimes I take a fall and I break bones. I just need to figure out why I break bones every time I take a fall."

She asks me if I've told my family. I tell her I haven't.

Why?

Because they would worry, and there's nothing they can do from the other side of the world. Plus, I already have a family here. My Argentine family who are looking after me.

"Roxy, you need to talk to my friend. The psychologist. Seriously. You don't have a family in Argentina. You've broken your bones in the backyard of a professional polo player, on one of his horses. It's normal the guy takes you to hospital and makes sure you have decent treatment. Anyone would do so. And he's got a reputation to guard. He can't be seen not to look after his clients when something happens. You're getting your mind all confused. Your family isn't in Argentina. It's in Romania. And they have no idea what just happened to you and they'll be mortified when they find out. And I'm not sure why you feel so confused about where your family is and about why you break bones. Both things are pretty clear to me. Please talk to my friend, the psychologist. I'll send you her number."

She doesn't understand. Definitely not. But she's very insistent and I feel dizzy from the painkillers and I promise her I'll talk to her friend, the psychologist, at least once. I've just fired one lady with a crystal and have one vacant spot. Maybe the psychologist will do.

FRIDAY 25TH NOVEMBER

I'm locked in a time loop with the same moves, same places and same faces. The movie goes on and I already know it. Only that I can't stop it. It plays over and over again.

It's one week after my surgery and I need an X-ray. Doc told me I couldn't travel back to Lobos, so I go to Hospital Alemán, one of the top private hospitals in Buenos Aires. It's the same place where last year I had a number of X-rays taken for my other broken arm. I'm checking in at the emergency room, telling them I'm a foreigner, I've broken a bone and I can't travel back to the hospital that saw me because it's out in the *campo*, so I came here for a check-up and an X-ray. Just like I did last year. The corridors of the hospital are the same, the nurses in their white uniforms look the same, the queues at the cashiers where I'm directed to pay are as long as they were last year. I see the same X-ray room, the same doctor's office with a different face. It's the same arm, only a different bone. What's new this time is the metal plate. It shows clearly on the X-ray, together with the eight screws that fit it to my bone.

I feel sick looking at the picture but I diligently send it to Doc via WhatsApp. I even manage a cheerful voice message.

"*Hola*, Doc. This is Roxy, your English patient."

I'm not really English, even though I have a British passport and come from London, but the English patient from the movie with the same name wasn't really English, either. I contemplate the rest of my message.

"As requested, please see attached …"

No, too formal. Doc is a sweetie and he's anything but formal. Reword.

"Here's the picture. It looks pretty scary to me. I hope you like it, though. I also hope you're going to tell me it's OK, because I've been in bed as you instructed for two days now and I'm getting bored crazy. There are games at the *Abierto* tomorrow. Can I please go and see them? Just see one game, it's not going to kill me, and then I'll be back in bed, I promise!"

Doc answers immediately. *"Hola* Roxy. *Cómo estás?"*

They always add the customary "How are you?" here. It's part of the greeting, even though I've just left him a detailed message saying precisely how I am.

"Soy tu medico argentino," he goes on. He's my Argentine doctor. Good sense of humor. I definitely like Doc. The rest comes via voice message. It's too long to type.

"The X-ray looks good. I'm happy with it. But you're not going anywhere. Back to bed. You hear me? No polo, no games, nothing. Bed. Polo isn't going anywhere. I'm sure it will still be there in a week or two." And then his voice goes quiet, as if he's really tired. "And please take it seriously this time. It's for your own good."

The message ends with *besos*, that is kisses, just like all goodbyes in Argentina.

OK Doc, I'll go back to bed, I text back. No more voice messages. I can't trust my voice to hide the disappointment of losing yet another weekend of games at the *Abierto.*

On my way back home I stop by the same café where I had a coffee every day last year, when I had my arm in a sling. There was a cute waiter there who always used to flirt with me, even when I was an invalid. He's still there, recognizes me immediately, and almost drops his tray when he sees me with the same arm in a sling.

"Again?" He points at my arm. "What happened this time?"

My loop in time continues. I'm trapped in a movie that keeps on playing and I can't escape, whatever I do. Same people, same faces, same places. I tell him I had a fall playing polo and I broke a bone. And can I get a coffee, please? Ideally not over-burned, and with cold milk, please. Cold as in from the fridge. They always burn the coffee here and it makes it taste bitter, and they always overheat the milk. It's hard to drink it like this once you've experienced the taste of an Italian coffee.

Then I go home, straight to bed. It's the third weekend of the *Abierto* and I can't go to any of the games. For a second I'm considering ignoring Doc's recommendations, but then I remember the pain I had last time I did so and I decide to be good now.

There's not much to do. No more phone calls. I still haven't told my parents. No reading. I can't, since I'm still dizzy from the painkillers. There's no one to talk to. I close my eyes and I try to meditate.

The phone rings just as I manage to settle my mind to follow my breath.

"*Ciao imbecille, come stai?*" I hear Marco's cheerful voice.

I can't get angry with Marco, not even when he disturbs me in the middle of my meditation, and not even when he calls me an imbecile, which is how he expresses love. I once researched this word and found out it comes from "weak" in Latin, which is actually a very good description of how I feel right now.

"I'm good. Meditating."

"What?"

"Meditating. Do you know what that is?"

"Like you're on the toilet trying to shit and you need to stay there a long time because it won't come out?"

"Marco, don't be an idiot. Meditation. A spiritual practice that involves trying to get in touch with yourself."

"You worry me. Really. This worries me, even more then the broken bone. Why the hell do you need to do this, freshly out of surgery?"

"Because I need to find out. Marco, I need to find out."

"What exactly?"

"Why I'm doing this. Breaking bones. What it means. Why it keeps on happening to me. What I can do to stop this from happening again."

"Roxy!" He's shouting now. Just like my other friend. I can't understand what makes them so irritated.

"*Imbecille*. I'll tell you why this is happening to you! Because you've got back on a horse. And you weren't actually able to stay on it. So you fell. Bullshit, that meditation. You break bones because you play polo!"

"Give me a break. You don't understand. It's my hobby. I love it."

"Maybe you should pick a hobby you're actually able to do."

"Oh, enough!"

I have a pain in my chest, and a friend shouting at me doesn't help.

"Marco, *guarda che sono fragile*. I'm fragile." I'm almost in tears. "I can't have this conversation right now, about why I play polo and whether you think I'm able to sit on a horse or not. If you want to talk to me, you have to promise me you won't tell me anything else about polo. OK? Not now and not for a while. Nothing." My voice is hoarse.

"All right. I won't say anything."

Thank God he gets it. I'm almost breaking down in sobs by this point.

"Promise?"

"Yes, promise."

"OK." I take a deep breath. "Marco, I can't deal with this right now—"

"*Va bene, imbecille*. You don't have to explain. No more talk of polo. Let's talk about money. I'm calling you because I'm flying to Buenos Aires tonight and I'm going to the bank next and I need to know how much cash you need exactly. I'll bring you the dollars."

"I don't know … I'm not sure."

"Roxy? Are you on drugs? What do you mean you don't know?"

"No. Yes. Painkillers. I'm not sure."

"Let's do one thing. I'm opening an Excel spreadsheet. Wait a minute."

Marco was an accountant before he became a management consultant and started traveling the world. As such, he loves numbers, and an Excel spreadsheet is always popping up at key moments of his life. Or mine.

"So tell me," he says. "Who do you need to pay and how much?"

I tell him everything I can remember. The hospital, the doctor's fees, the anesthetist, the X-rays I'm still supposed to take, the physio sessions that will follow at some point, the cleaner who will come every day and help me in the house. I have no idea of the numbers, but he helps me estimate. One by one, all my medical bills along with my expected living and recovery costs are entered into the spreadsheet.

"Ah, Marco, and a palm tree," I suddenly remember.

"A what?"

"A palm tree. We need to pay the cardiologist and he won't take payment. He's one of Patricio's cousins. It's complicated, this cousins business. So Patricio suggested we buy him a palm tree instead. The guy is doing up his garden."

"I can't put a palm tree into an Excel spreadsheet, Roxy!"

"Just fit it there somewhere. It's part of the costs."

Silence. I guess he's trying to find a place for a palm tree in his formula.

"Six thousand," he says after a while.

"What?"

"I'll bring you six thousand dollars. Tomorrow. And I'll come and take you out for lunch."

"*Grazie*, Marco."

I haven't seen him for a year. Last time I saw him was here, in Buenos Aires, when I had the other arm in a cast. I didn't need cash then and I wasn't alone. Rodrigo was there to keep me company.

I'm caught in a loop in time where the same things happen in the same places with the same faces. One face is missing, though. Rodrigo isn't here any longer. If one thing is different this year, maybe there's hope that I can find the pause button and stop this movie once and for all.

I go back to my meditation. I'm going to find a way to do it.

LATER THAT EVENING

I've been trying hard to focus on my breathing and think of nothing else. But my mind wanders and goes away … away from my breathing and the pain in my shoulder, away from the small stifling-hot flat and the traffic noises outside. It flies off with a sense of urgency that won't be restrained, landing back in England, on a fresh green polo field one late spring afternoon.

"Let's go-o-o!"

I see Jonny coming out of the stables, leading his big black horse by the reins, and I watch as he effortlessly lifts himself into the saddle in one big jump that doesn't involve touching the stirrups. How can he do this? I wonder once again. I would definitely break my neck in the process.

"You take it easy!" the Old Man says still holding the reins of my horse there, outside the stables, where I've just mounted my pony in a far less spectacular style than Jonny.

"You take it easy, you hear me?" He's now turned towards Jonny. "No stupid things, please. Just hit some balls, slow canter." And then to me again, "It's like this with polo. You need to get back into it slowly."

Yes, slowly. I know. It's been four months since I rode last, since I fell and broke my arm in a tournament in Argentina. But I've done tons of physio sessions and now I am ready to play again. Or so I think.

"We're not going to pressure you to play again soon. Only when you're ready. Only then." The Old Man's voice is mellow, his face expressionless.

I know he won't pressure me. But I want to play again. I want it more than anything in the world. That's why I'm back here, on his polo field. I'm here to train, to get back into the game. And Jonny is here to make sure I do.

We're both silent as we take the horses to the stick and ball field. This is unusual, because Jonny and I normally talk a lot. But today we're both thinking the same thing. Will I be able to do it again?

"Look at the ball," he shouts, as I miss it later. I pass by it in full gallop and lift my now-useless mallet back onto my shoulder. Jonny is riding behind and I know he will hit it now and he won't miss.

He hits. The ball is now in front of me again. I direct my horse towards it with one subtle lean of my body. Not with the reins. We don't really use the reins that much in polo.

"Look at the ball," I hear the shout from behind. "Look at it. Look! Look!"

Of course I look. But I miss again and then I hear him shouting once more.

"You didn't look!"

I am getting angry now.

"Yes, I did!" I shout back.

He picks up the ball again and sends it with one effortless hit well ahead of me. How does he do that? I wonder. Why is it that he so rarely misses a ball?

"Look at the ball. Focus. Concentrate. The ball. The ball. Nothing but the ball."

I see the ball and I make sure I keep my eyes well open as my horse gallops towards it. I swing and hit and keep my eyes on it. I really do. But I barely touch it and it only moves a few inches this time.

Damn. Damn that ball. And damn his shouting. It's going to come back now, any minute. It does.

"Look at the ball, I said!"

I stop my horse, out of breath and out of patience.

"Jonny, wait. Maybe it's the mallet. Maybe there's something wrong with my mallet. Here, have a look. Give me yours. Maybe I should try with your mallet."

He hits balls so well, every single time. Maybe he's got a magic mallet.

He smiles and brings his horse to a stop next to me. He hands me over his mallet.

As soon as I touch it I give it back to him with no further explanations. It's too heavy. Of course it is. His mallet would be too heavy for me. In polo, players choose their mallets carefully. A heavy mallet helps with longer hits but requires considerably more strength in the arm to hold it. My mallets are light—girls' mallets, as they call them—and that's because I haven't got Jonny's muscles. There's no way I can lift and swing his mallet.

"Roxana, listen." His voice is kind.

Jonny doesn't call me Roxy or Rosanna like the Old Man and most of the Argentines do. No idea why, but he's one of the few who always pronounce my name as it would be in my own country.

"It's not the mallet, you know this."

"But then what? What, Jonny?"

Maybe that's it, I think. Maybe I can't do this again. Maybe there's no way I can ever come back to play polo.

I'm discouraged. It's been close to half an hour now and I haven't managed a decent hit. Not even one.

"It's looking. You're not looking."

"Yes, I am. I swear I'm looking. I see it clearly."

"And what else do you see?"

"I see the ball, the horse, the field, the grass, the sky. My mallet hitting it. I see it all."

"You see, this is the problem. You see it all. When you really look," he goes on, "there's nothing else to see. Nothing. Just the ball. Only the ball. The ball and nothing else."

How can that be? I wonder, but I decide to try anyway.

The ball. The ball and nothing else. I approach another ball, my horse breathing heavily under me. The ball … only the ball.

My arm opens out to prepare the swing without me telling it what to do. I am not conscious of it. I've gone out of me and into that ball. I am the ball. I can see it clearly. White, pure white. The ball. The ball and nothing else! Everything around the ball turns grey as though it has disappeared, and for the first time ever I don't see the green of the field or the brown of my horse's ears. I don't see anything. Nothing else. Just the ball, lying in one big ocean of grey.

Time stands still.

And then I see it flying high in the air as if another me has just hit it and this time it is a great hit.

"Buena-a-a," Jonny shouts from behind.

It is the last hit of this session. The horses are exhausted. I am too. Sweating and panting just like my pony, I walk in silence back to the stables, next to Jonny.

The Old Man is there, waiting.

"So, Rosanna. You OK to play next week?" he asks with a grin.

And all of a sudden time is no longer standing still.

SATURDAY 26TH NOVEMBER

Marco arrives, as elegant as I always remember him. Dark jeans, crisp white shirt, thin black cardigan, polished leather shoes. Even abroad, Marco is Italian from head to toe, sense of fashion included. In his pocket he carries an envelope with six thousand dollars in cash.

He persuades me to get out of the house. I tell him I'm not really ready, but he drags me out and into the first restaurant we find.

"*Mi fai tenerezza.* I've never seen you so bad," he says, cutting my ravioli into small pieces so I can eat it.

For a second I worry he's going to open the polo discussion again, but no, he asks me about Rodrigo instead. I tell him the whole story and how it ended, exactly on my birthday.

"No surprises there," Marco says. "That story was dead before it started. It had no future. Only an *imbecille* like you could manage to drag it out for a year. It should have been done and dusted before you left Argentina last time."

"Yeah, it was over. But he came to Europe, and then—"

"And then what exactly changed? When he came to Europe?" he asks, with that mocking expression on his face.

"I fell in love. Again. This time it was for real. I believed him. I believed it was possible to have a life with him. So, I came here to be with him, to move in with him. To have children together."

He almost drops his cutlery on his plate. "What?" he cries. "Are you mad? You came here thinking to have children with this guy?"

"Yes. What's the big deal? He said he wanted children."

"I'm really worried about your mental health. I think you're not to be left on your own without adult supervision. This is even more worrying than breaking arms every year. You seriously considered having children with a guy fourteen years younger than you, who hasn't got a cent in his pocket, and who clearly wanted to be with you so that you can finance his move to Europe? Are you insane?"

He's almost shouting now. I'm worried people around are looking at us. Even polo didn't get this treatment.

"That's enough! I'm not with him any longer."

"Thank God for that." He eyes me with a critical look. "I've heard a lot of crazy things from you in all these years, but never something as bad. Seriously."

I'm tired of being lectured as though I were a schoolgirl. I change the subject, picking a safer one, and tell him about the days I spent in the *campo*, the beauty of the fields in full spring bloom, and the lovely people who looked after me, my Argentine family.

He tells me I should call my own parents. My real family, he stresses, and tell them what's going on with me.

Maybe this isn't such a safe subject, after all. He's now going to have a go at me for imagining I have a family in Argentina.

I'm not sure what to talk about next. Polo, Rodrigo, my

Argentine family—all get the same harsh treatment. And meditation isn't safe territory, either. I can't tell him I'm sitting on my sofa every single evening for a couple of hours with my eyes closed, trying to find out why this is happening to me and what I can do to stop the pattern. And I can't tell him the only thing that comes back when I do this are my polo memories. He would suggest locking me up in a mental institution, for sure.

But Marco has been my friend for fifteen years, and that means there's always something to talk about, even when the current circumstances are no-go territory. I tell him about a business idea. He laughs.

"Here we go again. Business plan number 230, probably."

There have been quite a lot of business ideas we've discussed along the years. Plans that never took off and that were replaced with other plans for other businesses that never took off, either. I'm the dreamer who comes up with ideas, and Marco is usually the one with the practical head who smashes them down with figures. It doesn't matter. I'm still the dreamer. And I still have ideas. Some things never change. I tell him about my new plan to organize executive teambuilding retreats using the farms in the pampas and their cattle-herding activities.

At least I don't get shouted at this time. And there's no more lecturing either. Only the old Marco is left, laughing at my business ideas as he kills them in cold blood, calling me *imbecille* every now and then. And I laugh too, despite the metal in my chest that hurts at every breath.

MONDAY 28TH NOVEMBER

New week, new me, I decide. I've had enough of lying in the bed and feeling sorry for myself. I have cash in my pocket, I need to sort out the hospital bills, and I need urgent advice about my life. Marco is useless with this, since he doesn't approve of my recent choices. One lady with a crystal has been fired, but there are still two to go, and I have an appointment set with lady number two this week and lady number three next month. There's no availability sooner than this. Lady with a crystal number three is in high demand.

I start the week well by breaking the news to my parents. It must be Marco's influence, but I finally find the guts to do it. My dad tries to be supportive. My mom cries. They want X-rays, reports, details. They'll get second opinions from doctors in Romania, they say. I send them all they want and tell them the surgery looks fine, and they calm down a little.

But I'm not telling them that I still get worried at night when I wake up sweating badly. The counting-lives exercise has not come back since that night at the farm, but the feverish sweat comes back regularly during the nights. I tell Marco about my fears when he calls in the evening to check how I am. He suggests I open the window at night, since it's the middle of a hot summer in Buenos Aires. Maybe this will sort out my night sweats, he says.

I don't open the window for fear of mosquitoes, and also because they're heavy sash windows and I can't lift them with only one arm. But I stop taking the painkillers. They make me feel dizzy and I need to have my mind clear. I need to meditate and find out why this is happening to me. No one seems to believe that I'm trapped in a movie that keeps on repeating itself and I can't find the pause button. And if I don't, next time I might just die.

I receive one more call. It's the Old Man asking me when I'm coming to Mar de Plata, his native town in Argentina, to train with him. Just like he did last year. I ask him if he's sitting down, just like I did last year when he asked me the same question.

"Why should I sit down? Rosanna?" he shouts, sensing there's something wrong.

I tell him I've had a fall and broken a bone. Just like I did last year. And once again I won't be able to come and train with him like I promised. At the end of the English season he had raised my handicap to minus one, which is supposed to be considerably better than a minus two. I didn't feel like a minus-one-handicap player though, and I thought that a couple of weeks' training with him in Argentina would sort me out. But there was none of this now.

My movie goes on and on, repeating the same scenes with the same faces, in the same places. I need to find that pause button. I really need to.

TUESDAY 29TH NOVEMBER

"Roxy! *Qué pasó*? What happened? How can you do this again?"

Sol freezes in the doorway of the hair salon and her face moves quickly through a whole range of emotions—pity, anger, shock, concern, disbelief. I wonder how she can carry all of these emotions at once. Her big blue eyes, carefully contoured with black liner, look at me in accusation, and judging from her tone of voice I'm not sure whether she feels sorry for me or wants to strangle me.

Sol knows very well what's happened. I made sure I sent her a message telling her the whole story, precisely because I didn't want her to react like this when she saw me with my arm in a sling.

"Come in." She decides to move away from the door and let me pass. "Sit down. Not there. Here." She points to the chair in front of the big mirror. "I'll make you *linda*, but before that you have to tell me what happened. Everything!" Her voice rises again and for a second I think she'll go back to screaming at me.

I tell her all of it—the fall, the surgery, the verdict of the doctors. There's nothing I can do but wait, I say. And all I need right now is clean hair.

But I can't have my hair done until I answer all her questions, and a lot more get asked. Sol, Madri, and a couple of clients all want to know what happened. When it happened. How exactly it happened. Which hospital I went to. What did they do? How much have I paid? You should be careful not to be ripped off. They will try to rip you off because you are a foreigner. How come I broke a bone again? How come I got on a horse again? How come—

"Roxy, I tell you what's happening." Sol takes a deep breath in. "It's that guy."

"Which guy?"

"The guy you dated."

"Rodrigo?"

"Yes."

"He has nothing to do with this. He wasn't even there. He doesn't know about it."

"It's him, I tell you," Sol says, with that look of certainty on her face that won't be defeated.

"What do you mean?"

"He's sucked your energy. Like a vampire."

"Sol, this is crazy."

"No, it's not. I know it. I've seen a movie about it. This guy has sucked all your energy and look what's happened. His life has got better and better since he met you. He traveled all over Europe last summer. Do you think this isn't a big deal? This is a very big thing for an Argentine. And you? Look at you." She points to some indefinite place in between my chin and my arm. "Look at all of this. Last year you broke a bone a week after you met him. This year you broke another bone a week after you stopped seeing him."

I'm laughing out loud by this time. "So, you think he's a vampire and he stole my soul?"

"Exactly. He stole your energy," she corrects me. "What's going on with you isn't normal stuff. Say what you want, but this isn't normal."

An old lady with short white hair who is waiting for her turn wants to know more about the situation. Sol gives her a full update on my love story with the energy vampire and why she's sure he's sucked all my energy, which now results in me breaking bones. The client nods her head in approval.

Madri comes up with a solution. "You need to go to church. Go pray. Sol is right. You've had black magic set on you. Don't take these things lightly. More could happen."

Madri sounds convinced. Everybody agrees with Sol's explanations. The conversation moves on from why this happened to what I can do to stop it from happening again. I'm starting to get chills down my spine. I'm not sure where this is going and I really only want my hair done.

"What church? The church isn't enough. I'll take her to a witch." Sol turns around to Madri, motioning me to move towards the washbasin. Oh good, at least something is now going to be done about my hair.

"Roxy, you need a witch, a white witch, to unlock this curse that's on you. Maybe church too, but the witch first. Definitely," she tells me, bringing the shower head over my hair.

Talking of churches with water pouring down my head makes me feel like I'm being baptized. I tell her the water is a bit too hot, but she ignores me as her mind is occupied with solving this mystery.

"And this family. This family you're always with when you break a bone. Is this not weird?" Madri continues watching Sol as she shampoos my hair.

"*Boluda*, they're the good ones," Sol answers. "They look after her. They're the guardian angels. They're not the ones with the black magic. The guy she dated, he's the one who stole her soul."

Her hands, full of shampoo, come up in the air, and she gesticulates animatedly.

"Yes, but why do you break bones with them every time?" Madri asks. "Can't you break bones somewhere else?"

"I broke bones in England, too," I say from the washbasin, but they ignore me.

"Maybe they have something to do with this, too," Madri continues.

Oh great, now my Argentine family will go to meet Rodrigo in the land of black magic.

I take a deep breath and think of a rational explanation.

"I ride horses when I'm with them and when I fall from horses I break bones, so maybe that's why I break bones when they're around," I say quickly before they can launch down this new path.

This convinces Madri and she's quiet for a little while, just enough to give Sol the chance to finish washing my hair.

"You're so lucky we did the color last time you were here." Sol moves on to more down-to-earth subjects as I retake my place in front of the big mirror. "We couldn't have done it with your arm in the sling. At least like this you can face everything with your hair in order." She says this as if it's the most important thing in the world.

I smile. Thank God there's no more mention of black magic. I don't want to think about anything any longer. No more reasons why, black magic, energy vampires or guardian angels. I want to put them all on hold.

But I can't just yet. Before I leave the shop, Sol produces a picture of a saint from her pocket.

"What's this?"

"San Benito. He fights off black magic," she says, with a serious look in her eyes. She turns the picture around to show me a small prayer printed on the back of the card. "Say this prayer every day. It takes only one minute. And on the twenty-first of every month spend some time praying to him. It's his day on the twenty-first. He'll protect you."

I nod and take the picture. She watches me critically, trying to assess whether I'll do as instructed.

"I promise, Sol. I promise I'll do it," I say in a hurry. "I'll do everything. I'll go to church, too. To the witch as well, if you really want me to. I'll do it all."

I just want to go home now, lie in my bed, and not think of anything. When I meditate I won't even ask why this is happening to me any longer. I'm already overwhelmed by the responses I get. Somewhere deep inside me, my rational mind battles with all these ideas. But, hey, who am I to question things? Ladies with a crystal, saints, black magic—I have no idea what's real and what's not any longer. Except for one thing. The piece of metal in my shoulder is real. At least I can be sure of this.

They give me a kiss on the cheek and let me go, but I can't hide in my home just yet, no matter how exhausted I feel. I've got a friend from London to meet up with, because she's in town for only a few days and she really wants to see me.

We sit down to have a salad for lunch and I tell her the whole story.

"Roxy, you're spending too much time alone in your home. And too much time talking to crazy Argentines," she says. "There is no black magic, no need for witches or miraculous pictures of saints. None of this. The simple truth, which you're not prepared to accept, is that you're addicted to doing things that harm you. Do you know how many people I know who have given up polo? Precisely for the same reason. They broke too many bones. It can be done, you know. It can be done. It's up to you."

With her words ringing in my head I finally go home, lie in my bed and watch the little picture of San Benito that Sol gave me. He's a monk with a long white beard, a walking stick, and a black cloak. He's not very talkative. He just looks back at me in silence.

Hola, I say. If you can do something about this whole mess, please do. I'm not quite sure what you can do or if you can do anything at all but just in case you can, please do. I'm too confused to even think about it right now.

December

THURSDAY 1ST DECEMBER

I wake up suddenly, but the dream is still with me. It's about polo, again. I don't fully remember it, but I stay there with my eyes closed, and other bits and pieces come into my mind, fragments of what my life used to look like.

I'm tired. Gravity is pulling. My wrists hurt, both of them. The one I broke three years ago and the one I broke six months ago. My stick is leaning down as though sucked in by the ground.

It's almost the end of the game. Come on, one more time.

Up. Stick up. I take a deep breath. Stick up!

But as we line up for the throw-in, my stick comes down again. Sticks are always supposed to be down for throw-ins. It's the last chukka. I feel so tired that for a moment I think I won't be able to hold myself in the saddle any longer. But there's no time for silly thoughts.

"Good luck, reds," the other team shouts.

"Good luck, blacks," we shout back.

We've been fighting them hard throughout this game, but it's polite to wish them good luck as we line up face to face for the last time. Polo is a gentleman's sport.

The ball is thrown in and time starts running again, just as we all do, eight ponies and riders running across the field, with the ninth horse, that of the umpire, leisurely cantering at the back.

Magic, I think. We need magic. Only magic can make us win this game. I look around and see the Old Man at the back of the field, where he plays as number four. I can't see his face. He's too far away. But I look back at him, desperately hoping he can help. We're losing and we have only a few minutes left, and we need some magic.

And then he does something. He plays one of his tricks on an inexperienced player from the other team, leaving the ball for him like an open invitation, and he moves his horse in such a way that the other player will break the rules if he tries to touch the ball. Most of the time his trick works. It does now. The unsuspecting guy touches the ball, the umpire whistles, and we are awarded a penalty shot. It's at sixty yards, quite a difficult penalty to score. And it's defended. I watch the four riders of the other team as they take their place in goal. I take mine, close to one of the goalposts. I'm supposed to try and push the ball inside if it comes my way.

But I am tired, too tired to even hold myself straight on a horse. Magic—please!

He does it again, the Old Man. He takes the penalty shot, of course he does. He circles his horse in a wide circle, far too wide, and he comes at the ball singing. Singing! No one comes at the ball singing in polo. But the Old Man does, as though he hasn't got a worry in the whole world.

I close my eyes. I'm supposed to keep them wide open and look at that ball and try to anticipate where it's about to go, but the tension is so high I don't dare to watch. I just hear the clear click as his mallet hits the ball and then I keep them closed for one more second. And when I open them again the magic has happened and the ball is through the goalposts. We have equalized.

We're back to the center of the field for a last throw-in. Only a few minutes left now. Will we do it? Magic! Once more, please. We can win this game. I had given up hope, but with that last goal we scored, I now believe again. Even if we have only three minutes left.

Magic. The Old Man, he needs to do his magic once again.

The Old Man, he's a legend. He used to do magic on a polo field and he did it time and time again. He scored unbelievable goals. He helped us win hopeless games. He coached us through impossible shots. He got me back to polo after my first accident and then again after my second one. And this was magic, too. The Old Man, he always got me back on the horse. He'll do it once more. I'm sure he will.

I stay in bed for a long time, my eyes closed, my mind filled with smells and voices. It all comes back to me—the games we shared, the conversations, the laughs, the craziness, the bond. I feel I'm back there on a polo field and I'm scared of how real it all feels.

I get out of bed eventually and go to the small restaurant where I had lunch with Marco. I'm meeting the Old Man today. He's in town for two days only and he wants to see me. I feel apprehensive about what he's going to tell me when he sees me all wrapped up in bandages.

But the Old Man knows better than to give me a hard time over my broken collarbone. He doesn't roll his eyes, doesn't pity me, and doesn't tell me I have a curse from an ex-boyfriend.

He sits down at the table in front of me and asks me matter-of-factly, "So, tell me how it happened."

I tell him. Just got on the horse, did one round of warm up, picked up a ball and started hitting it. I hit really well; I went the whole length of the field without losing it. Then I turned the horse, a sharp turn.

"Was the ground wet?" he interrupts.

"No, not at all. It hasn't rained for a long time."

"Then was it too hard?'

"Maybe a little hard, yes." I try to remember the exact sensation I'd had on that horse. A hard ground can usually be felt with every step the horse takes.

"Didn't I tell you that horses slide when the ground is too wet or too hard? How many times did I tell you this?"

"You did, yes, but—"

"And didn't I tell you not to turn sharply? Never to turn sharply? Not while you train, anyway?"

"Yes, you did." I remember well his "you're not on a motorcycle" comment.

I fall silent.

"So, you turned sharply, the horse tripped, and you fell," he concludes the story for me.

"Yes." I look down at the floor.

"Don't worry, such things happen." His voice has suddenly gone mellow, as if he's just realized there's no point giving me a hard time now.

"What do you mean? This was the most idiotic fall of all. No run, no speed, no game even. Just a small horse at a speed close to standing. How can this happen?"

"These falls are the worst." He smiles, but with a tired smile. "The ones that don't seem like a big deal. They're the worst."

He should know, after more than fifty years in polo and a few broken bones himself. He carries on questioning me.

"And now what happens?"

I tell him about the hospital, the surgery, the further surgery I'm likely to have when I get back home, in order to take the metal plate out.

"Why do you need to take it out? Leave it there, you can play like that. I had some screws in my leg for twenty years from a fall when I was young. Then, when I broke my leg again a few years ago, they found the old screws and removed them when they put the new metal plate in."

"So, you mean I should leave them there until I get surgery anyway for my next fall?" I can't help but smile at his advice.

"No! Rosanna, are you crazy?" He is horrified. "You won't fall again."

"How do you know?" I'm hoping for some miraculous reassurance.

"Don't think about it." He avoids the answer. "You won't fall. Not again. Not if you play with me," he adds.

This is true. I've never broken a bone while playing with him.

"But still, even you fell. You broke a bone and then you fell again." I'm still chasing my reassurance. I need him to do magic once again. To tell me something that will make me believe beyond a shadow of a doubt that I won't break a bone again, that I'll be all right. I absolutely need him to do this for me, and I'll chase him until he does it. Magic. He's good at it. He always does it on a polo field. But this time it doesn't come. Maybe it's because we're not on a polo field.

"I did have breaks," he admits. "But only twice. Once I broke my ankle and then my leg."

"And your collarbone? You said you broke your collarbone, too."

"Ah, yes. I forgot about that. That, too. Three times. Only three times."

I give up trying to find out how many bones he has actually broken. I ask him something else instead, the big question that is looming behind all the others.

"Tell me … tell me one thing. Please. Do you think I should play polo again?"

I watch him with my eyes wide open, as if I'm waiting for a life-or-death verdict.

He watches me, too. His eyes are kind, just as I always remember them. I detect a hint of sadness inside.

"Rosanna, how can you ask me this question?" He shrugs. "How can I tell you to play again when I see you like this?" he continues. "And how can I not tell you to play when I know how much you love polo?"

Just what Patricio had said. Maybe I should stop asking this question.

"Don't ask me." He echoes my unspoken thought. "Make your own decisions."

"But do you think I'm a good player? Why do I keep on falling? Maybe my riding isn't good enough. Maybe I need to train more. Maybe—"

"There's nothing wrong with your riding," he interrupts. "If there was, I would tell you."

I know he would. He's screamed enough times on that polo field for me to know he saw everything I did wrong and wasn't afraid to tell me.

"Then, what? Why?" My tears bubble to the surface. "Why does this happen to me?" I just hope he won't tell me, like Sol, that it's black magic.

"Bad luck," he says instead. "That's all."

Mala suerte, or bad luck, is a favorite phrase of Argentines. They use it to explain everything that can't be otherwise explained.

Silence. We're both thinking of the bad-luck explanation. And it must be a huge one to account for five broken bones in three years.

"I wish I'd called you before. You know, I thought about calling you at the beginning of that week. When you fell. I wish I'd done it. I could have called you to tell you to come to Mar de Plata. If I'd done it, maybe you would have been all right now." The strain in his eyes almost brings tears into mine. He cares. He always has.

"There's no way you could have known," I tell him. "And even if you had called me, I might not have come. I had an appointment with fate. Or maybe it was just *mala suerte*, like you say."

"Maybe." He smiles. "But what can I do for you right now? Is there anything you need?" His practical mind has already moved forward. The past is gone. In polo one always needs to focus on the next move.

"Yes, there is. Actually, there's one big thing you can do for me. I have too much luggage with me here. Would you mind taking my polo equipment back to England when you go?"

"No problem. I'll leave it in the tack room. It will stay there waiting for you. For when you're ready," he adds.

I'm not sure when or whether I'll ever be ready, but I'm feeling relieved. I have way too much stuff with me here, and the idea of getting rid of one big polo bag with all my equipment makes me feel lighter.

"Maybe I'll play again." I smile. "And you know what? My friends here told me there's something I can use if I play again. It's like a vest you attach to the saddle and it inflates when you're thrown off the horse. It cushions the body, so it doesn't break. Maybe if I wear something like this I won't break bones if I fall."

He looks at me with a blank expression and then when he finally gets it he starts laughing, one long, roaring laugh that he doesn't mean to hide.

"Oh, Rosanna," he says finally, when he gets his breath back. "That was really funny. Let's get the bill."

And so I get it. My Michelin-man solution to polo bone-breaking isn't even worth a comment.

FRIDAY 2ND DECEMBER

From the other side of the line her voice sounds professional and calm. She's not sweet and soothing like lady number one, not at all. Lady number two is an astrologist and she delivers her reading of my astral chart in a clear and concise way.

She tells me I have a strong karmic connection with Argentina and specifically with the people I meet here. Accidents are likely to happen to me in this country. Planet Mars is strong on my chart when I'm here and this brings about impulsivity and possible injuries. It's a bad idea to play polo here, because I might break another bone.

I tell her I broke bones in England as well. She listens politely, doesn't comment and carries on with her analysis of my astrological chart.

"And what do you mean by karmic ties with the people I meet here?" I ask skeptically.

"They are people you have been connected to in other lifetimes. People you have unfinished business with."

"And now I've met them in order to finish some sort of business?"

"Probably," she says.

"And what exactly is this sort of business about?"

She says the stars don't tell her this bit of information.

"But who exactly are these people? The guy I dated? Sol, my hairdresser? My friends from Lobos?" I carry on trying to get to the bottom of this unfinished-business story. Maybe that's why I wanted to have a business in Argentina.

"Probably all of them," she says.

"So, does this mean I have to do things with them? Like set up businesses?"

She says it's not about businesses as we know them today. It's more like unfinished issues, and that there's nothing specifically I have to do. I just need to be aware that I have strong bonds with these people because I've met them before.

"But what does this have to do with polo?" I ask again, stubbornly.

"Nothing to do with polo specifically. But it may have to do with accidents. The accident aspect is well present in your chart."

"I still don't get it."

"It's the karmic ties with these people and the land that bring you back here. This is why you feel at home here and meet people you feel like you've known for a lifetime. And while you're here, you have accidents involving horses because that's what shows on your chart in this location."

She then tells me something about Chiron, one of the stars, I think, and about it being half-man and half-horse. Hang on, how can a star be half-man, half-horse? No, Chiron isn't a star; it's actually a comet, and that's just the myth behind its name. I'm not sure I get it, but I feel reassured to hear about horses.

I don't like her conclusion though.

"If you get back on a horse, you're likely to break a bone again," she says at the end of a long explanation.

"What do you mean? I have to stop playing polo?"

"Yes," she says. "You have to stop playing polo."

"That can't be."

"It is."

"Why?"

"Because you're moving from a warrior energy to a goddess energy. Look, it's in your chart. It's a big time for change in your life and you have to let go. Do you understand? Let go. Stop doing what you did before and move to embrace the new."

Let go. These words hit my stomach with the precise punch of an experienced boxer. Let go! No-o-o. Not just now. Not yet. Impossible. I just had lunch with the Old Man yesterday. He's going to get me back on a horse, I know he will.

I take a deep breath and tell her that it isn't going to happen.

"Then you will break a bone again," she says. "Or you might die next time."

"What do you mean I might die? I don't want to die."

I have a strong feeling that this lady with a crystal will end up just like the first one. Fired.

"You choose what you want to do." Her voice is calm on the other end of the line. "I can tell you only one thing, and I see it very clearly on your chart. If you get back on a horse again in Argentina, you'll have another accident. Please take this seriously and stay away from polo."

"For how long?" I've almost stopped breathing.

"For a while. At least a year. Then you'll see what you want to do. But not now. Definitely not now. Go away, go and heal. Somewhere else. Go somewhere where you're not in this energy. Change place, change country, change continents. You need to go away and heal, and this is more than just for your shoulder. You need to heal your soul."

Then she goes back to talking about Chiron and the wounded-healer energy. I'm not listening any longer. I just hear some disparate words that I can't link into any meaning: endings, patterns, the third time something happens, listening to what the Universe is trying to tell me, letting go, healing.

We run out of time before I can make sense of what she's saying. At exactly 3 pm my lady with a crystal tells me she has another appointment and says goodbye.

I'm left there for a long time on my sofa, thinking of one thing only. She said I need to let go of polo, and I'm just not ready to do it.

SATURDAY 3RD DECEMBER

One day later and I've dismissed the call with my lady-with-a-crystal number two as if it never happened. I'm finally going to the *Abierto* today, for the first time this year. I'm meeting Gabriela and Patricio there and there is no way I can seriously think about polo killing me while I enjoy watching an exquisite game in the company of my polo-playing friends. One thing has to go, so the lady with a crystal and all her warnings vanish from my mind. Other more important things come in to replace her. Things like what I'm going to wear.

I contemplate the long row of dresses and all twenty-five pairs of shoes nicely arranged in my bedroom. At least I had the foresight to unpack all my bags before breaking my bone. Now I have everything ready. All the useless dresses that I can't fit into because of my sling, and all the glittery heels now rendered useless by the same sling. Maybe I've slightly overpacked.

Two hours and twenty unsuccessful attempts to fit into anything decent later, I give up. I put on the same bright blue top—the one with a wide neck cut large enough for me to get into legs first—and the same beige miniskirt that Gabriela finds way too mini. She and I have different tastes in fashion.

We also have different tastes regarding horse names, I think later as we sit in the tribune waiting for the game to start and I hear her brainstorming names. It's spring here and Patricio has just had a full string of new foals born to his polo mares.

"*Traicionera. Mentirosa.* How about these two?" Gabriela asks.

I can think of better names for horses than Traitor and Liar.

"Maybe *Curiosa*?" she carries on.

Curious. This one is slightly better.

"And Sugar. I love Sugar. For a gelding."

We're making progress here, I think, and then I offer a suggestion.

"How about sweetening up the names of the mares, too? Something like Love, Joy or Peace?" I laugh at her puzzled face.

"Fucking boring." Gabriela dismisses my attempts. "The whole point about polo horses' names is they must be fun."

Yes, fun. I've heard a lot of fun names. 7 Up was my favorite. It was one of the Old Man's ponies.

"We already have a Dracula," Patricio adds.

When I first came to their farm and stayed for Christmas, Patricio had a new foal. He decided to call him Dracula in memory of the vampire stories about Transylvania that I'd entertained them with over countless dinners. Now Dracula is three years old and about to start his polo training.

"I have a better one," Gabriela exclaims. "*Bandita*. Perfect name for the one born today."

I nod. Let's stop at Bandit. If she carries on her train of thought, the poor horse might be called Serial Killer or something.

I watch the game with a mixture of sadness and irritation. I'm tired. It's the first time I've ventured out of the house for such a long time, and the painkillers I've reverted to taking for this occasion have made me dizzy again. My arm doesn't hurt but I'm feeling fragile, incredibly fragile. Patricio gets it and he goes up and down the stairs in front of me just to make sure he can catch me if I stumble. His concern brings up a mixture of emotions. I'm touched and irritated at the same time. I don't want to be an invalid any longer, I really don't. But I don't want to climb the stairs alone, either.

Everything at the *Abierto* is just the way I remember it. Men in white shirts and baseball caps move swiftly around with girls on their arms wearing long, brightly-colored summer dresses. I know this world well. I thought it was my world. I'm not sure any longer. Ah, and those baseball caps. I don't know what it is about the baseball caps, but they really irritate me. I haven't thought about them before but now I do. I can't seem to concentrate on anything else. Thank God Patricio doesn't wear one.

"Rosanna?" I hear a voice next to me as I walk around the Chandon bar at the end of the game, a glass of Campari Orange in my only usable hand. Emi, the owner of the polo club where I broke my arm last year, is standing next to me, paralyzed with shock, his mouth wide open and his eyes fixated on my sling.

"What—?" He motions to my arm. He doesn't say anything. He can't say anything.

I can't say anything either, since his sudden appearance makes me choke on the drink I was just sipping. I cough and wave to him to wait for me to regain my speech.

He waits. He probably needs to regain his speech as well.

"*Hola*, Emi," I say when I finally get my voice back.

"What— what happened. Again? Last time I saw you, you had an arm in a sling. Last year. And now again?"

He's shocked. He shouldn't be. I remember last year, as I was lying in the grass on his polo field waiting for an ambulance that took a long time to come, he told me he had broken many bones and he gave me full details of each of them.

"Yes. Again." I try to smile but the smile doesn't want to come out.

All of a sudden I feel very tired.

"What happened?" he asks dryly. "Polo?"

I nod. "Yes. I fell. Stupid fall during stick and ball. Not even a tournament this time."

He says he's sorry.

Me too, I'm about to add, but then I say nothing. There's nothing more to say.

"Where's Patricio?" he asks me suddenly, as if he needs to go. Immediately.

I wave around the crowd towards the corner where I last saw my friend taking his son to play with the other children. A group of boys were playing with foot mallets and a ball—just like polo but with no horses.

Emi utters a *cuídate,* take care, and leaves to find Patricio as if pressed by a sudden emergency. Before he goes, he tells me he's having a party on Friday at his *estancia*. It's the finals of a tournament he's organized. I should come. He'll sort out the details with Patricio, he says.

Of course he will. As an invalid woman I'm not expected to be able to arrange anything for myself. Not even going to a party.

With Emi gone, I'm left with my thoughts. The music in the Chandon bar is loud, but I can still hear Gabriela talking to a group of Irish people who are all playing polo. They're lovely people. One of them tells me he's broken a collarbone too, and it's not a big deal, I'll recover. And I'll play again. And who knows, I may play with them next year. I nod. Yes, maybe. And then the words of the lady with a crystal ring in my ears once again. *If you get back on a horse, you'll fall again and this time you might die.*

I can't deal with this right now, so I push the words down where they belong, far from my conscious mind, leave the Irish, and go for a wander. Everywhere I look I see the same faces and the ever-present baseball caps. People I know, people I don't know but who I'll eventually come to know if I hang around long enough. The polo family, my polo family, the one I'm supposed to now leave forever and replace with—what the hell am I supposed to replace this with? I'm now irritated at lady-with-a-crystal number two, who tells me to do impossible things but doesn't tell me how I should do them.

"Roxy!" Patricio shouts on my right. "Come here. Come! I have to show you something!" He makes his way towards me through the crowd and I see he's bringing another guy with him, a dark-haired, well-built guy in a blue striped shirt and jeans. No white linen and no baseball cap, thankfully.

"I have someone for you," he shouts as he approaches, dragging the guy along.

Patricio is my chief matchmaker in Argentina and I've heard a lot of comments about the suitability of his many cousins to become my boyfriends. Still, I've never seen him so excited to introduce me to someone before. Who is this guy?

"Roxy, come, you have to see this. You have to meet my friend Jorge."

"*Hola*," I muster.

"*Hola*," he answers. I have the weird feeling he's uncomfortable.

"Come and look. Look here." With a quick gesture, Patricio starts to unbutton the guy's shirt. Right there in the middle of the crowd under my shocked eyes. Is he going to strip this potential match naked for me to have a good look at him?

"Jorge had a fall just like you and surgery just like you. Three weeks ago. Look how well he has healed." Patricio finally answers my silent question.

The shirt is now unbuttoned and the collarbone of the named Jorge revealed. Patricio is pointing to Jorge's scar, all excited. "Look how well he's healed and he doesn't even wear a sling."

I look at the guy. He's slightly embarrassed by the whole fuss, and his shirt is half open. The scar looks great though, neatly closed off, just a thin white line on his shoulder. I don't yet know how mine looks. I haven't seen it yet.

"Broken collarbone?" I ask.

He nods. "Yes, in four pieces. Metal plate with seven screws."

Mine was broken in five pieces and I have eight screws. I guess I win this contest.

"Wow, you're doing well," I say, pointing to my sling. "How come you're out of your sling so fast?"

"I just took it off before coming here today. It didn't hurt that bad. People don't know, though, and keep on slapping me on the back." He grins. "It hurts like hell every time someone says hello."

I can imagine it does. The customary Argentine greeting between men involves a kiss on the cheek and sometimes a hug and a slap on the shoulder. I feel sorry for the guy.

"Don't worry," he says as he buttons his shirt back up. "You'll be all right. We'll both play again. Collarbone fracture, a classic with polo falls. No big deal."

I nod. He goes. Patricio stays there, his eyes beaming.

"You see?" he says. "You'll be all right. Did you see how well he looks?"

"Where the hell did you find him?" I ask him, amused. Patricio's ability to find answers to my unspoken worries has never ceased to amaze me.

"And did you find Emi? He was looking for you."

"Yes, I did. He told me he was shocked to see you in a sling again."

"I bet he was. What else did he say?"

"That maybe you fall because you ride with the stirrups too short."

That was something new. I'd never heard this explanation before. Short stirrups allow greater movement in the saddle, but if your muscles aren't strong enough it's easier to lose your balance and fall.

"So he says maybe you should ride with longer stirrups next time. Or maybe you shouldn't ride at all."

I look at him, but he's not joking. His face goes back to that impossible-to-guess-what-he's-really-thinking-about expression I know so well.

This is exactly the question in my head. Maybe I can change one little thing and I'll be all right next time. Or maybe there shouldn't be a next time at all.

TUESDAY 6TH DECEMBER

My stitches come out at the hospital in Lobos under the precise movements of Doc's hands as I watch his face, deep in concentration. I can't see my wound. There are no mirrors in the room. I can see only his face, but I can't read his thoughts.

"It looks great," Patricio says, and then he stretches his iPhone out and takes a picture. He and Gabriela are there with me in the small emergency room at the hospital and they talk to me constantly to distract my attention from what's going on.

Doc is chill. His face is calm and he doesn't seem to register the constant chatter of my friends, their pictures, or my muffled cries.

"It looks good," he says eventually. "It's healing well."

"Will it look all right? In the end?" I ask, as if this is all that matters.

"This girl is looking for a boyfriend." Patricio feels the need to add an explanation. "She wants to make sure the boys will still like her," he adds.

"It'll look like it's never been there." Doc smiles encouragingly.

"Can I see it?" I say, with all my courage mustered.

"Not now. Tomorrow. I'll put a fresh bandage on it now, and tomorrow you can take it off yourself. No need to cover it up any longer."

I'm instantly relieved that I don't have to see it just yet.

"And now what happens?" I ask.

"Nothing. You go home and you rest. In two more weeks you take the sling off and you start physio. For about a month."

"And then?" I hesitate, but I have to ask. "When can I play polo again?"

"We'll see about that." He shrugs. "I can't tell you just now."

Just like I can't tell myself either.

WEDNESDAY 7TH DECEMBER

I'm supposed to take the bandage off but I can't bring myself to do it. Patricio sends me a text message in the morning asking me if I've done it.

Not yet, I text back.

Do it now, he replies. *Otherwise I'll send you the pictures I took yesterday.*

Don't!!! I answer in panic. *Just give me some time, please!*

I go to the bathroom determined to take off the little bandage. It's not a big deal, I tell myself. I've got other scars on my body, other memories of other surgeries, other broken bones, and other cuts. But it doesn't work. Whatever I tell myself, I just can't do it. I stay there for a long time in front of the mirror, alone with my scar, which I'm too scared to see.

There are things others can help with. Have helped with. But there's one thing they can't do for me. They can't look at that scar for me. I wish someone could.

I'm about to give up, but I hear the sound of an incoming message on the phone, which I've left in the living-room. I guess it's

Patricio sending me the pictures, and the fear of seeing them makes me do it. I take the bandage off and take a good look at the ugly, swollen cut that stretches all the way across my collarbone.

You and I will need a long time to get acquainted with each other, I think.

THURSDAY 8TH DECEMBER

I'm hiding in the house, putting cracked-nipple cream on my scar. I asked for arnica cream at the pharmacy but the only type they had was for lactating mothers, and I bought it because I'm a big fan of arnica. It's done wonders for my previous cuts.

I have no water left, no food, and no fruit. I try to get *empanadas* delivered, but they don't answer the phone. It's a national holiday today and the shops are closed. People are celebrating. I hide. With the bandage off I can't hide my scar any longer, but I can hide myself.

I'll come to terms with it, I tell myself. Eventually. But for now I just don't want to think or do anything. I've been swallowed up by a big black void that tells me there's nothing left in my life.

I stay with it the whole day. The void. And then once I've felt it all, in the hour just before dark, I open my laptop and I start to write. I go on late into the night without noticing that the day is gone. One by one, words come out and pages start to fill. I write about polo and passion, about bones, breaks, and trying to find the road to recovery.

FRIDAY 9TH DECEMBER

I had a dream last night. A powerful one. It wasn't about polo this time. I woke up sweating with the memory of it imprinted in my mind. I was on a train and the train was going fast. All of a sudden the brakes came on and it stopped, in a loud noise of metal rubbing against metal. I got off the train and walked a little bit ahead, following the tracks for only three or four meters, no more. And then I saw it—a huge precipice opening up in front of the stopped train, the tracks disappearing into nothingness. I woke up thinking this was close, really close to death. But the train has miraculously stopped and I'm alive.

I get out of bed with a new determination. I venture out to the beauty salon next door. I paint my nails blue. I have a facial and I wax my legs. I do everything I can to convince myself that I'm alive and I'm still a beautiful woman.

Tomorrow is the final of the *Abierto*. I have to look great for this. It'll be the last final I'll ever see. Tomorrow is my one big goodbye to the polo world. The train has stopped. And I have got off it. I'll look my best, despite the arm in the sling and the ugly cut on my shoulder.

I select the dress, bright yellow. The very same dress I wore three years ago for the finals of the *Abierto*. It was my first trip to Argentina, the first time I saw the finals. It's the most appropriate dress for the last time I'm going to see them.

I won't be able to get it on alone, since it's got a zip at the back and I have only one mobile arm, but I'll call my cleaner to help. I then select the earrings, gold with long black feathers; the shoes, flat black sandals; and my handbag, black as well, to match my sling.

We always choose our colors carefully in polo. We share the same team shirts, but the helmets are very personal, and the color scheme that goes into them is like a fingerprint for a polo player. Mine is light blue and white.

But tomorrow my colors will be yellow, black, and blue. Yellow because it's the color of power and I'll need all the power in the world for this battle. The blue nails are for Rodrigo. I'd promised him we were going to see this final together. One more promise that would never be fulfilled. All throughout our romance last year I wore the same bright blue nail varnish. He said he loved it. So I put it on today again, one last time. For him and for all that could have been between us and never will be. And black is for Ellerstina, the team of Facundo Pieres, my polo idol. That's because I support them and because they're playing in black tomorrow. And also because black is the color of mourning and I'm quite sad. And, moreover, my arm is in a black sling and it makes sense to match all my other accessories to it.

All kind of complicated, but polo is a complicated game too. I prepare everything with the same care as if it were my polo equipment before a game. And then when all is ready I get back into bed and cry.

Tomorrow I'll be a warrior one more time. But tonight I'm still alone in the house, feeling scared and vulnerable and trying hard to not think of one long, ugly scar that will stay with me forever.

SATURDAY 10TH DECEMBER

Hola, Rosanna! I'll wait for you at the entrance to the stadium before the game.

I wake up late with the sound of the incoming text message. It's good news. The Old Man is going to be there, and then my friends from Lobos will arrive and I'll sit next to them in the tribune, watching the last finals of the *Abierto* I'll ever watch. Good. I might be a warrior in a yellow dress today, but even a warrior needs some support when going into battle.

How on earth will I tell the Old Man I have to give up polo?

This question clouds my mind all morning. Eventually I decide to discard it as I get into the taxi taking me to the *Catedral de Polo*— the huge stadium in the center of the city where the *Abierto* takes place. I won't tell him anything today. No need to. And after all, who says I need to give up polo forever? Maybe I can just give it up for a little while and it'll be enough.

The stadium is bursting with people. Everyone is here for the finals. The whole world of polo has one meet-up point every year— the finals of the *Abierto*. I meet the Old Man by the entrance, but I can't see my friends anywhere. I get a message from Patricio telling me they'll be late. No surprise, they always arrive at the last minute. It's a long drive from Lobos. Then I get another text. They've left the tickets at home and they'll have to buy new ones, probably in a different stand. The Old Man's seat is far away. *Sola*. Alone. I'm going to have to do this all by myself.

This realization sinks deep and I feel a sudden urge to cry. I've never felt more alone in my whole life. The bright yellow dress can do nothing for this. I'm going to watch the final alone.

I take my seat next to the empty seats of my Argentine family. The older couple on my right clearly support Ellerstina and I'm grateful to fate for this small sign of favor. *Sola*, but still supported by my tribe. The guy wears the classic attire of an older Argentine gentleman who comes to watch polo. White linen shirt, panama hat, beige chino trousers. Loafers, no socks. The lady wears a white linen dress. The man's shirt is nicely tucked into his trousers, not hanging out like that of the younger guys around. Younger men mostly wear jeans, not chinos. There appears to be a clear-cut line between these two male dress styles somewhere around the age of forty-five. Women display a variety of summer dress with no differentiation in age.

On the field below, a military fanfare plays the national anthem. Everyone stands up and the Argentines join in the singing. I only catch one word repeated again and again. *Libertad*. Freedom. Then a rider brings in the flag of Argentina and is greeted by the applause of the audience. Once the ceremonies are done, the two best teams in the world—*La Dolfina* and *Ellerstina*—line up facing each other for the final of the biggest polo competition in the world. In the stands, everyone holds their breath as the umpire throws in the first ball. This game is broadcast on national TV. A whole nation watches its warriors going into battle.

"*Vamos, Ellerstina,*" the lady to my right shouts. I too hope they'll win. Every year they make it to the final and every year they lose against the best team in the world and its captain, Adolfo Cambiaso, the best polo player in the world. My polo idol Facundo plays with his brothers and one cousin, all of them with the same surname—Pieres. Polo, in Argentina, is a family affair.

I watch the incredible speed of the play, so quick I don't even notice the fouls, and I listen to the old gentleman explaining them to his wife. I see one of the Pieres brothers take a fall, his horse's hooves landing all over him, and I fear he'll never stand up. Two ambulances rush to the field at once, but, no, the guy is fine, and he gets back into the saddle to the applause of the audience. I don't even have time to wonder how many bones I would have broken in a fall like that, because the game has picked up again and it's fast and beautiful.

I watch the effortless grace they display under the biggest pressure there is in polo, playing the finals of the *Abierto*, and I cheer for them. I cheer in Spanish and in English, whichever comes first. Goal after goal, *Ellerstina* is ahead of *La Dolfina*, and by the middle of the game it looks like they might actually make it.

The older gentleman next to me jumps off his seat in excitement after an amazing goal by Facundo. Then he turns to me and apologizes.

"Sorry, darling, I don't want to hit your arm with emotions running high and everything."

I tell him not to worry. My collarbone is the problem, not the arm in the sling. He probably wonders what the hell I'm doing there, an invalid and all by myself. No one comes to see the finals alone.

Cambiaso circles his pony to take a penalty shot just in front of a stand filled with the opposing team's supporters. I remember exactly how it feels when you have to take the penalty in a game. Although you've practiced the same shot thousands of times, emotions run high, as the gentlemen to my right would say, and sometimes this means you'll miss. But no, he being the best player in the world, he doesn't let emotions play with his shots. He scores a perfectly clean goal.

By the start of the seventh chukka the game is equal, and everyone holds their breath. The players come back into the field on fresh horses. Facundo is on Open Candy Kiss. I love the name of this horse. All the names of his horses start with Open, and I remember Patricio once telling me this is the name of the stallion he uses to breed them.

For a second I close my eyes and I remember how it feels to ride back into the field with your teammates at the start of the last chukka, when you're too tired to hold yourself straight in the saddle. When the score is equal. The pressure you feel when you know you might win or you might lose and there's about a fifty-percent chance of either. I remember the knot in the stomach, the pain in the body, and the pride in the heart that makes you carry on. I remember the sense of camaraderie and connection to your horse and your teammates as you all ride out in the field together. I'll never forget that feeling.

Facundo and Cambiaso, the two best players in the world, line up one in front of the other. The stands fall silent, the umpire throws the ball in once again, and the players start their graceful and impossible dance.

In a quick sequence, *La Dolfina* score three goals, one after the other. There's a deep silence around me. It's going to be very difficult for *Ellerstina* to equal that. The gentleman next to me talks aloud to one of the players.

"Nico, son, you see what happens when you're in a hurry? Take your time before you hit. Take your time!"

But Nico is obviously too far away to hear the advice of my neighbor and he loses his ball once again. I'm looking across the field for the purple hat of my polo idol, but not even Facundo can save the situation, and another goal is scored against them.

Ellerstina fight beautifully until the last moment, when the sounds of the bell mark the end of the final. They fight hard, although they already know they're losing, and they knew it long before they heard the bell. They fight to the end, because this is what you do in polo. You play your best. For your teammates. For the audience. For the sport. For your pride. You always play your best.

I'm never going to feel this again. My eyes fill with tears. The couple on my right probably assume it's because *Ellerstina* lost. Oh God, how can I carry on with my life without polo?

The stands where *La Dolfina* supporters sit go insane. It's another victory for the best team in the world and another defeat for my heroes. But they're young, much younger than the other team. Their time will come.

Mine won't, though. Mine has passed. I swallow hard trying to ease the tension in my throat and keep my tears at bay. People start to leave but I don't move from my seat. I stay there, frozen, watching the prize-giving ceremony from high up above. The cup is presented to *La Dolfina*. The defeated guys graciously withdraw from the podium, leaving the winners to spray champagne. They make their way to their corner of the field, where they are surrounded by their friends and family and encouraging hugs. Even in a macho country like Argentina, where a man will never cry for breaking up with a woman, it is absolutely proper for a polo player to cry at the end of a final he's lost.

And when all the people have left the stands and the ceremony is over, I slowly make my own way down the steps, taking care not to trip, because there's no Patricio around to catch me if I fall. I'm sad for my idols. They really tried and they were close. I tried, too. I really tried with polo, with Argentina, with finding love and settling here. And I was close, too. But then, like the Old Man would say, what use is it to be very close if you haven't won the game?

I go to the Chandon bar but I still don't see my friends. I have no idea where they are. I can't reach them on their phone. I see the Old Man talking to some players from my club in England, but I don't want to hear any more comments about the bad luck I've had and about how quickly I'll recover and play again. I let them enjoy their beers and I go for a wander. *Sola.* Again. Maybe I should go home.

But I can't. Gabriela finds me in the crowds.

"Where the fuck have you been? We have been looking everywhere for you!"

We queue up to get a Campari Orange each and Gabriela tells me about the drama of the forgotten tickets. I don't tell her about my little polo-giving-up drama, though. I can't really talk about it, not yet. We drink another Campari Orange and then I tell her I'm going home. I don't tell her that if I stay longer I might start crying.

I have a small problem, though. I can't get out of my bright yellow dress and earrings without help, and I doubt my cleaner would be available at close to 10 pm to help me undress. I ask Gabriela to open my dress just before I get into a taxi.

"Are you crazy? What are you going to do half-naked in a fucking taxi? Do you want the driver to rape you? We'll drive you home."

They drive me home and in the entrance door of the block Gabriela opens the zip of my dress and takes off my earrings.

"Don't worry, I can manage from here." I wave them off. They have a long drive back to Lobos and I have only two flights of stairs in my bright yellow dress with an open zip at the back and tears that refuse to be held back any longer.

I walk into my flat, drink some water, and go straight to bed. I must be gentle with myself after surgery, I remember. And this one is quite fresh. I've just had polo cut out of my heart today.

My tears finally come out in the darkness of my bedroom and I cry for it all—for the final gone wrong, for feeling alone, for the arm that has started aching again, and for that lost feeling of riding a horse on a polo field, surrounded by my teammates, my heart filled with the joy of the game.

I will never feel that way again.

THURSDAY 15TH DECEMBER

The last few days have gone by in a blur. I've locked myself in the house and I've started writing with the same ferocious intensity I used to keep my tears at bay. The *Abierto* has finished, and with it my last contact with the game. Patricio and Gabriela have gone back to their farm, with no more reason to come to Buenos Aires. Rosario, my Argentine sister, calls me daily to find out how I am, but I'm not prepared to admit to anyone how much I'm hurting.

I'm not even sure what exactly is hurting. My shoulder is painful. That's easy to identify. The weather has changed in Buenos Aires and the storms have come—big electrical storms with heavy rains and strong winds that last for a few days. The screws in my shoulder hurt with the weather change, just like Doc warned me they would. But something else hurts even more, something hidden deep inside. Maybe it's the polo passion that is clinging to me, not really ready to go, or that damn word. *Sola*. Alone. Once again, I'm alone in Buenos Aires, just as I started out last year.

After the past few days of this deep pain with no name, I decide I've had enough. I send an email to the psychologist my friend recommended. Lady with a crystal number four, I decide to call her. Number one was fired. Number two talked nonsense about a comet called Chiron. Number three was unreachable, so I'd better get myself a new one.

The new lady connects with me on Skype, as agreed, and tells me she can't see my face. Of course she can't: I've switched the camera off. I don't really need to see the faces of my ladies with a crystal. And why would she want to see me? I tell her I haven't taken a shower in two days and I have one big, ugly cut on my shoulder. Better if she doesn't see me.

It doesn't work like this, she says. She has to see me. Seriously. If she doesn't see me, we can't talk.

I switch the camera on, reluctantly. None of my other ladies with a crystal asked to see my face. I'm really not that sure why she does. I'm also not sure she's going to last very long. We're starting off on the wrong foot, I can tell already.

She smiles and says, "Hi." She doesn't seem disturbed, neither by my dirty hair nor by my long scar. She's a very smiley woman, about my age, with long brown hair and dark red lipstick. She greets me like she already knows me.

"Tell me about it. The accident, the breaks," she says.

I tell her as much as I know. I say I play polo and I break bones one after the other—my wrist, my arm (both arms, actually), my shoulder blade, my collarbone.

"I can see these breaks are getting closer to your neck," she remarks casually.

This is really not what I want to hear right now.

"Tell me, why do you do this?" she carries on, not leaving me too much time to think.

"Why do I do what?"

"Self-harm," she says.

I was right not to like her. She's crazy. And she clearly doesn't have a clue.

"I don't self-harm," I explain to her patiently. "I play polo. People who play polo break bones. It's just like that. Some die, too. Polo is like that."

"People who do drugs die, too. Sometimes," she says.

"Are you telling me playing polo is like taking drugs?" I am now seriously irritated. Maybe I should cut this call short.

She doesn't answer.

"Tell me why you play polo," she asks instead, this time in a natural tone.

"Because I love it. Because there's nothing like it. Because it makes me feel alive."

"Even if it nearly kills you?" she asks, in the same casual voice.

"Maybe just because of that," I admit. "The excitement. The

adrenaline. And something else, impossible to describe. Connection. It gives me a connection—to the horse, to my teammates, to the other people who play polo. There is this big feeling of belonging."

She waits for me to finish. "People who do drugs feel they belong, too. With other people who do drugs."

Ah, the bitch! She just patiently lets me speak and goes back to her broken-record story.

"Look, you don't get it. I've never done drugs in my whole life," I shout.

"Not chemical drugs, you mean."

"No, any type of drugs. Polo isn't like drugs. Polo is healthy. It's nice. It's a sport, for God's sake. It's exercise. I've never felt healthier in my whole life than since I started playing polo. It makes me feel good." I try to explain but I have this nagging feeling I'm wasting my time.

"It also breaks your bones."

"That was just an accident. It doesn't mean anything. I can still play and be all right."

"How many bones did you say you've broken so far?"

Five. I don't need to count them. I keep silent.

She summarizes her understanding of the situation. "So, you've chosen to associate yourself with a group of people who get regularly injured by doing something they love. And you feel connected to them. And this sense of connection is stronger than the sense of self-preservation."

She will definitely not last long. She and I are on different pages. I glance at the time and realize we've got only ten minutes left of this session. The first and the last one. For the sake of my friend who recommended her I am trying to keep the anger in my voice in check. There's no need to fire her. I'll let the ten minutes pass and I'll never talk to her again.

"Polo isn't like drug addiction," I repeat patiently.

"No, it's not," she admits. "It looks so much better from the outside. I bet a lot of people envy you when you get on that horse and ride onto the field with your teammates."

How does she know about the feeling of riding onto the field together?

"Maybe they do. That isn't the point. That isn't why I do it. It's the connection. I never get this connection anywhere else. But anyway, the point is, now I don't have it. And I want it back. But for this I need to resolve the question about why I break my bones. It's very important."

"Why?"

"So I can play again and not break bones anymore," I say. "What do you think I should do about it?"

"That's for you to decide," she says. "I can't tell you."

Great. Just like Patricio and the Old Man. They won't tell me what to do, either. She's a lady with a crystal, though. She's supposed to tell me what to do. This is what ladies with crystals are paid for.

I hang up. It was a waste of time. I'm irritated and angry and I have no idea why. Fragments of that conversation continue to go through my head but I try hard to brush them away.

My phone is silent afterwards. No more calls. After a while people lose interest in a broken bone. They want to help but they can't really. Alone in the house I go back to writing, in a desperate attempt to silence the unanswered questions that are bubbling up inside me. Karmic ties, drug addiction, black magic, bad luck, and everything else I've been told all mix up in my head in one big, thick porridge. It's quite hard to digest.

With the picture of San Benito watching over me from the shelf where I've placed him, I open my computer and I write about my polo passion.

His eyes are shielded by the dark goggles. He looks like a knight, all

covered in armor. I can't see his eyes. I can't see if he's looking at me right now. But the tone of his voice leaves no doubt.

"You!" His mallet comes down, pointing at me. A rider has no free hands to point at anything. "You take it!"

No, no, no. I cringe inside. No, please, Jonny, no. I plead silently, hoping he can read my thoughts.

I say nothing. My eyes are shielded by my own dark goggles. He can't see them either. Thank God he can't read the terror I'm hiding.

"Roxana." His shout comes back. "You take it, I said."

He's the captain of our team. I should do what he says.

"Spot or thirty?" The umpire asks again, and this time he demands an answer. You can't let an umpire ask this too many times, otherwise he might just decide that there will be no penalty at all, and the unbelievable luck that landed on our team will just disappear.

If I am to take the penalty, I should answer. But my mouth is frozen and nothing comes out.

"Spot or thirty?" The shout comes back one last time.

"Thirty." Jonny answers for me. This means he's choosing to have the ball placed at the thirty-yard line in front of the goalpost, instead of on the spot where the foul occurred. It's an easy shot from the thirty-yard line. Undefended. All one needs to do is get the horse in a slow canter, circle wide, then come to the ball, stay relaxed, look at it, at the ball, really look at it, swing, and hit. And score. All the rest doesn't matter at all if one doesn't score.

And we need this goal. We desperately need it. The score is equal and there are about two minutes left in the game. The clock has been stopped as we prepare to take the penalty, but it will start running again as soon as the ball is touched. If we score now, we have a very big chance of winning this game.

"You take it," Jonny shouts again. "You can do it. You've done it before."

I shake my head. No, no, no! I've done it before on the training field with him. I've done it countless times, more times than I can remember. But I can't do it now. Now it matters, now it will make the difference between winning and losing the game. I just can't do it now.

My right hand is shaking as I hold the mallet. I don't trust myself to do this.

"Roxana." Jonny brings his pony close to me. Why can't he call me Rosanna like all Argentines do?

"This is the game we play. You have to do these things. Don't be afraid."

"I will miss. What happens if I miss?" I whisper. He's now close enough to hear me.

"Come on, whites!"

The ball is on the thirty-yard penalty spot. The riders of the other team are behind the goal, lined up on both sides of it as they should be, leaving it open, undefended. It's going to be an easy penalty.

"One minute," Jonny shouts back. And then he turns again to me. "You will do it. Trust yourself. You can do it. You'll do it. Just like you've done it with me on the training field. I know you can. And if you fail, no pasa nada."

"No, I can't. Please, Jonny, I just can't." I cringe.

"Take the penalty now or you lose it, whites!" the umpire shouts mercilessly, oblivious to my little drama.

I take a last look into Jonny's dark glasses and shake my head, while a tear comes out hidden by my own glasses.

"Number 2, you do it!" Jonny shouts without looking back. He's still looking at me. I don't see his eyes but I can read his frustration. The hours he spent training with me on that field, the countless penalties I took, the many times I scored. It was all meant so that I can use it now. In a game. When it matters. Now, when I'm bailing out like the little coward that I am.

But in my heart I am relieved. The other player, number 2, he'll do it. He's a much better player than I am. He has a better chance to score. We all have a better chance to win this game if he takes it.

I don't even see it when it happens. I'm still looking at Jonny's dark goggles, trying to guess how upset he is with me.

But I hear the shout of the umpire, "Hit in, blacks!"

And I know this means my teammate, the number 2, the much better player than me, has just missed, and we're now not likely to win the game.

"See? No pasa nada. We all miss sometimes," Jonny tells me, moving his horse off to go and take his position for the hit-in by the other team.

Maybe he's not upset with me, then, I think. But the bitter taste in my mouth stays with me for the rest of the day. It tells me I had a chance to score and I didn't trust myself enough to take it.

MONDAY 19TH DECEMBER

I start to cook the broccoli in the steamer I bought in my first week here. I've never been good at cooking, but I'm quite proud of my recent attempts. Gabriela has been trying to convert me into a cook for some time now and she has no idea she's almost succeeding, even if only to a beginner's degree. Steamed vegetables, I can do this. It's quite easy actually—just wash them, cut them, place in the steamer, and press a button. Wait. Eat. Maybe I can get this cooking thing.

While the broccoli is steaming in the kitchen, I prepare for another call. This one is big, really big. Today I'm talking to lady with a crystal number three, the one who's really hard to get hold of. I have a big hope that she'll unlock this puzzle for me finally, once and for all.

I pick up a pen and write my questions one by one.

Why do I break bones?

What can I do to not break bones again?

Hmm. Better to rephrase this.

What can I do to play polo again and not break bones?

Do I really need to give up polo? Just to double-check the advice of lady number two.

Do I really need to leave Argentina? This one is because the same lady said something about karmic connections to this country. Maybe I can play polo safely if not in Argentina.

I pause and take a look at my list. Actually, it would be better if I played here. Jonny comes back in January. I could train with him. My arm is already out of its sling and I'm starting physio next week. I could recover by mid-January.

I pick up the pen again and write with a new determination.

What do I need to do so that I can still play polo in Argentina?

And then one more, just because I remember my hairdresser's voice.

Is Sol right about black magic?

For a second I contemplate adding something about self-harm, but I decide not to. That can wait. And I don't think I'll ever speak again to lady number four, anyway. What I really want to find out now is how I can still play polo and not break anything.

Lady number three listens in silence to my long list of questions. Then she tells me I already know the answers. They are all inside me. I didn't expect this. I booked a session with her precisely because I can't find any answers inside me.

"Close your eyes and focus on your breathing," she says.

I do as instructed. It takes some time because my mind gets in the way, telling me I'm wasting my precious time. I would be better off using this time to ask my questions.

But lady number three won't have any of this. She just guides me to connect with my breathing and then she guides me to connect with the earth, to feel deep, long roots from each of my feet going down into the earth, reaching its very center.

I'm not sure how long I have to spend doing this but eventually I stop thinking about the time. I'm now turned inwards, feeling my breathing as it goes in and out of my body. I am relaxed, expanded, still. Nothing really matters any longer.

"Good. You're there." I hear the voice on the phone and for a second I wonder how she knows where exactly I am.

"What do you feel?"

"Still," I answer.

"Very good. Keep this feeling. Now tell me what your body feels."

"My body. Hmm." I move my awareness away from my breathing. A ray of light travels inside me, shedding light on various parts of my body. The feeling of stillness remains with me. Slowly, I search around inside my body.

"I feel pain in my shoulder." I've arrived at the metal piece.

It's raining outside. My shoulder always hurts when it's raining outside. My mind tries to get in the way and offer this perfectly logical explanation.

"Good. Focus on your shoulder. Take your time. Feel it, feel around it." She keeps quiet for a few moments. "Now ask your shoulder what it needs."

"My shoulder doesn't talk," I answer, with my eyes still closed.

"Yes, I know," she says patiently. "This is what your mind says. Leave the mind on one side and focus on the shoulder. What does it want to tell you? What does it need? Just allow the answer to appear."

Silence. With my eyes closed I focus all my attention on my shoulder and on the feeling of pain coming from it. The only other thing I'm aware of is my breathing. Even the lady with a crystal seems to have vanished. I'm not sure how long I stay there in silence.

"Healing." The words leave my mouth before I have time to think them through. I'm not sure who has spoken them.

"Does your shoulder want to play polo?"

"No."

"Where does your shoulder want to go?"

"Somewhere warm and peaceful."

By now I'm not even questioning my answers any longer. I just let the words rise within me as if they're being spoken by someone else. Maybe they are. Maybe my shoulder is really talking through my mouth.

"What does it want to do there?"

"Take it easy, move slowly. Rest. Be in pain for a while."

My mind kicks back in suddenly and it feels like I've gone slightly insane. I open my eyes and snap out of this silliness. In a fraction of a second, the stillness is gone too.

"Can't be. It's a joke, right?"

"It's the truth," she answers. "It's a part of you that's talking."

"Well, there are other parts of me who want to stay here and play polo," I tell her, unconvinced.

"Let's take a look at them, too," she says. "Close your eyes again."

I'm not sure who we're about to talk to this time, but I pay a lot of money to have a session with this lady, so I do as instructed. It's difficult to reach the same stillness as before. I try to concentrate on my breathing, as she says.

"Ask to see what holds you here," she says.

"What do you mean, to see? I've got my eyes closed."

"See in your mind. Imagine."

"You mean I can imagine anything I want?"

This is more difficult than talking as my shoulder. At least I know exactly where my shoulder is. But now it's just darkness. And the air going in and out of my lungs in the middle of all the darkness.

"Yes, just see what comes to you. Focus on your breathing. Don't think about it. Just let the images come to you."

I breathe in and out. She's silent. Nothing comes. Again, breathe in, breathe out. My mind is trying to tell me this is bullshit, but I ignore it. Again. Breathe in, breathe out.

The wind of the *campo* is suddenly on my face. The smell of it hits my nostrils. It's fresh grass and earth, a pungent smell, just like after a rain shower. Maybe it's coming from outside, I think for a second, but no, it can't be, there's nothing but a road full of traffic outside.

"What's coming to you?" she asks.

"It's weird. The smell of the *campo*."

"Good. Anything else? Focus on your breathing."

"There isn't much else. The smell of the earth. A strong smell."

"So, you're strongly connected to this land," she says.

"You mean I have karmic ties to this country?" I suddenly remember lady number two.

"Karmic or not, you have ties. That why you've come back several times and you're finding it hard to leave."

"Do I really have to leave?"

"Ask your shoulder, does it want to stay in Argentina?"

I don't need to close my eyes and focus on my breathing again to know the answer to this one. My shoulder doesn't want to be here or to get back on a horse. Not for now, at least.

"So, I need to go away," I say, my voice mellow. It's not really a question any longer and she doesn't answer.

"How can I go away when I feel so connected to this place?"

"That's because of the ties you have with this land. Well, you cut them."

"How do I do this?"

"You ask the land to release you."

"You mean I go and have a conversation with the *campo*? My friends will lock me up in a mental institution."

"You'll find a way. The solution always comes when one is ready."

I don't really feel like talking any longer. I feel the pain in my shoulder, and the smell of the *campo* is still in my nostrils. I keep a long silence and she keeps quiet too.

"So, polo—never?" I ask after some time.

"Never is a very long time," she says. "Let's just say not for now."

"And go where?"

"This is for you to decide. Somewhere warm and peaceful where you can take it easy and be in pain for a while, like your shoulder said. Somewhere you can heal."

I don't argue with this verdict any longer. I feel calm and grounded. Maybe it's because of focusing on my breathing. Or maybe she did a little magic. I rarely feel that calm and grounded when I meditate by myself.

I thank her and we hang up. There's nothing else I need to ask and the time is up, anyway. It's clear what I need to do. The only thing that's not clear is whether I'll be able to do it.

TUESDAY 20TH DECEMBER

I start my physiotherapy sessions at the same Institute for Sports Medicine, Recovery, and Rehabilitation where I've already recovered from two previous breaks. They know me there. They greet me as if I were an old acquaintance. I tell them I broke a collarbone this time. They find my records, all the notes they had taken about my left wrist and about my right wrist. They don't tell me I'm crazy. They don't tell me I should give up polo, either. They're used to sports people getting injured, recovering, and then getting injured again. They also don't tell me that if I do it again I might die.

They take a long look at my X-rays and my scar and tell me I have to start with the beginning.

"*Hay que trabajar la cicatriz,*" they say, and I burst out laughing instantly.

We have to work on the scar. They mean touch it and loosen it up. This will hurt initially but it will desensitize it. It'll make the skin normal again. It'll take away that awful, ever-present sensation of extreme vulnerability I have every time I accidently touch my scar.

Working on the scar was also a joke I shared with Rosario. Last year when I came here determined to find love, Rosario talked me out of my finding-love plans and convinced me to change them to just having some fun.

"Don't trust Argentine men," she told me then. "Don't get your heart broken. If you have a scar in your heart from previous relationships and you need to heal it, just use them to work out the scar, to desensitize you. Just have some fun!"

So I did. I worked on the scar left by the surgery I'd had on my left wrist. And at the same time I worked on the scar I was carrying in my heart. I had physio sessions here. And I kissed football players in discos. I thought that would help me not feel so vulnerable any longer. And then I met a guy fourteen years younger than me and I thought that was just for fun too, part of working the scar. But this one didn't go according to plan. I ended up falling in love and thinking that I might really have a life with him. And he loved me too, or at least that's what he said.

But all this is gone now, replaced by one long wound to recover from. I let the thought go as I concentrate on the hand of the physio guy pulling and rubbing the scar on my shoulder. It's very uncomfortable but I know it's good for me.

As I make my way home, the memory of the conversation with the lady with a crystal number three is still with me, but now, after my fresh visit to the physio center, my conviction that I need to go away starts to shake a little. Maybe I don't really need to go, not just yet. Maybe I can simply do enough physio sessions to recover properly and then play some polo again.

To stay or not to stay, this is the question. Or rather, to play or not to play.

I reach home, put some vegetables in my steamer, and while they cook I decide to take a very rational approach to these questions. I will draw a proper pros-and-cons list, like I would do in a consulting project.

I take a blank sheet of paper and start writing. Shall I stay in Argentina, go to physio, allow my shoulder to recover, and play polo with Jonny in January? Or shall I go away and forget about polo for a while? I draw two columns and list all the advice I've received.

First, the ladies with crystals. Lady number one doesn't count, but numbers two, three, and four all go under the Cons.

Same for my non-playing friends, Rosario, Sol, Marco, and various others.

Under the Pro column I put various people I met at the *Abierto* who told me I should recover and play again as soon as possible. Except for Emi. He said he wasn't sure if I should play, with longer stirrups, or not at all. So he's entered into a third column headed Maybe. Patricio, Gabriela, and the Old Man go in there as well, since they said they wouldn't advise me either way.

Hmm. I contemplate my list, which is now heavily skewed on the Con side. I don't really like what I see. There's something in me that still wants to do it.

And then I remember my new lady with a crystal, number four, who talked about self-harm, and for a second I contemplate adding this to the Con list. But I don't. It sounds too strong. And my Con side seems weighted enough without it. Plus, she can't be right.

I leave the list and go to check on the vegetables and rice cooking in the steamer. I'm hungry and I need to eat quickly because in exactly thirty minutes from now I'm going to see Gabriela and Patricio, who are finally in town today. They told me they'd pass by and pick me up to go for a coffee.

And then it happens. Something happens and it makes me think for the first time ever that maybe my newest lady with a crystal, number four, is right.

As I check on my vegetable steamer, I place my left hand on the hot lid with boiling steam coming out of it. I place my full palm on it and let out a long, loud scream as I feel my hand burning.

I can't believe I've done this. My mind races, trying to push down the pain that comes from my burning hand. Why have I done this? How did this happen?

With tears pouring down my face I rush to the bathroom, turn on the tap, and let the cold water run all over my burned hand. The pain is deep and intense, and brings up all the memories of the other recent pain, my broken shoulder.

Alone in the bathroom, I cry with my hand under the cold, running water.

Why? Why? Why do I do this to myself?

And then the answer comes. Because sometimes it's just about asking a question enough times.

Self-harm.

She was right.

I stay there for a while, letting the cold water pour down my arm, but the pain intensifies instead of decreasing. My palm feels like it's on fire.

I call Gabriela. She doesn't answer. She's in the habit of misplacing her phone regularly. I'm always surprised when she answers or texts back straight away.

I call Patricio. He picks up, immediately.

"I burned myself," I scream.

"Roxy, what's going on? Where are you?" His alarmed voice sounds like he's next to me.

"In my flat. I can't believe I've done this. It's my palm. On the steamer. It's not serious. I don't think so. But it hurts like crazy."

Sobs. I'm crying. I am not sure if it's for the pain or for feeling such an idiot.

"Put it in cold water. We'll be there in ten minutes."

With Patricio there's never a need for too many explanations. He just knows.

"Don't worry," he adds. "We're going to be there soon. We'll look after you."

I put the phone down. They're going to look after me. Again. Once again. The enormity of this thought shocks me even more than my burned hand.

But I've got no time to dwell on this. They arrive and I have to go downstairs to let them in. There's no buzzer in the flat. I go down the stairs from my flat on the second floor holding a big piece of ice in my swollen red hand. If I don't hold the ice it still hurts like mad.

"Roxy, I can take you to the hospital," Patricio says, after examining my hand. "If you want, we can go now. But they won't be able to help you. I don't think so. All they'll tell you will be to put your hand in a bucket of ice. Burns are like this. They carry on burning for a while afterwards."

I know. Tears are still rolling down my cheek.

"How the fuck did this happen?" Gabriela is shocked. "Show me. What have you done? How could you do this?"

"I touched the lid of my steamer. I don't know why. I just touched the lid."

She shakes her head, speechless. Very few things can render Gabriela speechless.

In the end we decide there's not much we can do about it. The thought of going back to a hospital fills me with horror. I guess it fills them with horror, too. They have had far too many instances of taking me to a hospital. And Patricio is right. There's nothing the doctors will be able to do for me, anyway. A burn carries on burning for some time afterwards.

They leave me in my flat with my hand sunk deep in a bucket of cold water mixed with the ice that Patricio had diligently broken into small pieces for me. They instruct me to keep my hand there for the rest of the day.

And for the rest of the day I do so. Seated on my sofa I watch my two useless hands—the right one freshly out of its sling, weak and painful, not yet able to hold even a glass of water; the left one, freshly burned, sunk deep into a bucket of ice.

And for the rest of the day I have only one thought on my mind.

Self-harm. This is what it looks like.

WEDNESDAY 21ST DECEMBER

"Roxy! You did what?" Sol's eyes are open wide, her mouth trembling in shock.

There's silence in the shop. Her two clients are quiet. There's always more than one client in Sol's shop, even though she works alone. People don't mind waiting here. Madri is silent, too. She's stopped washing the hair of one of the ladies. They all watch me in silence.

"Not a big deal." I'm too tired to try to explain anything any longer. "It's just a cooking accident. It will heal."

"No-o-o, Roxy. I told you. I told you, and you didn't want to hear." Sol slowly regains her voice.

"What? You told me what?"

"I told you this is black magic and you have to do something about it." She's now fully recovered her voice. "I told you, didn't I? I told you a few weeks ago, and you, you did nothing. And now this!" She picks up my left wrist, turns the hand upwards and takes a good look. The palm is still red raw, and some blisters on my fingers have already filled with liquid. I can't touch anything with this palm.

Here we go again. I shouldn't have come. But I had to. I can't wash my hair with one arm just out of a sling and another one freshly burned.

I try to tell her not to worry, but my voice is drowned by the instant release of all the other voices in the room. Sol says over and over again that she can't believe it.

Madri shouts from the washbasin. "The church! I told you, you have to go to the church! I was right. The church! It's not too late!"

The lady whose hair is being washed lifts up her head and takes a good look at me. Or maybe she's concerned about Madri waving her hands full of soap above her. The other client, seated on the chair in front of Sol, turns around and wants to know what's happening. As if she guesses there's something really dramatic going on, Sol's youngest, a charming little three-year-old girl, stops playing with her mother's phone, which she's managed to drag onto the floor, and starts crying. Nobody minds her, though. My news has priority.

I'm starting to think I should have sent Sol a warning message in advance, just like I did when I broke a bone. But it did little to help then.

"Sol, it's OK. Really. It will pass."

"No, Roxy, this time it's serious. You must call the witch! Today. No more delays."

"Not the witch, *boluda*," Madri jumps in. "First she has to go see the priest."

She turns to me. "You go now. Find a priest. Right now. He must do something; he must talk to someone up there." The hands full of shampoo are now pointing towards the roof of the shop. "Someone up there must be able to help with this situation. Jesus, a saint. Anyone. Don't know who, but the priest will have to find someone who can sort it out. This is serious stuff."

"What priest, *boluda*? This is too deep, even for a priest. What can a priest do?" Sol shouts back, unconvinced. Then she turns to me. "You probably need to have sex with a priest for him to reach deep enough."

Madri doesn't take this lightly. Lack of respect, she says. The client on the chair asks again to be told what happened.

"Exorcism, this is what you need," Madri says, as Sol tells the client the whole story involving black magic, my soul being stolen by an ex-boyfriend, which has resulted in one broken shoulder and now one burned hand.

"Go to the church, find a priest and ask him to exorcise you. There's one church here, the first street on the left. Don't waste any time," Madri carries on.

The mention of the church makes Sol turn towards me again.

"What did you do with the picture of San Benito? The one I gave you?" she asks in an accusatory tone.

"I still have it, Sol. I promise. It's on my table."

"Did you read the prayer on the back?"

"Yes, once."

"Why only once?"

"I keep him there. He's watching me from the table every day. Really."

The client in the chair, who has now been brought up to speed with all details, nods her head in agreement. She tells me to take these things seriously.

Sol continues to watch me accusingly, as if somehow I'm to blame for all this.

"Today is the day of the saint. The twenty-first," she says. "Roxy, promise me you'll go home and light a candle and pray to the saint. Here, I've got one for you."

She disappears through the door at the back that hides a little kitchen and returns holding one big red candle.

"Promise me, Roxy. You must pray to the saint until this candle has finished burning."

I want to laugh but I'm touched by her concern.

"OK, I promise." I try to calm her.

"And go to church," Madri jumps in.

"I promise that too."

Anything they want. I'll promise anything. I desperately need my hair washed and I'm ready to do anything for it.

The mood in the shop lifts slowly. The little girl has stopped crying. I take my place at the washbasin and Madri's expert hands begin soaping my hair. I close my eyes, enjoying this bliss, and don't even think of saying anything as I hear Sol continue debating the merits of the church vs. a witch.

"Maybe she should go to both," Sol agrees, conciliating with Madri. "One of them might be able to sort it out."

I leave the shop with my hair feeling silky and one big red candle sticking out of my bag.

On my way home I pass by the church Madri mentioned and I try to continue my walk, but the feeling of guilt catches up with me. I made a promise to her. Reluctantly, I go inside. There's nobody there, no priest, no one. Just the empty benches and a sense of timeless silence. Well, at least I tried.

I go home and I keep my other promise, the one I made to Sol. I light the red candle. It doesn't want to be lit. I try again. It burns for a few seconds, then it dies down. San Benito watches me accusingly from the table where I placed him.

"Yes, I know. I've ignored you, but I'm doing my best. It's not easy, not when you have two hands close to non-functioning."

He doesn't answer.

I manage to light the candle eventually and I watch it burn. Now what? Ah, the prayer. Let's do the prayer. I pick up the saint, turn him around, and read the short prayer printed on the back. Deliver me from the evil spirits, it says. Wow, Sol is really taking things seriously here. Maybe this saint can solve my problems and then I won't have to worry about breaking bones again.

I turn the card to look at the saint again, but he doesn't want to tell me anything. I place him next to the burning candle and look around, trying to find something to do. The candle is going to burn for a long time and there's no way I can talk to the saint for so long.

Then I remember the Old Man, my polo trainer. He'll be leaving for England on Friday and he promised he'd take my equipment. I have to get my bag ready for him. But then if my polo bag goes back to England, so do my polo dreams. For now at least. I won't be able to train with Jonny here in January if I send all my stuff back to England.

I stay there for some time, watching the red candle burn. I don't think of anything. I try to argue with myself, but I know it's useless. I've lost this game. I can't play polo with a shoulder that still hurts, no matter how much I want to. Well, that's it, then. I'll take a break from polo for a while.

Under the flame of the red candle I bring out all my polo gear. My mallets, my boots, my helmet, my Oakley glasses, my knee and elbow pads, my belt. I put everything in the bag, one by one. There's a lot of space left. The bag is huge. I once tried to lie in there myself and found out I could.

I fetch my white jeans—the ones I use for polo and the ones that aren't for polo. Everything that looks like white jeans reminds me of polo, anyway. I put them in the bag and I add my blue jeans as well. That's because in Argentina people ride in blue jeans. I don't want to have them around, either. I put in the *alpargatas*, the traditional cloth shoes with rubber soles that the grooms wear. A lot of players wear them after a game, when they take off their heavy boots. I just received a pair as a birthday gift from Rosario. I love them, but they have to go too. They remind me of polo. I then put in all my polo T-shirts, all the ones I train in and all my brightly colored Polo Ralph Lauren T-shirts that I wear casually. There will be nothing that reminds me of polo for a while. I contemplate the bag. It's only half full. Why do they make polo bags so big?

I go back to my wardrobe and take out all the sexy nightgowns and underwear Rodrigo liked so much and the dresses I wore when I went out with him. One by one, every piece of clothing that reminds me of either Rodrigo or polo is placed inside the bag.

Two hours later I watch the end result with a smile. The big black bag is zipped up and is resting like a whale with a full tummy in the middle of my living room.

I turn to my red candle. That will do, don't you think?

But the saint isn't answering. He just watches me silently, with that stern face framed by the hood of his black cloak.

Well, I hope he approves. I've done my best. With every little thing that went into that bag, a little piece of my heart was cut away. I'm not sure there's much left of it, anyway. I bet it looks like the remains of that red candle, which is now almost all burned down. So he'd better approve and start lending a hand here. There's more work to do and I'm not quite sure I can do it all by myself.

THURSDAY 22ND DECEMBER

I wake up from a long, deep sleep, with no dreams. Not even polo dreams. I jump into a taxi and get going with my to-do list. I'm going to buy gifts today. I'm going back to the farm for Christmas and my Argentine family is quite big.

"Where are you from?" The taxi driver asks casually, just after I give him the address.

I'm giving up the hope I'll ever pass for a local. Not to taxi drivers, anyway. I tell him I'm from Romania.

He asks me how many square kilometers Romania has.

No idea. No one has asked me this before.

And what's the population of Romania?

"Errr, not sure. Twenty-three million, I think. Or maybe less. I heard it's been decreasing these past few years. Why?"

He tells me I should know these things. They're important.

He tells me that Argentina has a total surface of 2,780,400 square kilometers but that this is misleading, because a large part of it—1,461,597 square kilometers, precisely—is made up of a part of Antarctica, which is technically another continent, so this means Argentina itself, without Antarctica, is only about half the size.

"Still a hell of a lot of land," I tell him. "And how about the population?"

He tells me 41.5 million.

I wonder if he's a retired geography teacher or just a weirdo. Or maybe he makes up the numbers in his head.

He says I should remember these things, they're important. And then he tells me that the ice crust on the Antarctic is four kilometers deep and that this is the biggest reservoir of fresh water in the world, and that it's divided up amongst a handful of countries only. Do I think this is fair?

"No, it's not fair," I agree.

"It's not fair," he echoes. "And you know why? Because fresh water is precious. It makes up only three percent of the surface of the world. How much fresh water do you have in Romania?"

I don't know if he expects the answer in liters or tons or percentage of the surface of the country, which I don't know anyway.

But the great thing about taxi rides in this city and the related conversations is that they both tend to be relatively short.

"We have arrived," he tells me shortly. "Here's your address. Please remember these things." He turns around to give me the change and looks me straight in the eye. "I tell you so that when I die, someone is here to remember them. And to tell others."

I get out of the taxi with this absurd pain inside, thinking that the weird taxi driver will die and he'll have wasted his efforts on me, because I still don't know the total surface of Argentina. Or that of my own country.

I can't do much about my missing geography knowledge, so I decide to focus on buying Christmas presents instead. By evening I'm done. I've even finished wrapping them, despite the painful blisters in my left hand and the heavy thoughts that cloud my mind. This is the last one, the last Christmas I'll spend with my Argentine family.

I don't know that yet, I tell myself, trying to silence the thought.

But it comes back and tells me I know, that I'm going there to the *campo* one more time so I can finally leave.

"How is this going to help me leave?" I ask the annoying thought.

"You'll cut your ties with it, just like lady number three said you should."

"Yeah, right. And how am I going to do it? Shall I pack one big knife, just in case?"

The thought ignores my irritation and tells me it's going to be done without knives but the cut will be equally sharp. These ties will go, whether I'm ready or not.

"We'll see about that," I mutter, and I get all the presents nicely lined up in one big plastic bag in the middle of my living room, next to the packed polo bag.

But later, as I meditate and ask the same question, I get a new answer. And this time I have to trust it, because it comes from a place of silence and warmth and it's light like a feather, the way all true answers are.

"Just go there tomorrow," it says. "What needs to happen will happen. And everything will be all right."

FRIDAY 23RD DECEMBER

I get a taxi to the airport and arrive just in time to meet the Old Man at the check-in counter of British Airways. He checks in my thirty-kilogram polo bag with no sign of surprise. It's an oversized bag and it goes through a special desk, but they don't charge extra for the weight. Great!

"What's in there?" he asks, watching it going away on the belt. "In case I get asked."

"Polo stuff," I say. I omit to mention the sexy nightdresses. I hope the customs officers won't ask him to open the bag, so he'll never find out he's carrying away my smashed dreams of love in addition to my smashed dreams of polo.

"I'll leave it in the tack room at the club," he says. "It will be there for you when you're ready for it."

If I'm ever going to be ready for it, I think. I give him a big, long hug.

"*Gracias, Viejo.* You really make my life lighter, you know."

I really don't know that many people who would agree to take a thirty-kilogram bag from South America to England without even bothering to check what's inside.

"*De nada.*" He smiles. "*Cuídate.* Take care. And Merry Christmas!"

I watch him go through the security gates with a mixture of gratitude and uncertainty. Of all the polo trainers I've had, he is the one who has really taught me how to play this game. He taught me to love it. Now he was the one taking my polo gear with him, back to England. Was this an omen?

I let this question drop in the big pile of unanswered questions I carry inside me these days and get back in the taxi, hurrying towards my next appointment of the day—a check-up with Doc at the hospital in Lobos.

Doc greets me with a kiss on the cheek and a very large smile. This guy should meet Sol, I think. They're both about the same age, late twenties. And they both smile non-stop. They would make a handsome pair together. Doc mentioned he had a baby, but not a wife, and there's no wedding ring on his finger …

Stop it! I tell myself. You're becoming a matchmaker, just like the Argentines.

"*Hola, mi medico argentino*!" I say instead. "Want to see how well I can move my arms? Look at this!"

Before he can say anything I lift both my hands up and touch my palms on top of my head and then bring them down together in that great *namaste* yoga pose that looks so cool.

His smile vanishes from his face immediately.

"Stop," he shouts. "Stop this! Didn't I tell you not to lift your arms above the shoulders?"

"Yes, you did, but I can do it! Look, I can do it again. It doesn't hurt."

"No, I don't want to see! I don't want you to do it again. Don't! You hear me? Don't. It's too soon."

"But I can."

"I don't care what you can or can't do. I don't care, you hear me? I said you're not supposed to do it and you should listen. At least this time, listen."

He's not smiling. He's angry. I haven't seen Doc angry before.

"Rosanna, you should listen to me. I know what I'm talking about!"

He pauses. I don't say a thing.

"You had a bad fracture," he continues. "Your bone was broken in five pieces. I spent a lot of time trying to put these pieces together. The middle pieces have no connection to any blood supply any longer. They'll take a long time to recover."

"But you said the X-ray was good."

"Yes, it was, but there are times that you can't rush. Cellular recovery times."

"But my physio said—"

"I don't care what your physio said." The anger in his voice comes back. "I'm your doctor and I tell you to go slowly. For two more weeks from now you lift your arms only to shoulder level, then slowly upwards, ten degrees higher per week, no more."

I keep silent. There's no way I'm getting back to polo soon with this routine.

"These physios are brutal," he adds. "I know how they work. All they want to do is push and force. They want sports people back on the field as soon as possible. I go slowly. I go by bicycle, not in a Ferrari. But I get there in the end. Safer."

The mention of a bicycle makes me smile.

"All right, I get it. I'll listen to you," I promise. "But talking about the bicycle, I have something for you." I reach into my bag and take out a small perfume bottle with a silhouette of a polo player on the box.

"To remind you of my bicycle," I tell him. "And Merry Christmas!"

I kiss Doc goodbye. He lets me go with no further lectures, but by the time I meet Gabriela in the middle of the town I'm already exhausted. I've had far too many emotions for one day.

Gabriela doesn't ask about my bones or burned hands and I'm grateful for that. She tells me it's going to be a packed afternoon since we need to go to the kids' school *fiesta*.

"An end-of-term party with lots of Nativity stuff for Christmas and that type of thing, you know. Argentines like to make a big fuss about everything, Christmas included."

Actually, I think Argentines are extremely low-key about Christmas. In London the festivities usually start in early October and go on for three months, with Christmas carols, decorations, and so many Christmas parties that one wants to hide away from it all. In Argentina I spotted the first Christmas decoration in the shops only about a week ago.

"You don't have to come if you don't want, but we're going. The whole family."

I tell her I wouldn't miss it for the world.

The three boys who live at the farm all go to a primary school about twenty minutes' drive from the farm across a dirt road. If it rains heavily, the school closes, since the road becomes impossible to drive on. But it hasn't rained for some time now, so we get there without any incidents, the whole family loaded in three cars.

The school is in the middle of a village that consists of ten houses, a church, and a communal hall. We go to the school, but they tell us the *fiesta* will take place in the communal hall. We go to the communal hall, but it's still empty. Someone tells us that it's going to start in the church. We go to the church, a beautiful Romanesque-style building with a tall tower and a line of palm trees in front of it, but there's nothing happening there either.

"We're probably too early," Patricio concludes. The *fiesta* was supposed to start at 7 pm, but no one starts things on time here. The boys are let out to go and play in the schoolyard and Patricio carries on driving.

"Where are we going now?" I ask.

"Nowhere. Just killing some time," he says.

His drive comes to an abrupt stop some twenty meters further on, right in front of a huge plum tree heavy with ripe yellow plums. We all get out of the car.

"What's happening here?" I feel like I'm part of a movie I don't understand, which requires constant translation.

"Nothing. The plums. Have you seen plums like this before?"

No, I haven't. The tree is so loaded it looks like it's going to fall down. We start eating some, picking them straight from the tree. The tree is just in front of a small house, and an old woman comes out to greet us.

"Do you know her?" I ask Gabriela, choking on a large yellow plum.

"No, I don't. But don't worry, darling, we're not robbing her. We're just eating some plums."

Patricio strikes up a conversation with the old lady, who motions us to carry on eating the plums.

"I can't gather them, anyway, and the birds end up eating them," she says.

They're delicious. I imagine what a great marmalade Gabriela would make from them.

I'm not quite sure what we're doing there, stuck by the tree in front of the woman's house, but no one seems to be in any hurry to go anywhere. Patricio asks the old woman if she knits.

Of course she does, they all know how to knit here. As I eat three more plums, the woman goes back inside the house, coming out again with a big basket filled with knitted things for sale.

"Do you know her?" I ask Patricio this time, as Gabriela takes a look through the contents of the basket. "What are we doing here?"

"*Tranqui*. We're just spending some time and eating plums. Waiting for the school *fiesta* to start. And no, I don't know her. But now we all do. *No pasa nada*."

Gabriela picks up a cute pink baby top. She buys it for very little money. It's for a friend whose new baby daughter was born just a few days ago.

The woman is now very pleased she's made a sale and asks us to eat more *ciruellas*. No, no more plums for me, I'm about to explode.

Patricio carries on eating while Gabriela tells the woman she's looking for someone to knit a dress for her just like this. She goes through her phone in search of a particular picture. I move towards the car, my belly full of plums, the cool evening breeze bringing up the smell of earth and grass in my nostrils.

I love the *campo*. I love the people living here. How on earth am I going to leave here and never come back, like these crystal ladies say I should?

Stop thinking, otherwise you'll cry, I tell myself. And there'll be no way to explain to my friends why I'm crying just after I've had the most delicious plums in the world.

We leave the old woman and her plum tree eventually, because we notice cars starting to gather in front of the church. The school *fiesta* is about to begin.

The church is surprisingly large inside, with benches nicely arranged on both sides, a small altar with a painting of Jesus in the center, and a statue of the Virgin to the left.

The kids are dressed up—the girls in large, colorful skirts, with their hair braided up, and small ponchos hanging on their shoulders; the boys in large ponchos and hats, and khaki *bombachas*, the traditional *gaucho* trousers that remind me of Facundo, Patricio's groom. They look like the *gauchos* of the last century. Maybe this is what the *fiesta* is about. I'm just not sure why it's starting in church.

Families enter the church and take their seats on the long wooden benches. For a while nothing happens. They all wait in silence. There is no priest, no one to start the service, only the silent statue of the Virgin overlooking the whole assembly. I sit between Patricio and his niece. Gabriela is two seats away on my right. The rest of the family line up on the same bench and on the one in front as well. There are many people in this family. Seated there, on those benches, I feel I'm part of them.

Then an old lady walks up to the altar, turns to the audience, and announces that we have a problem because the priest can't make it. He's got a flat tire apparently, and he's too far away. He'll never make it on time. We need to improvise. She says she'll conduct the prayers for tonight.

I'm expecting only a short prayer before we carry on to the communal hall, but it turns out to be a full Catholic Mass, conducted by a woman who isn't a priest, but who apparently has the blessings of the local resident priest to step in for him. She knows what she's doing. She recites all the prayers by heart, and the congregation answers, obediently. I believe it's not the first time she's acted as a substitute for the priest.

And then she takes the cup from its sacred place on the altar. I can't believe she's going to do the sacrament of the Holy Communion as well, but she takes her role seriously. Everyone stands up and holds the hands of their neighbors. The words of the most well-known Christian prayer rise up in the church, spoken by everyone around me in Spanish. I say them in Romanian, standing up as all of them do and holding hands with them.

One by one the Spanish words are echoed by my whisper in Romanian:

Our Father, who art in heaven,
Hallowed be thy name …

I say Amen at the end. This is the same in Spanish and in Romanian.

Then the congregation goes on to recite the Creed, but I don't know this prayer and it's a long one. Instead, other words come into my mind from nowhere and I say them one by one too, only this time I say them silently in my head, my heart pounding in my chest and a rebel tear rolling down my cheek.

God, please help me. Help me heal my bone and never break another one again.

And if I need to, please help me go away from here—from this campo, *from these people, from the feeling that I'm part of them. Cut my ties with this land. Help me go away and stay away.*

Amen, I say, just as the rest of the congregation reaches their own Amen.

That's it. The hands that hold my palms right and left let go and we sit down again and watch the new priestess giving the Holy Communion to a long queue of people. I'm not one of them. I'm not Catholic, after all.

Patricio turns to me and says, "Wow, this was a full mass. Sorry, I didn't know we were supposed to have a mass, otherwise I'd have warned you. Hope you didn't mind."

"Not at all," I manage to say. "It was just what I needed."

And then I remember my thought at the end of my meditation last night.

Just go there. What needs to happen will happen.

I guess it did, but is that all? My mind starts to question, as it always does. You mean you just say a prayer and that's it? You'll no longer break bones? You can go away from Argentina and from polo just like that? Come on, let's be serious!

I don't know. The pounding in my heart is still there, my palms still hold the memory of their hands, and my tears are just about to start again because I've been part of their circle on this long wooden bench. I've been part of this family and I've just prayed silently to go away from them forever.

After church everyone heads over to the communal hall for the actual *fiesta*. Outside, a huge fire has already been lit and an impressive quantity of meat is grilling nicely on it. It takes a long time to do a proper *asado*—I learned this from the Old Man at his polo club in England—so it's no wonder they put the meat on the fire before the *fiesta* actually begins.

The kids go to their teachers and get ready for their parts. They all have a role to play. There are about fifty kids in this school, I'm told, and that includes the nursery school too, which means fewer than seven per class.

Everyone is seated on plastic chairs lined up towards a side of the hall that is doubling up as the stage. The lights are switched off. A girl with an incredibly deep voice starts singing "Ave Maria," and for a second I feel I'm back in that church, and I wonder if I should say my little prayer again, just in case.

But my mind is silenced by the beauty of the song and I don't think of anything any longer. I just soak it all in—the dark silhouettes of the people seated in silence, the vastness of the hall with its doors and windows open so that the outside breeze can cool the air, the beautiful voice breaking into the silence, and the warm feeling of my Argentine family all around me.

The last note of the song hangs there in the darkness and then the lights are switched back on and the Nativity scene unfolds on the stage. A heavily pregnant Mary comes out, holding Joseph's arm, and they cross the stage slowly, while another voice begins the ageless story. I spot a pillow under Mary's robe, which accounts for the big belly. Joseph is wearing *alpargatas* and a poncho. He looks like a *gaucho*. A stray dog wanders into the scene, but nobody minds him. There are quite a few stray dogs in the hall, circulating between the plastic chairs.

The kids come in and perform a few traditional dances. I spot little Patricio waving enthusiastically to his parents, and Gabriela jumps up from her seat and starts taking pictures. The dance finishes and we're back to the nativity scene, where Mary has, meanwhile, given birth and now holds a real baby in her arms. I wonder whose baby it is and why it's not crying. It looks quite tranquil there on the stage.

The dog on the scene has now retreated to a corner, probably intimidated by the dances. The small kids from the nursery classes enter hand in hand, led by their teacher. They sing a few songs and clap their hands. They all wear cute, little, colorful ponchos.

Then we're back to the Nativity scene and we see the three kings arriving to pay homage to the newborn baby Jesus. I guess they must be teachers from the school, because the kids start laughing when they appear with their paper crowns and fake beards. The narrator explains about the three kings coming from a faraway land, bearing gifts for little Jesus.

Two more stray dogs become involved in the scene. Some of the kids start petting them. But there's no time to play with the dogs, since there are now more dances, from the older kids this time. Boys in full *gaucho* attire dance with the girls in bright, long skirts and braided hair who I spotted in church. Santos is one of them. At ten he's already a big boy, well qualified for a proper dance. His mum and dad take pictures, too. He smiles back but doesn't wave. He's focused on his dance. It seems complicated but he doesn't miss a move.

I'm expecting some more Nativity scenes, but we're done. Mary and the baby vanish from the stage, the kids all mingle, and the teachers hand over small pieces of *pan dulce*, the traditional Christmas cake that looks like a muffin with raisins inside.

"That's it, darling," Gabriela says. "Done. You have successfully survived an Argentine school *fiesta*. Now we can relax, have a drink and some food."

The part about the food is going to be difficult. I remember the huge *asado* cooking outside. It's likely to be meat and meat only. And I'm right. I end up munching on a piece of bread, which Patricio has topped up with some mayonnaise and a look of pity.

"Roxy, stop this vegetarian nonsense and try some meat. You're in Argentina."

The kids jump in with lots of encouragement, and his niece hands me over a big piece of meat in between two loaves of bread.

"Come on, Roxy. We want to see you eating meat."

This would be the very last piece of my Argentine makeover. I wonder what will happen if I do? Will the prayer I said in church suddenly be erased and I'll remain here forever, part of them? Will I miraculously find a way to stay with them and play polo again, but not break anything any longer?

I'm tempted to take a bite just to try my luck, but then I remember I haven't eaten meat for over twenty-five years now and I probably can't digest it any longer. And the last thing I need right now is to have Patricio rush me to the hospital with indigestion.

I content myself with eating the bread and mayonnaise instead and talk to one of the schoolteachers. She tells me that they have no funds, no money at all, but they do their best with what they have, and that the *pan dulce* distributed to the kids has been baked by the teachers. She gives me one and I eat it immediately, grateful for this big improvement on bread and mayonnaise.

Parents, teachers, kids, and stray dogs mix happily all around the big hall. Patricio and Gabriela go to talk to other people. I wander outside, where more meat is being added to the huge grill and other people chat in groups, drinking beer or soft drinks from plastic cups and eating bread and meat, occasionally topped with mayonnaise. The kids play in large groups, running around on the grass of the courtyard by the fire and outside on the dirt road. The music flows out through the open windows and doors, and luckily it's not Christmas carols. London shops have made me allergic to Christmas carols.

I walk around, a small glass of orange juice in one hand and the remains of the bread and mayonnaise in the other, and I breathe it all in—the smell of the grilled meat, the sounds of laughter and Spanish conversations, the shouts of the kids, the breeze of the night. I take it all in and hope it will live there in me forever and remind me of this magic night in the pampas.

And no words in any prayer in the world can stop me feeling part of this.

SUNDAY 25TH DECEMBER

I wake up with that unexplainable feeling of joy that always hits me when I open my eyes and hear the sounds of the *campo* in the morning. I don't even mind the concert of birds, all going insane in the early hours of the morning, just around sunrise. The noise usually dies down after a while and I love this second morning sleep that I fall into, just after the birds settle, when I know there's still plenty of time until I need to get out of bed.

A couple of hours later I emerge from the guest room in my friends' house, the same room where I sweated with fever and worried about dying after surgery. It seems like centuries ago. I go straight to the kitchen in search of a coffee. The best part of their lifestyle is that they mix perfectly the latest joys of civilization with the roughness of the *campo*. And one needs civilization—an espresso machine in this case, like the one on the kitchen counter.

With my cup of coffee in one hand I leave the house and decide to pay a visit to my old acquaintance, the quinoto tree. Just to check if it's still got some of those delicious little orange-like fruits, and also because it might be some time before my friends wake up. I haven't heard a single movement inside the house.

But I'm wrong. Just around the corner I spot Patricio some twenty meters away, fully dressed in rubber boots and all, holding a rifle, which is pointed towards a hole in the ground. Under his feet, a hose pours water into the hole.

"Good morning! What on earth are you doing there?" I shout.

"The bastard will come out! And this time I'll kill him!" he shouts back.

"What?" I'm now suddenly alarmed. "Who do you want to kill?"

"The armadillo. It's been digging holes in my backyard for a few days now and this time I'm not going to miss him. When the water inundates his den he'll come up and I'll shoot the bastard."

"Stop!" I'm not sure what's going on but the thought of starting Christmas Day with the killing of an innocent animal fills me with horror.

But he doesn't look like he's heard me.

"Stop, please. Please don't!" I scream, with my hands over my eyes. I can't bear to watch. If he does, at least I shouldn't see it. I know I'm screaming like a hysterical woman, but I can't stop it. The life of a poor armadillo is at stake.

"Please don't! Spare him. Please!"

Patricio lifts his head and looks at me. "Roxy, are you crazy? This bastard is digging holes in my yard. I have to get him."

"Please!"

"OK, calm down."

The rifle comes down. I'm hardly breathing.

"All right, I won't kill it. But come on, you have to help me out. Hold this." He hands me the rifle.

I run and take the rifle from his hand. If he has no rifle, he can't kill.

"Take care, it's loaded," he says, and I freak out. I hold it gingerly, trying to keep it pointing towards the ground.

"I'll catch it and put it in the car and we'll throw it in the fields far away from here. Are you happy now?"

"Yes, yes. Thank you." I whisper.

Exile is a much better option.

"The bastard should thank you." Patricio throws me a smile. "You're saving his life. Now go back and turn the tap on completely. I'll wait here to catch him when he comes out."

I run back to the pump and turn on the tap, keeping the rifle still pointed down. Behind me, I hear a victorious shout and when I turn around I see Patricio's hands reach inside the den and come back out, holding the tail of what appears to be a mini-version of a crocodile mixed with a hedgehog.

It doesn't bite, though. I remember Rosario had told me that when I saw one at her farm. She also told me that this animal can be found only in the Argentine pampas and that it's a distant cousin of I don't remember which prehistoric animal.

"Turn the tap fully on," Patricio shouts.

He's holding the animal by the tail but can't get him out. The armadillo is less than half a meter long but it weighs quite a lot and is holding on with all his might to the walls of his den.

"Once his hole is full of water, he'll let go," Patricio says.

I stay there by the tap awaiting further instructions, with the rifle in my hand, watching my friend holding the bum of an *armadillo*. I'm not quite sure how we got into this situation.

A few more minutes and Patricio's prediction comes true. The den fills with water, the animal stops grabbing hold with its front legs, and my friend emerges victorious from the fight, carrying the animal tail up.

"Look at the bastard. He has no idea how close he was to dying this morning. Switch the tap off, we're done."

I do as I'm told and then walk over with him towards his pickup truck. He throws the animal in the back of it and the *armadillo* starts running round, wildly trying to escape. But there's no way, the sides of the pickup are too high. He's trapped. Eventually he gives up and freezes in one corner.

Patricio tells me to hold the rifle a little bit longer while he gets rid of the mud from his fight with the armadillo, then tells me I'm crazy to intervene in what is a normal farm-life scene, and he's even crazier to listen to me.

"It's Christmas Day. Maybe we shouldn't start it with a killing," I say in my defense.

Gabriela emerges from the house with a cup of coffee in her hand and jumps into the discussion in support of the armadillo's life. Outnumbered, Patricio gives up arguing, takes his rifle from my hand, unloads it, and takes it back into the house.

"Only Mali understands me," he says.

Gabriela's small terrier has gone insane, barking at the car, sensing there's an animal inside. I bet she wants to kill the armadillo, too.

I finish my cup of coffee, thinking there's a lot more to the life in the *campo* than just waking up to the sound of the birds.

We leave for the big farm to have a proper breakfast there with the rest of the family. Just before we go, Patricio goes to check on the sheep. He says a new lamb was born yesterday. I go with him, hoping to see the lamb. We search for it everywhere, but the sheep all huddle together in one corner of their enclosure and there's no trace of a newly born lamb.

"Maybe the foxes took it last night," Patricio says. "There's nothing we can do about it."

That's one life saved and one life gone. The *campo* likes even numbers.

We get in the car, the three of us and the dog, with the armadillo still unsuccessfully trying to escape from the back of the pickup. We drive straight across the fields, leaving the dirt road to one side. It has rained in the night—not enough to turn everything into mud, but just enough to bring up the smell of the earth. The same smell of grass and clay that I remember so well.

We drive amongst the cows, all watching us with their immobile eyes, and we reach the horses. They come towards the car. They're always curious, the horses. Patricio holds his hand out and the horses come over to touch him. On my open window on the back seat I try to do the same, but they don't come over to touch me. Maybe they know who's the boss.

We drive away from the horses and when Patricio decides we're at a safe distance from their house he stops, picks up the armadillo by the tail, and throws it out of the car. The dog locked inside barks like crazy.

"Shall I let Mali out now? We can see who's faster, Mali or this bastard."

"No, don't!" Gabriela and I scream with one voice, united in defense of the armadillo.

As if sensing his life is at stake, the animal quickly regains his bearings after being unceremoniously dumped in the bushes, and starts running away as fast as the short legs under his long crocodile-like body allow him.

Run, mate. Today is your lucky day.

"Lucky him." Patricio echoes my thought. "If it wasn't for you, Roxy, he wouldn't have lived."

I'm feeling good about myself.

But later, as we're having breakfast at the farm, I don't feel that good any longer. The rest of the family can't believe I've prevented the killing of that terrible animal who digs up holes in the lawns.

"Roxy, life in the *campo* is like this. You can't afford to let your feelings get in the way."

I detect a hint of reproach in their eyes. But Patricio laughs and the kids laugh too, all finding it very funny that I felt compelled to save the life of that armadillo.

I think of it for the reminder of the day—that weird, long animal with scales all over his body as if he were a crocodile. I'm happy for him. He'll still carry on living here, hiding in the bushes of the pampas and digging other holes, hopefully far away from Patricio's backyard and his loaded rifle. He'll still be here, even when I'm gone. The *campo* likes even numbers.

January

New Year's Eve came and went in the *campo*. The same *campo* I prayed to leave.

What am I waiting for? The thought comes back annoyingly, just as I return to Buenos Aires. I have no answer, so I decide to get busy instead.

First, I have to finish my book, the one I wrote about my Argentine adventures of last year. It was waiting for me with a pile of corrections diligently suggested by my editor. I'm going to do it, I told myself, and I turned on my computer with a fresh determination to get this book over with and the love story as well.

My editor liked the book, she said, but it needed a lot more work. Some of the characters were great, others not so convincing.

"Let's say Rodrigo, for instance. You don't really say a lot about him. All he does in the book is look into your eyes and say *linda*, which makes you look rather stupid."

I have to laugh when I read this comment. Maybe that's all he did.

Her next note goes further.

"Please rewrite. Get back your memories about this guy and find out what really attracted you to him. Make him human. I want your true feelings here. The reader will want to know him better."

And how can I do this right now when I'm trying to let him out of my heart? But this isn't my editor's problem. This is the trouble when you write about your own life. Maybe I should write fiction from now on.

I carry on reading her notes and I'm not sure if I should laugh or cry.

"*His nice arms were coming out of his black T-shirt*—well, of course they're going to come out of his T-shirt, right? Where exactly do you expect arms to be? Please rephrase. And enough with these general adjectives. Nice doesn't mean anything. Give me more. What else can you tell me about his arms? Warm? Sexy? Strong?"

I spend some time there on my sofa, with my laptop open and my thoughts wandering aimlessly. I can do this better, I tell myself. Only if I manage to recall the sensation of Rodrigo's arms from the dungeon in which I've locked these memories.

I'm not sure I'm ready to do this—to let myself feel, I mean. I've spent quite a lot of time these past few weeks making sure I wasn't feeling much. Not about him, anyway. But I can't make progress with this book if I don't work on her comments and there's no way I can rephrase my empty descriptions if I don't allow myself to feel.

The day is slowly turning into night and I'm still on my sofa, tears running down my cheeks and the memory of Rodrigo's strong arms and soft whispers all around me. And when I'm done crying I pat my eyes dry and start writing again.

FRIDAY 13TH JANUARY

Almost a week later I'm happy with the results of my rewrite. The second draft of my book is almost finished and I've done my best to keep my editor happy.

My mood is low, though. I'd locked myself in the house, and writing about my recently ended love story made me feel like a total failure. But immersing myself in writing was a great way to keep the leaving thought at bay. I know I have to leave. Soon. But not just now. And not while I still have no idea where to go next. I've done a little bit of internet research and found an Ayurveda sanatorium in India that apparently does wonders for post-surgery recovery. I've never been to India before and never done Ayurveda, this ancient Indian holistic medicine system that looks to integrate the mind, body, and spirit aspects of healing. But one way or another, once Doc discharges me, I'll have to go somewhere. And back to work in London isn't yet an option, not while my shoulder still hurts like crazy.

I decide to take a break from these thoughts as I prepare to spend the weekend at the seaside with Rosario and two girls from her family. I'll make up my mind when I come back.

We start driving around midday, all fitting nicely into Rosario's sister's car—four girls, and one big basket filled with all the contents needed for *mate*-making. We have one large thermos filled with boiling water, one bag of *yerba mate,* and one perfectly round brown leather cup with silver edges and a matching silver straw. That's because in Argentina no one gets in a car for a six-hour journey without a *mate* supply.

The music is on. We listen to Mana, the Mexican band. I haven't heard them in almost ten years. How does time go so quickly?

We drink *mate,* each one taking turns to empty the cup which gets refilled and passed on to someone else. We sing along with Mana, a dramatic song about love and horses, about how his departed lover will one day understand their love was real. And then she'll miss his kisses.

My eyes fill up with tears.

I don't want to think about him. Not about Rodrigo or his kisses. And not about horses and reins, either. And both things in one song are a little bit too much. But Mana doesn't care about my little private drama and the song goes on and I have no escape but to join in with the girls as we sing along in one big, long scream.

Ping. Message on my phone, just as Mana has finished trying to rein in his love. It's Doc. He sends me a thumbs-up once again, in reply to the last X-ray picture I sent this morning.

So, all good? I text back.

Yes.

Full range of motion?

Yes.

Any more X-rays?

No. That was the last one. You're out of medical supervision now.

Out of medical supervision. No more Doc. No more hospital, no more —tears well up again. Damn these tears. I should be happy, not sad.

But keep in touch, he texts back. And damn these Argentines who can always guess my thoughts. *Tell me how it's going. And take care.*

Gracias. I will. You take care too!

I'm going to miss you, Doc, but I don't text him. I bet he knows it, anyway.

I take another sip of *mate*. I'll never leave this place if I start drinking *mate* like them.

THURSDAY 19TH JANUARY

The thought hits me again, with the same precise hammering motion, the second I enter my flat in Buenos Aires.

How come it's still here? It's been hiding the whole weekend. I drank *mate* with the girls, enjoyed the beach with strong winds and cold waters, and baked in the sun. I haven't thought of anything. But I'm back now, and the bastard thought is back, too.

You said you're going away, it says. *When are you going?*

Deadlock. I have no answer and have run out of excuses. So I do what I usually do in such situations. I book an appointment with a lady with a crystal. The trouble is, there aren't many options left. Number one has been fired; number two is useless, since she's going to deliver the same astral chart reading as last time; and number three is hard to reach and requires booking well in advance.

So I email lady number four for an emergency session. The psychologist. She's available but only in the afternoon, she says. Damn. What am I going to do until then?

And then it hits me. The ridiculousness of the situation hits me full blast, and it happens that morning in my flat in Buenos Aires, as I contemplate the next five hours of having to wait to talk to my lady with a crystal.

I can't go on like this. I can't go on expecting others to make decisions for me. Enough. At the age of forty-two it's about time I made my own decisions. And maybe it's about time I started looking after myself, as well.

I sit down at the table and open my computer next to the picture of San Benito, still standing beside the remains of the burned-out candle.

In the next thirty minutes I do it all. I book a flight to London, leaving on Saturday, arriving Sunday. Then I book another one, leaving in the morning from London, a few hours after my flight from Argentina lands. This one is for Abu Dhabi for a stopover, then on to Kerala, in southern India, to an airport I can't pronounce. Thiruvananthapuram. I email the Ayurveda place I'd found online a few weeks ago and ask to book a three-week stay because their website recommends twenty-one days for a full treatment.

Then I close my computer, and with a blank mind I stay there seated at the table for a while, watching the picture of San Benito. Saturday is the twenty-first, I think, out of the blue.

"Your day. I'm leaving on your day. You had something to do with this, didn't you?"

He says nothing. He just watches me, his old face with a long white beard looking very serious. He's silent. But in the depth of his eyes, I detect a little smile.

Well, it's done now. I sigh. It's going to hurt like crazy to go anyway, so it's better if I do it just like this, without too many days to think about it.

I'm going on Saturday, I text Rosario. *Just booked my flight.*

Oh noooooo. Roxy! When am I going to see you again?

This I don't know. I don't know if I can bring myself to go to Lobos one more time. It already hurts bad enough from a distance.

I break the news to Sol next.

Roxy! We're going out tonight. Your bye-bye party. You can't go without a party!

OK, I text back. Let us party. Maybe it will help soothe this stabbing pain inside.

But the pain inside laughs and tells me there's nothing in this world that can help. By 3 pm, when I'm finally due to speak to my lady number four, I'm almost in tears.

"What have I done?" I sob. "I've booked my flights and they're non-changeable and I'm not ready to go!"

She looks at me calmly from the other side of the Skype screen.

"Yes, you are," she says.

"How do you know?"

"Because you booked those flights. No one forced you. No one told you what to do. You did it. Alone."

Yes, I did. Maybe that's why it's so hard now.

"But the pain inside. It hurts!"

"Of course it does."

"Why?"

"Because leaving a place where you've been loved always hurts. But it's time to go. You've made the right decision. A part of you knew you had to go, that's why you've booked those flights. A part of us knows. It always knows, even when the rest of us refuses to believe."

"But I'm not ready," I tell her stubbornly. "What if I still have things to do here?"

"Do you feel that you do?"

The only thing left for me to do here is to get back on a horse. The answer in my mind is scarily clear. I don't say anything.

She asks me where I'm going.

"To India. An Ayurveda sanatorium for three weeks of treatment."

"Sounds great to me," she says.

Yeah, right. What does she know?

I hang up the phone, feeling as empty as I did at the start of the call. Maybe I should really fire her. Not only does she not tell me what to do, but also she has no solution when I tell her I hurt like hell.

There's one more person I need to let know that I'm going— Patricio. Gabriela has already gone to Europe to visit her mother in Switzerland, but Patricio is back at the farm. I text him saying I'm going on Saturday.

Bloody hell! he answers. *So soon? I hoped to see you before you go!*

He tells me there's a party tomorrow. His dad turns seventy and the whole family is going to be there, at the farm. I should come. I tell him I'll let him know tomorrow if I can make it, since it's my last day in Buenos Aires and I need to pack. If I finish on time, I'll come.

But I know I won't. Because if I go there one more time and spend a full evening eating and drinking and making merry with them, there's no hope in hell I can tear myself away the next morning and go away to India, to the other side of the world, knowing I might never come back. I simply won't be able to, and I'll stay there forever, at their farm, not wanting to let go, because I love them and I love the *campo*, too.

No, I'm not setting foot in that party.

LATER THAT EVENING

I dress in a tight black top and a very short black skirt with glittery white and golden beads embroidered on the front. I get into my gold platform heels and grab a small black handbag. My hair is up and I've got heavy make-up on. Sol would approve.

She does. She greets me with a cry of surprise as I walk into the restaurant at exactly 11:30 pm, a decent time to have dinner in Argentina.

"Roxy! You look like a queen. Finally! Enough with these flat sandals and boring T-shirts. You finally look like a *reina*."

If I'm a queen then she's a princess. She's dressed all in black—high heels, embroidered top and satin shorts, all covered with a long silk cardigan, which adds a casual note to her look. Sol has a talent for picking up pieces that I would never dare to wear and combining them in an unexpected but exquisite look.

Madri gives me a big hug as well. She's dressed in black too—a silk transparent shirt under which I detect a push-up bra, long leather trousers, and impossibly high heels. Madri must be well over sixty. I'm wondering how she can still walk in such high heels.

The restaurant they picked turns into a disco as soon as people finish eating. The transformation is swift. At some point after midnight the music gets louder and people stand up from their chairs and dance right where they are, around the tables still full with the remains of the dinners that busy waiters rush around to clear. Once the tables are empty they're used for dancing, and I watch Madri in shock as she climbs onto ours in her skyscraper heels.

"Sol! Your aunt! What if she falls from there?" I shout in her ear, trying to make myself heard above the pounding music.

"*Tranqui,*" Sol shouts back. "She does it all the time. She'll be fine."

We dance to the sensual music, and because it's a Latino tune and Latino dances are not meant to be danced alone, before I know it I'm dancing with the guy in the blue shirt from the table next to ours, while his friend approaches Sol. A third guy is contemplating climbing onto the table next to Madri but then decides against such a risky move, and Madri retains the use of the whole table for herself.

I throw a look every now and then at Madri's heels but they're still securely planted on the table, and she gives me a thumbs-up from above. I decide to stop worrying about her and try to keep up with Sol instead. She laughs at my timid dance moves and tells me to loosen up; *bachata* is a sensual dance and this is how it's done. She shows me the moves, to the delight of her dance partner who embraces her even more tightly.

"Who's this guy?" I shout in her ear again.

She shrugs. Doesn't know and doesn't matter, most probably.

I try to imitate her sensual moves but I can't. I'm too embarrassed and I end up lightly touching the hands of the guy I dance with, who probably wonders what he's done wrong and why I don't embrace him like my friend does with his friend.

In the meantime Madri has jumped off the table, drinks one big glass of sangria to cool off, and then continues her dance with a very young guy, probably close to the legal age limit, the same one who previously tried to climb onto the table with her. She's good with *bachata* moves, too.

"Roxy, don't worry. We have this in our blood. We're born with these moves. You're doing well for a foreigner," Sol shouts encouragingly.

I carry on trying to shake my bum just like Sol instructs me to, and then my dancing partner starts smiling and dares to come a little bit closer, and before I know it I'm locked with him in one long embrace, and I bet he would have kissed me if it wasn't for the bright lights in the restaurant. They didn't dim the lights when they turned the music on.

"It's better like this," Madri tells me as we stop and have another glass of sangria. "Why have the lights off? Better to see who you're dancing with!"

A man in his late fifties approaches and takes Madri for another dance. He wears a black T-shirt with big white letters that say, "Tonight and every night." I'm not quite sure what that refers to. He's got a big belly but he dances well, and Madri swings around under his skilful guidance. Sol carries on with her suitor, who is wearing Timberland boots and rough jeans and looks like a builder, but a sexy one, considering his typical unshaved Argentine look. The boots don't seem to hinder his *bachata* moves.

I stop, dizzy, and tell my dancing partner I need to have a glass of water. He guides me towards a chair, takes a seat next to me, and pours wine from the bottle on their table.

"No, not wine. Water. I need some water."

He tells me it's a waste to drink water when there's nice wine available, but he manages to find a glass of water and gives it to me together with the glass of wine. For after the water, he says.

I take a look at him for the first time since we started to dance. He's in his early thirties or maybe late twenties, has short hair and wears jeans and a black T-shirt. Just like Rodrigo. Except his hair isn't black but dark blond, and his face is more round than Rodrigo's square features, and he doesn't have the unshaved look. Too bad, I think. I always liked guys with square faces and unshaved beards.

He tells me his name is Eugenio, which means "well born" in Greek.

I'm impressed by his knowledge of languages, I tell him.

He's impressed by where I come from, he says. He hasn't yet met anyone who comes from Romania.

Out of the corner of my eye I spot Sol, kissing the sexy guy with builders' boots she's been dancing with. I bet she's not disturbed by the strong lights.

I finish my drink, turn to Eugenio the Well Born, and let myself go dizzy again, guided by his expert hands to the sounds of the *bachata*.

At 3 am Sol tells me she has to leave because tomorrow is a working day for her, and she has to get up at 7 am. Like she does every day. The three of us leave the restaurant followed by the two guys Sol and I have been dancing with. Eugenio the Well Born tells me he would like to drive me home. I tell him it's not going to happen.

"Why not? Here in Argentina we don't complicate things," he tells me.

Madri sticks an elbow into my ribs and tells me to go home with him.

I tell her I can't. I'm leaving in two days' time.

"What has this to do with it? It's gonna be just a *tachengo*."

"A *tachengo*?" I repeat, uncertain.

"Yes. I mean a *touch and go*." She carefully pronounces the English words.

I burst out laughing as poor Eugenio watches me, not really sure what's going on. A *tachengo*. Just the way my story with Rodrigo started last year. Here's my opportunity to do it again. And maybe I won't leave. Maybe I'll just stay here with him and forget about my flights. Hmm. Tempting. Very tempting.

Out of the corner of my eye I catch Sol and her suitor whispering, probably having the same type of conversation, but everything ends very quickly in one big cry.

"My car! Where's my car?"

Sol panics, but then Eugenio says his car has gone as well, and they all conclude that it must be the *gruga*, the car-clamping patrol, who have passed by and decided to collect their unlawfully parked vehicles.

The missing car suddenly wakes me from my *tachengo* train of thought. No, this movie is finished. I've already pressed the pause button. There's going to be no *tachengo* tonight and no repetition of a story I've already lived.

I jump into a taxi and head home, while the four of them—Madri, Sol, her sexy suitor with builder shoes, and Eugenio the Well Born—all cram into another to go and collect their cars from the police garage.

"Text me when you get home, OK? *Bombona!*" Sol screams through the open window of her taxi. "Let me know that you have arrived safely. I don't want to worry about you!"

Another person who looks after me, I think, as I finally arrive home and take off my impossibly high gold platform shoes. Maybe it's an Argentine thing.

It must be because of the sangria but I forget to text her, and I'm awakened by a series of pings two hours later.

Are you OK???

Yes, yes, sorry. Sleeping, forgot to text.

I fall back on my cushion, the sounds of *bachata* still going round in my head and the sangria still pulsing through my veins. I'll need a lot of sleep to get over it.

FRIDAY 20TH JANUARY

But no amount of sleep can save me from the harsh hangover that hits me in the morning. And there's one more painful thing to deal with. Today is the day of goodbyes. In Argentina this is a big thing. One needs to say goodbye properly.

I start with Sol because I need to get out of the house, and because I need to get updates on how the rest of the evening went for her.

She greets me with her perfect make-up on and her usual big smile.

"Girl, how can you look so well? So rested? How many hours of sleep did you get in the end?"

"Three," she tells me, but this isn't such a big deal because she sleeps only between four and five hours a night anyway. She gets home around 9 pm from work, and by the time she's finished putting all her three kids to bed and has cleaned, cooked, and prepared everything for the following day, it's usually well past midnight.

Sol tells me how she finally rescued her car from the police station. The handsome guy with builder's shoes who danced with her all night ended up paying half of the fine for her. Because he likes sharing things, he said.

"A perfect gentleman," Sol says, her eyes dreamy.

"Are you going to see him again?"

She smiles. "He's already invited me out on Saturday."

I smile too. The guy was handsome. I wonder how this is going to end. I won't be here to know. I'm leaving tomorrow.

I tell them I can't stay long. It's my last day ... the bags ... and ...

There's no need to explain anything. We keep it short. Well, as short as one Argentine *despedida* can be—one big hug for her and one for Madri, a few *cuídates,* a lot of *cuídates* actually, and some tears. Tears are quite normal for an Argentine *despedida.*

Sol slides a bracelet around my wrist.

"*Que la Virgen te proteja, Roxy,*" she says. "And that she makes you come back here," she adds.

I leave the shop and look at the small picture of the Virgin of Lujan, the patron saint of Argentina, which is hanging from an orange leather bracelet.

"May the Virgin of Lujan protect you too, Sol," I say in my mind.

I go home and find my cleaner waiting for me in tears. The landlady told her I am to go tomorrow. I give her a big hug too and walk her around the flat, showing her all the things I'm going to leave there because I can't carry them back and that she can take if she wants. All my toiletries, a few books, a yoga mat and roll, all the laundry detergents, an impressive quantity of vitamins and supplements, and my treasured vegetable steamer. Her eyes light up at the sight of my vegetable steamer.

She goes finally and now there's only one *despedida* left. The last one, the most difficult one. I can't disappear without a proper goodbye to my Argentine family. But I can't go there tonight either.

I pick up the phone and call Patricio. I tell him it's impossible to get there tonight. And this time it's not a lie. There are two big empty suitcases lying open in the middle of my living room and there's no way I can finish packing in time. But I'll come tomorrow, I tell him.

"I'll come in the morning to have a coffee with you all."

"Forget it, Roxy. That's crazy," he says.

"No, it's not. My flight leaves at 2 pm. I have to check in at 12. I can leave home at 7 am, be at the farm by 9, spend two hours with you, then leave at 11 and be in the airport by 12. I'll do it."

And there's nothing in the world that will stop me from doing it.

LATER THAT EVENING

Marco calls me in the evening just as I've finished packing. How he knows it's time to show up because I'm going through a difficult time, l have no idea. He just knows.

"*Ciao, imbecille!* What are you up to this time?"

I tell him I've called his usual taxi driver, Luciano, to book him for my long trip tomorrow. He's the same taxi driver Marco sent to pick me up from the airport three years ago when I first arrived in Argentina without knowing anyone here.

He tells me he knows; Luciano has informed him about my trip, that's why he's calling me. I wonder if Marco has instructed the driver to send him regular updates about me.

"So, it's your last evening in Buenos Aires. How are you feeling?"

"Hung over," I tell him. "It's better this way. I'm not thinking about anything. I don't want to think about anything. Marco, it hurts like crazy if I think about things."

"You've always had this rather exaggerated tendency to feel too much," he comments, in his usual dry voice. "Taking things out of proportion. What exactly is it that hurts now? Your shoulder is better, I assume."

"Yes, *freed from medical supervision.*" I quote Doc's words. "But Argentina, these people, my family here… All these people who have given me so much love. It's everything. I'm going and I have no idea where and no idea when or whether I'll be back."

I don't dare to mention polo and my question of when and whether I'll play again. Not to Marco.

"Let's start at the beginning. Where exactly are you flying to tomorrow?"

"I'm going to London for five hours, then to Abu Dhabi for three hours, then to this place in India I can't pronounce for three weeks and then I don't know where next."

"How about going back to your home in London to do some work? I imagine you're spending your savings like crazy now. When will the money run out?"

I smile. Marco is always an accountant at heart.

"Not for a while. I still have some time to go before I need to work on another project. And talking about money, you still haven't sent me your bank account details. So I can transfer back the money you brought me."

"I will, don't worry. There's no hurry."

"And what if I disappear in India and you never hear from me again? You'll be left six thousand dollars short."

"How you manage to live like this, only you know," Marco says, deciding to ignore my disappearing-in-India scenario. "But maybe it works for you. Maybe you've found your balance, in the middle of all this apparently unbalanced life. Maybe your life is supposed to be like this."

This isn't the usual Marco speech. He would normally urge me to go back to work, tell me I'm ruining my career, and ask for the phone number of my dad when he feels I'm in urgent need of adult supervision. He's not supposed to encourage me to carry on drifting God knows where.

"It's not that bad," he continues. "You have a shoulder to heal and this is your priority now. Maybe they can sort it out in this Ayurveda place. What do they do there anyway?"

I tell him I don't know a lot about it. I'll have massages with different medicated oils. There are lots of oils, apparently. Oils they pour on your body and your head, make you sniff up your nostrils and then some more weird treatments. Vomiting. Enemas. Detox for the body, they say. I only read a little bit on the internet.

"Roxy!" I hear worry in his voice. "What are you getting yourself into this time?"

That, I'm not sure. But I'll find out soon.

SATURDAY 21ST JANUARY

Luciano is in front of my flat at 7 am sharp, as agreed. I tell him we need to buy *medialunas*, lots of them. There are likely to be close to fifteen people at that farm. He tells me he knows the best place in town for this and that it's already open.

With the car filled with two huge bags of pastries that give out an irresistible smell, we drive out of the city and take the road towards the airport. It's the same road that goes to Lobos, the road I know so well. It feels like I'm going home, not away. I'm going home to the little farm in the middle of the pampas.

Patricio calls and tells me to come to his place first. The party went on very late last night, and people in the main farm are still sleeping.

"Rosario and her boyfriend are here as well. They stayed over last night. In your room," he adds. He means the guest room. Not mine any longer.

I arrive by 9 am as planned. Luciano parks the car in the shade of a tree in Patricio's backyard, close to the place where I saved the life of the armadillo, and politely declines all offers to come inside the house. He prefers to have a nap in the car, he says.

Patricio waits for me on the porch. He has red eyes. He slept only a couple of hours. He tells me they had a great party last night and that I should have been there. Then he goes inside the house to make some coffee. For a few minutes I remain outside alone and take a deep breath in, the familiar smell of the *campo* hitting my nostrils. In the fields, I spot the cows peacefully grazing in the distance. Nothing has changed since the last time I was here. In the pampas, time stands still.

It stands still for the next couple of hours too, as we talk and laugh and have lots of *medialunas* and about three cups of coffee each, just to fight the hangover, as Rosario says. Then we get into the cars and drive up to the big farm because I have only thirty minutes left, and saying goodbye takes a long time in Argentina.

We drive through the wooden gates, on which hangs a signpost bearing the name of the farm, and onto the small dirt road that curves around the polo field, and I try hard not to look at it because I don't want to cry. Not yet. We drive past the big arch that holds the bell, and I see the dogs coming to welcome us as we park the cars close to the porch.

The kids are playing outside already and they all come to give me a kiss. I tell them I have *medialunas* for everybody, and for a second I'm tempted to sit down and have another cup of coffee, my fourth one this morning. But then Luciano tells me he's received a text message from Marco asking him to make sure I don't miss my flight, and we have to leave because there's going to be traffic on the way to the airport.

I have no time to think about Marco and how he managed to remember the time of my flight from God knows what country he's in at the moment, because the rest of the people come out of the house with sleepy eyes and slow movements and they all give me a hug too.

I tell them this is a hello and goodbye hug in one because I can't stay—I've got a flight to catch.

"Why are you going?" Patricio's niece asks, looking at me with big round eyes. "Don't go, Roxy, stay a little bit longer."

I tell her that if I stay I'll get back on a horse and that's probably not a good idea right now, so I'd better go.

She tells me they've got bicycles at the farm too. I don't need to ride horses.

We all laugh and Patricio tells me he'll name one of his foals *Bicicleta*. Bicycle. In memory of my story. And maybe this will convince me to ride again.

I'm dangerously close to tears again and I don't answer but carry on with my hugs, silently praying I'll make it back into the taxi without making an utter fool of myself.

"Roxy. You can come back. You know this, right? Any time," Patricio tells me as he walks with me towards my car. "Any time. Horse or no horse. It doesn't matter. We're here. And take care in India, please. I won't be there to look after you."

Maybe this is it, I think. Maybe all it takes to change the karma is that I start looking after my own self.

"See you this summer, in Europe," I tell him.

I won't cry, I will not cry, I tell myself. Not in front of them, anyway. I'm almost there. Only Rosario left to hug in the open door of my taxi as Patricio leans through the window to give Luciano precise instructions on how to get to the main road.

But my Argentine sister hugs me with that intensity that tells me she knows, she knows I'm not coming back here, even though I didn't say all the silly things that are going through my mind. She just knows because she's like that, my Argentine sister. She reads me well.

"Roxy, I love you. We all love you. We will always love you."

"I love you too," I whisper.

I barely make it into the car before the tears take over. Thankfully no sobs, just long, heavy tears running down my cheeks one by one, without end.

"It's all right to cry when you say goodbye," Luciano tells me in his professional voice, throwing me a glance through the rear-view mirror. "We all do it here. We feel these things here, in Argentina."

I carry on crying silently on the back seat, the taste of my tears mixed with that of the dust that instantly rises up behind the car as we hurry past the wooden gates of the farm and carry on down the dirt road that cuts across the fields.

I spot a group of horses in the distance and for a second I have this silly idea of asking Luciano to stop so I can say goodbye to the horses. But that would make me cry even more, and maybe I need to get back to my senses.

And then I remember one word that Patricio said just before I left and that makes me stop crying. *Bicicleta.*

Another foal will soon be born in these fields. She will be a mare, descended from one of his best polo-playing mares and the stallion he likes to ride in tournaments and which he always keeps tied up with a long rope, apart from the rest of the horses. The foal will have a surrogate mother, an older mare who isn't playing any longer and who will receive the embryo implanted in her womb so that the real mother can carry on playing polo.

The little foal won't know all this when she's born in the fields, maybe in the middle of the night, or maybe just at sunrise, because there's a special energy in the air of the *campo* just around sunrise. I know it because I felt it, too. She'll come out of the womb with big round eyes wide open and shaky legs, but then she'll stand at once, because she's a horse and this is what horses do. They like to run.

She'll grow up in the fields surrounded by other mares and other foals, and the cows and the sheep and occasionally the dogs will gather round too, maybe following Santos as he takes a ride on his small horse called Illusion. She'll learn to find the best grass and the water-holes, she'll listen to the silence of the night, and to the concert of frogs after a heavy downpour. She'll feel the scorching heat of the midday sun on her delicate skin with its short hair and she'll learn to take shelter under the trees, just as the rest of the horses do. She'll feel the cool breeze of the night and the freshness of the rain, but she won't feel cold. Temperatures never drop to freezing point in the pampas. She'll spend her days running around carefree next to her adoptive mother, and she'll play with the other foals and have a happy childhood.

When she's about two years old or so—a well-grown teenager—people will come and touch her gently and she will be led by a rope to the polo lines so she can watch the other horses playing polo and see there's nothing to fear. She'll stay there with them for a while, just watching, learning, getting used to people talking and touching her. And then she'll be sent away to the breakers, like a sort of boarding school, where she'll be taught about the saddle and the reins, and she'll slowly learn what it is that those strange creatures called people want her to do. She'll then come back to the fields she was born into for long holidays where she won't be expected to do anything, just to run around with the other horses, so she can settle again and digest everything she's learned. And then when she's about four and accustomed to the saddle and the reins, she'll come back to the polo field in front of the farmhouse. Facundo will talk nicely to her and pat her and show her a polo mallet and a ball. And she will let Facundo ride her because he has that special skill of making all horses behave like sheep around him, and he does this kindly, not forcefully, because the people who have real skill never need to force anything. He will ride her on a polo field and let her get used to seeing the mallet swinging past her eyes and the ball flying in the air.

She'll learn this game slowly and it will take a couple of years before she's ready to play.

And then, one day, she'll walk proudly into the field, all kitted up with leg bandages and rubber protectors, with her mane shaved and her tail nicely braided. She'll wear all the complicated tack a polo horse gets kitted out with, the many leather stripes that hold the saddle in place and the four reins held in the left hand of the player who rides her. She'll walk with a purpose and know what she has to do because of her long training, and also because the blood she carries has the genes, the polo-playing genes. Her mother and her father played polo and her grandparents too, and all the generations that came before them. And she'll do her duty well, because she's a polo horse and her name is *Bicicleta*.

She won't know it, but she'll also carry a part of me with her, the part that I leave here today and that I may come back one day to claim. One day, when the time is right, when her training is done and mine too, and after all that still needs to happen will have already happened. One day when it's time for a new beginning. But until then, I leave her here. She'll stay for me.

And when she plays, she'll play for me.

Epilogue

The good thing about breaking a bone is that you must make time to heal. And once you start on this journey there's no way of knowing where you'll end up.

I went to India thinking I was there to heal my shoulder. The Ayurveda sanatorium felt like a small boutique resort, nestled up a hill overlooking the Arabian Sea. I met the three resident Ayurveda doctors and gave them my latest X-ray. They looked at it briefly then put it aside and started on a long list of questions. I laughed out loud when they asked me if I had any addictions, and answered polo as if it was really funny. One of the doctors smiled kindly and told me it was just a standard questionnaire. I liked her instantly, with her beautiful colored sari and long gold earrings. She had a red dot on her forehead and smiled continuously, just like my doctor in Argentina. I decided to call her Lady Doc.

I spent the next three weeks being massaged and bathed in oil. I drank weird potions. I had oil poured on my forehead for hours with rhythmic movements that managed to bring any thoughts to a standstill. I was washed with what they called medicine water, and my shoulder was soaked in green oil and bandaged every day under the careful supervision of Lady Doc. She told me to stop worrying and that Ayurveda means the Science of Life.

"Trust it," she said.

I did. I let them do all they needed to do and I trusted it was for my benefit. And when the time came to go, Lady Doc walked into my treatment room as I enjoyed my last massage and asked me how everything had been. I told her everything was great and my shoulder much improved. I would have liked just one little thing to have been different. She asked me which one.

"The massage. It's lovely, but I would have preferred it to be stronger. I asked for a stronger massage but never got it."

"Yes, we know," she assured me. "Your therapist has been given very clear instructions. We told her she was to be gentle with you. We also told her that you would ask for a stronger massage. And she wasn't to listen to you."

"You knew this?" I asked, astonished. "You read my thoughts even before I had them?"

She smiled. "You're here to heal. And we're here to look after your body."

Even if I didn't, I added silently.

I left India refreshed, restored, and with a fully functioning shoulder, able to cope with the most difficult yoga poses, which I diligently repeated each morning just after sunrise, under the careful supervision of a yoga teacher. He had a funny phrase he kept on repeating every morning. "Past is history. Future is mystery," he said. "Present is gift." I left with this phrase still ringing in my ears.

I went to Thailand afterwards. Why here? Because a lady I met at the Ayurveda sanatorium told me there's an excellent yoga resort on the island of Koh Samui and I wanted to continue my yoga recuperation. I contacted the place but it was fully booked, so I searched for other yoga places instead.

This is how I came across Eve's site. She was a healer, she said. She also said she had a yoga class each morning and did karma clearing ceremonies. This caught my attention immediately. Maybe I should clear up this bone-breaking karma, I thought, as I booked a one-week stay, not anticipating where this experience would take me.

Mama Eve welcomed me with open arms. She lived in a small house at the end of a street in a village on the west side of the island. She had five dogs, just like my Argentine family. She had another client, a young blond guy who went there for the same rituals. Maybe he had troubles with his karma, too.

In the days that followed I slowly got it. You lose something, you get something. The Universe is always fair. I might have lost my Argentine family but I found a Thai mother. And a Norwegian brother.

William and I stayed with Mama Eve for a week and diligently followed all her instructions.

"You will both get better," she said. "You came here because you were meant to. It's part of your journey."

Mama Eve knew about these things because she was a shaman. This would qualify her as a new lady with a crystal, except she had no crystal. Just a very strong-smelling and incredibly bitter detox drink, which she made sure we drank under her careful supervision every morning at 5:30 precisely and then again just before dinner.

She prayed for us every day, just before the yoga, and we listened in silence to the words of the ancient language we didn't understand, sitting cross-legged on the floor behind her, in front of the Buddhist and Hindu altars she kept in her yoga room.

It was there that I dared to get on a bicycle again, because she said that I should. I told her about the falls and the broken bones. She said it happened because I had no balance in life, but it was time to get it back. So I learned to ride a bicycle again, slowly, behind William, on the road that led to her place. We rode them every day and when the week was done, my fear had gone.

And then, when all the prayers were done and all the cups of the detox drink ingested, she gave us one apple and one banana each and sent us back into the world. We were to start by spending a few days on a beach.

"Go together," she said. "Look after each other." Then she told William he was to go up into the Himalayas and told me I was to stay on that beach for a while. I wasn't sure how we could look after each other with these different sets of instructions.

We spent a few days on the beach and talked a lot. William told me about drug addiction. I told him about playing polo. He described to me in detail what taking various pills felt like. I told him about the adrenaline of the game. And then we realized we had both done things to our bodies that we were not proud of. But we also made the same commitment—that we would heal.

But healing is a hard business. He wrestled with one big decision—go back to his country and his group of friends, and do the same things he had done before. Or go forward, up the Himalayas, as Mama Eve said he should.

I wrestled with mine—get back on a horse or stay away for a while.

We had one last swim and one last dinner on the terrace overlooking the sea and then I watched him go, in the middle of the night, with a wet towel around his shoulders, his head up, facing his doubts. He was to board his flight to Nepal in the morning. I told him he was like Luke Skywalker from *Star Wars* in search of his sword, and that it took courage to go forward. He laughed and called me Princess Leia. I guess this makes us soul brothers.

He went on his path and I went on mine. I stayed on that beach for a while and wrote this book and with it wrote my goodbyes to all that I loved and have to now let go—polo, Argentina, and all the wonderful people I met there.

I'm not saying that everyone who plays polo is an addict and should give up. But I was. This is my story, and everyone's story is different. There's beauty in this sport—I've seen it, and it will stay with me forever. But I'd turned it into an addiction, and it took me a while to realize that.

It was on this beach that I received an email from Rodrigo. He'd not been in touch since we broke up, so his email took me by surprise. It was a short, sweet one. He said he knew he'd never see me again, but he's grateful for all that we had, and that I've been the best woman of his life. I smiled, felt my heart warm up, and forgave him instantly. Argentines, they just know how to make a woman smile!

Maybe life is like this. Like catching a bus, as William said. It can lead you in one direction or, if you catch another, it will take you somewhere else. Maybe there's a logic in all this, or maybe not.

But there's one thing I've learned. No matter which bus you catch or where it's going, look around. There will be others there with you, on that journey. People who will touch your heart, just as you touch theirs. People who will share your love and give you theirs. There will be someone to tell you *cuídate* or *no pasa nada*, someone to give you a hug or encourage you when you think you can't go forward. Because, in the end, we're all travelers on this one journey called life.

And it's the love we share that makes it worth living.

Lamai beach, Koh Samui, Thailand, March 2017

Post scriptum

Ah, and one more thing. It's kind of weird.

It started with Mama Eve. She opened my palms during one of her karma clearing ceremonies and drew some strange symbols with her fingers.

"Go put your hands on people," she told me afterwards.

I told her she'd got it wrong. I don't put my hands on people. I am a management consultant, for God's sake. I only do things for which I have a diploma.

So, I've got it. A diploma, I mean. I registered for a Reiki course in London and then discovered that the symbols she drew into my hands were the exact Reiki initiation symbols. I still had no idea what this meant, though.

But then something else came along—a shamanic course in the energy medicine of the Incas, and circumstances in my life aligned so that I went to that one, too.

And then, well. …I'm still not sure where all this takes me. But I have a little suspicion.

I think I'm about to find my own crystal.

About the Author

Roxana Valea was born in Romania and lived in Italy, Switzerland, England, and Argentina before settling in Spain. She has a BA in journalism and an MBA degree. She spent more than twenty years in the business world as an entrepreneur, manager and management consultant working for top companies such as Apple, eBay, and Sony. She is also a Reiki Master and shamanic energy medicine practitioner.

As an author, Roxana writes books inspired by real events. Her memoir *Through Dust and Dreams* is a faithful account of a trip she took at the age of twenty-eight across Africa by car in the company of two strangers she met over the internet. Her following book, *Personal Power: Mindfulness Techniques for the Corporate World* is a non-fiction book filled with personal anecdotes from her consulting years. The Polo Diaries series is inspired by her experiences as a female polo player—traveling to Argentina, falling in love, and surviving the highs and lows of this dangerous sport.

Roxana lives with her husband in Mallorca, Spain, where she writes, coaches, and does energy therapies, but her first passion remains writing.

www.roxanavalea.com

Next in
The Polo Diaries Series

Seven and a Half Minutes (The Polo Diaries Book 3)

Roxy looks for love … but polo is calling her.

Before Roxy found herself "Single in Buenos Aires," she was a single girl in London in search of true love. The third installment of the Polo Diaries series takes us back to that time, and we follow Roxy as she hires a love coach to help her navigate the dating scene. But the love coach comes up with an unexpected assignment: reconnect to a long-forgotten passion. For Roxy this means horses. Within weeks, she finds herself playing polo, thanks to a series of unforeseen events.

Torn between her desire to become the best polo player she can be and the dream of falling in love, Roxy steps fully into the exciting and demanding world of polo, where injury and recovery mix with hard training, and where celebrating the victory of a tournament comes at a high price. Will Roxy eventually become the polo player she dreams to be? And with polo being such a demanding sport, can there be any space left for love?

Single in Buenos Aires (The Polo Diaries Book 1), 2019

Roxy plays polo… but dreams of love.

Forty-one-year-old polo player Roxy arrives in Argentina with a to-do list that includes healing from a polo injury and falling in love with a handsome Argentine. From polo boots to tango shoes, the adrenaline of riding horses to glamorous after-game parties, Roxy learns to navigate this unfamiliar landscape with the help of new friends who teach her to take life as it comes. But will she find true love? Over three months in Buenos Aires, nothing goes according to plan, and yet, all the items on her list mysteriously get ticked off in the end. Just not the way she had imagined.

Fans of the Bridget Jones series will love the blend of humor, travel, and romantic comedy at the heart of *Single in Buenos Aires*, all topped off with the unforgettable flavor of life in one of the most sensual and passionate cities in the world.

Personal Power: Mindfulness Techniques for the Corporate World, 2018

This book is about your power. The one you were born with, the power that is always in you waiting to be used. Blending concepts of psychology, mindfulness and practical spirituality with the author's over twenty years of experience in the corporate world, it presents a simple yet powerful seven step framework to connect with your power and use it to manifest the life that you want.

You will learn to ground, cleanse and protect your energy. You will tap into what you already know and learn how to make decisions using your power base. You will be reminded how to direct your energy to manifest abundance and to reflect on and constantly improve your process.

If you want to achieve a sense of self-determination and inner peace while still working in a hectic corporate environment, and wonder how some people do this effortlessly, this book is for you. www. personalpowercorporate.com

Through Dust and Dreams, 2014

At a crossroads in her life, Roxana decides to take a ten-day safari trip to Africa. In Namibia, she meets a local guide who talks about "the courage to become who you are" and tells her that "the world belongs to those who dream."

Her holiday over, Roxana still carries the spell of his words within her soul. Six months later she quits her job and searches for a way to fulfil an old dream: crossing Africa from north to south. Teaming up with Richard and Peter, two total strangers she meets over the internet, Roxana starts a journey that will take her and her companions from Morocco to Namibia, crossing deserts and war-torn countries and surviving threats from corrupt officials and tensions within their own group.

Through Dust and Dreams is the story of their journey: a story of courage and friendship, of daring to ask questions and search for answers, and of self-discovery on a long, dusty road south.
www.throughdustanddreams.com